V

CLASSICS

474

Molly Keane (1904–1996) was born in County Kildare, Ireland. Hailed as the Irish Nancy Mitford in her day, she was a leading playwright of the 1930s, with her work directed by John Gielgud. Between 1928 and 1956, she wrote eleven novels under the pseudonym M. J. Farrell 'to hide my literary side from my sporting friends'. The death of her husband brought about a break in her career, which was ended in 1981 by the publication of *Good Behaviour* under her own name. It went on to be shortlisted for the Booker Prize.

Novels by Molly Keane

The Knight of Cheerful Countenance
Young Entry
Taking Chances
Mad Puppetstown
Conversation Piece
Devoted Ladies
Full House
The Rising Tide
Two Days in Aragon
Loving Without Tears
Treasure Hunt
Time After Time
Good Behaviour
Loving and Giving

GOOD BEHAVIOUR

MOLLY KEANE

Introduced by Maggie O'Farrell

A VIRAGO
MODERN CLASSIC

VIRAGO

First published in hardback in Great Britain in 1981 by André Deutsch Ltd
First published in paperback in Great Britain in 1982 by Abacus
Published by Virago Press in 2001
This paperback edition published in 2025 by Virago Press

1 3 5 7 9 10 8 6 4 2

A CIP catalogue record for this book
is available from the British Library.

ISBN 978-0-34901-960-4

Typeset in Goudy by M Rules
Printed and bound in Great Britain by
Clays Ltd, Elcograf S.p.A.

Papers used by Virago are from well-managed forests
and other responsible sources.

MIX
Paper | Supporting responsible forestry
FSC® C104740

Virago Press
An imprint of
Little, Brown Book Group
Carmelite House
50 Victoria Embankment
London EC4Y 0DZ

The authorised representative
in the EEA is
Hachette Ireland
8 Castlecourt Centre
Dublin 15, D15 XTP3, Ireland
(email: info@hbgi.ie)

An Hachette UK Company
www.hachette.co.uk

www.virago.co.uk

INTRODUCTION

Molly Keane hadn't published a word for twenty years when, so the story goes, a visitor to her house chanced upon a manuscript languishing in a drawer. The visitor was actress Peggy Ashcroft, the novel *Good Behaviour*; she read the manuscript and urged Keane to submit it for publication.

It's easy to see why Ashcroft might have been immediately struck by the book. *Good Behaviour* has a quiet, measured confidence to it. You can feel, from the first line, that this is an author at the top of her game. The characters are glass-clear, the dialogue piercingly accurate, the pacing leisurely yet muscular, the prose deceptively delicate, carrying the resilience and sting of a scorpion. Quite simply, there isn't a word out of place.

Critics have long speculated about the hiatus in Keane's career, suggesting she was unable to work after her husband's death or that the unfavourable reception of her 1961 play gave her writer's block. I've always found it refreshing that Keane refused to be drawn on what lay behind her prolonged wordlessness. Why should she explain herself, especially when the work that broke the silence was of such searing quality?

On its appearance in print, *Good Behaviour* was seized upon as an astonishing late flowering for its septuagenarian author. Malcolm Bradbury called it 'an extraordinary tour de force'; elsewhere it was 'a distinguised comeback' and 'a masterpiece'. Shortlisted for the 1981 Booker Prize, it narrowly missed out on winning to Salman Rushdie's *Midnight's Children*.

Molly Keane had a variety of names. She was born Mary Nesta Skrine in 1904 in County Kildare to a 'rather serious hunting and fishing, church-going family'. She was educated, as was the custom in Anglo-Irish households, by a series of governesses and then at boarding school, where she said her 'unpopularity, that went to the edge of dislike, drove me into myself.' Life at home wasn't much better: 'my mother didn't really like me and . . . my father had absolutely nothing to do with me.' Distant and awkward relationships between children and their parents would prove to be a recurring theme for Keane. She began writing as a teenager in order, so she claimed, to supplement her dress allowance, producing numerous novels and plays under the name M. J. Farrell. She said in an interview with Polly Devlin in 1983 that the pseudonym was essential because, 'for a woman to read a book, let alone write one, was viewed with alarm; I would have been banned from every respectable house.' She married Robert Keane in 1938 and had two daughters. Then came the famous two-decade silence and then *Good Behaviour*, the first novel she published under her own name.

It begins with a murder. Aroon St Charles is struggling for supremacy over her mother's lunch tray with the servant, Rose. Aroon has prepared a rabbit mousse for Mummie but

Rose objects, saying that 'rabbit sickens her'. Aroon pulls rank – 'I can use the tone of voice which keeps people in their places' – serves her mother the mousse, at which point Mummie protests, vomits and dies.

Rabbit mousse. Is there a more unappealing dish to be found in fiction? But worse is to come. Just when you think Keane is about to round off her perfect opening scene, mesmeric in its impact, she sends a parting shot over the bows. As Aroon leaves the deathbed, she instructs Rose to put the mousse over some hot water, to keep it warm for her own 'luncheon'. It's one of the most appalling moments in the book. Surely, *surely*, you think, she can't eat it now?

This is matricide most foul, but with a veneer of gentility. Oh, to be so well-bred, so refined as to be killed by a dish of food. As with most things in *Good Behaviour*, Mummie's death is an issue of deeply ingrained social mores. Rabbit in Keane's world is a food more suitable for the lower echelons of society (and children: 'the cook sent up [to the nursery] whatever came easiest, mostly rabbit stews,' Aroon notes). It is available to all from the fields; it is not procured from butchers, sanitised and billed-for. Mummie's shrinking refusal of the mousse – she would, quite literally, rather die than eat it – is an act of propriety, of protest, of self-elevation. It is her final act of 'good behaviour'.

Good Behaviour is Keane coming back, as if from the dead, with a novel much concerned with the infinitesimal calibrations of society and kin. The Anglo-Irish occupied a strange position in 1920s Ireland, the time in which the book is set. A breed apart, poverty-stricken yet proud, they were struggling to keep their niche in a changing country.

Aroon's flowing recall of her past offers glimpses of this

peculiar, hermetic world. Boys are beaten for reading poetry, grocers are called 'robbers' for sending in their bills, dogs are fed chicken while the servants are forced to eat laundry starch to stave off hunger, terrified children are put on horses at a remarkably young age, a nanny is dismissed for drunkenness but still given a good reference because to do otherwise 'would have been unkind and unnecessary'. The proper way to conduct oneself in all matters is to employ selective silence: Papa has affairs with the staff right under Mummie's nose but nothing is said; a beloved governess commits suicide but nothing is said; the son of the house is killed but nothing is said. 'We exchanged cool, warning looks,' Aroon says, after her brother's funeral: 'which of us could behave best: which of us could be least embarrassing to the others?'

The unspoken hangs like smoke in the rooms and corridors of Temple Alice. What is uttered are small asides, loaded with venom: 'They say whales can live for months on their own fat – do they call it blubber?' Mummie observes to Aroon, while outlining her economy drive, which boils down to neither of them having anything to eat. Food is a constant flashpoint between mother and daughter. Aroon feels herself to be ugly, enormous, ungainly, taller than is acceptable, 'bosoms, swinging like jelly bags,' forever cursed as the plain daughter of a beautiful mother. Much of the emotional heart of the book is Aroon's overwhelming urge to love – and be loved. All around her people are forming partnerships and allegiances, but none of them include her. Her mother with her father, her father with Rose, her brother Hubert with his friend Richard, and then her mother with Rose. Aroon is always on the outside looking in, always the unwanted hanger-on, the gooseberry.

The most painful thread running through the book is Aroon's misplaced love for Richard. This is where Keane's skill with an unreliable narrator comes into play: the reader realises pretty quickly that Hubert and Richard are in love with each other. But Aroon is convinced that something exists between her and Richard, remaining ever alert for signs, joyous at her inclusion in their outings, heart-rendingly unaware that her brother is using her to put their father off the scent. She is baffled by an evening when she arrives unannounced at their room to find Richard belting up his dressing-gown 'with exacting discretion' and Hubert 'wrapped in one of those great rough bath towels', both distinctly unenthusiastic at seeing her. When she leaves them, she hears them 'begin to laugh, relieved giggling laughter'. The experience leaves her 'puzzled and anxious . . . [with] a mistrust in happiness.'

Keane pulls up short of making Aroon the faultless martyr. The book is too subtle, too dark, for that. Aroon is offered an escape from icy, comfortless Temple Alice in the form of Kiely, the solicitor. '"When you need someone," he said, "will you think of me?"' Aroon, in extremis, proves herself to be her mother's daughter, dismissing him with 'one of Mummie's phrases': '"You must be out of your mind," I said . . . I was, after all, Aroon St Charles.'

Molly Keane is often categorised as a comedic writer, a satirist of drawing-room chatter, of interminable balls and horrendous social gatherings. But to view her as a kind of Hibernian Noel Coward is to do her a disservice. Yes, her books are shot through with painful parties and awkwardly inane dining-table conversation, but her themes are vast, universal, Shakespearean in their reach: inheritance, survival, familial love, intergenerational strife, bereavement, betrayal, marriage, adultery, murder. She writes better than anyone else about the mother–daughter relationship, in all its thorny, fraught, inescapable complexity.

The title of the novel is ironic, because the way these people conduct themselves is nothing short of execrable – and also mutable. 'Good behaviour' at the start means keeping oneself upright and benign in the face of adversity. By the end it has become a byword for enacting cruelty and revenge on your nearest relatives, all, of course, with the utmost subtlety and discretion.

In the closing scene of *Good Behaviour*, Aroon learns that her father has bequeathed Temple Alice to her, not Mummie. It is at once a relief and a terror to see Aroon finally come into her own, to step out of the shadow, the threat of lovelessness. She surveys the cowering, shocked partnership of Mummie and Rose: 'Empowered by Papa's love I would be kind to them. Now I had the mild, wonderful power to be kind, or to reserve kindness.' We, of course, have already been witness to where that power and kindness ends. Keane gives her masterpiece a beautifully looping structure that turns back on itself, like a Möbius strip, linking the beginning with the end. When Aroon says, 'remember that I'll always look after you,' we know what she means, and so does Mummie. You can almost smell the rabbit mousse coming.

Maggie O'Farrell, 2011

CHAPTER ONE

Rose smelt the air, considering what she smelt; a miasma of unspoken criticism and disparagement fogged the distance between us. I knew she ached to censure my cooking, but through the years I have subdued her. Those wide shoulders and swinging hips were once parts of a winged quality she had – a quality reduced and corrected now, I am glad to say.

'I wonder are you wise, Miss Aroon, to give her the rabbit?'

'And why not?' I can use the tone of voice which keeps people in their places and usually silences any interference from Rose. Not this time.

'Rabbit sickens her. Even Master Hubert's first with his first gun. She couldn't get it down.'

'That's a very long time ago. And I've often known her to enjoy rabbit since then.'

'She never liked rabbit.'

'Especially when she thought it was chicken.'

'You couldn't deceive her, Miss Aroon.' She picked up the tray. I snatched it back. I knew precisely what she would say when she put it down on Mummie's bed. I had set the tray myself. I don't trust Rose. I don't trust anybody. Because I like things to be right. The tray did look charming: bright, with a crisp clean cloth and a shine on everything. I lifted the silver lid off the hot plate to smell those quenelles in a cream sauce. There was just a hint of bay leaf and black pepper, not a breath of the rabbit foundation. Anyhow, what could be more delicious and delicate than a baby rabbit? Especially after it has been forced through a fine sieve and whizzed for ten minutes in a Moulinex blender.

'I'll take up the tray,' I said. 'When the kettle boils, please fill the pink hotwater-bottle. It makes a little change from the electric blanket. Did you hear me? Rose?' She has this maddening pretence of deafness. It is simply one of her ways of ignoring me. I know that. I have known it for most of my life.

'I see in today's paper where a woman in Kilmacthomas burned to death in an electric blanket. It turned into a flaming cage, imagine.'

I paid no attention to the woman in the blanket and I repeated: 'When the kettle boils and not before.' That would give me time to settle Mummie comfortably with her luncheon before Rose brought the hotwater-bottle and the tale of the woman in Kilmacthomas (who I bet did something particularly silly and the blanket was quite blameless) into her bedroom.

Gulls' Cry, where Mummie and I live now, is built on the edge of a cliff. Its windows lean out over the deep anchorage of the boat cove like bosoms on an old ship's figurehead. Sometimes I think (though I would never say it) how nice that bosoms are all right to have now; in the twenties when I grew up I used to tie them down with a sort of binder. Bosoms didn't do then. They didn't do at all. Now, it's too late for mine.

I like to sing when nobody can hear me and put me off the note. I sang that day as I went upstairs. Our kitchen and diningroom are on the lowest level of this small Gothic folly of a house. The stairs, with their skimpy iron bannister, bring you up to the hall and the drawingroom, where I put all our mementoes of Papa when we moved here from Temple Alice. The walls are papered in pictures and photographs of him riding winners. Silver cups stand in rows on the chimney-piece, not to mention the model of a seven-pound sea trout and several rather misty snapshots of bags of grouse laid out on the steps of Temple Alice.

Mummie never took any proper interest in this gallery, and when her heart got so dicky, and I converted the room into a charming bed-sit for her, she seemed to turn her eyes away from everything she might have remembered with love and pleasure. One knows sick people and old people can be difficult and unrewarding, however much one does for them: not exactly ungrateful, just absolutely maddening. But I enjoy the room whenever I go in. It's all my own doing and Mummie, lying back in her nest of pretty pillows, is my doing too – I insist on her being scrupulously clean and washed and scented.

'Luncheon,' I said cheerfully, the tray I carried making a lively rattle. 'Shall I sit you up a bit?' She was lying down among her pillows as if she were sinking through the bed. She never makes an effort for herself. That comes of having me.

'I don't feel very hungry,' she said. A silly remark. I know she always pretends she can't eat and when I go out makes Rose do her fried eggs and buttered toast and all the things the doctor says she mustn't touch.

'Smell that,' I said, and lifted the cover off my perfect quenelles.

'I wonder if you'd pull down the blind –' not a word about the quenelles – 'the sun's rather in my eyes.'

'You really want the blind down?'

She nodded.

'All the way?'

'Please.'

I went across then and settled her for her tray, pulling her up and putting a pillow in the exact spot behind her back, and another tiny one behind her head. She simply refused to look as if she felt comfortable. I'm used to that. I arranged the basket tray (straight from Harrods) across her, and put her luncheon tray on it.

'Now then,' I said – one must be firm – 'a delicious chicken mousse.'

'Rabbit, I bet,' she said.

I was still patient: 'Just try a forkful.'

'Myxomatosis,' she said. 'Remember that? – I can't.'

I held on to my patience. 'It was far too young to have myxomatosis. Come on now, Mummie –' I tried to keep the firm note out of my voice – 'just one.'

She lifted the small silver fork (our crest, a fox rampant, almost handled and washed away by use) as though she were heaving up a load of stinking fish: 'The smell – I'm—' She gave a trembling, tearing cry, vomited dreadfully, and fell back into the nest of pretty pillows.

I felt more than annoyed for a moment. Then I looked at her and I was frightened. I leaned across the bed and rang her bell. Then I shouted and called down to Rose in the kitchen. She came up fast, although her feet and her shoes never seem to work together now; even then I noticed it. But of course I notice everything.

'She was sick,' I said.

'She couldn't take the rabbit?'

Rabbit again. 'It was a mousse,' I screamed at the old fool, 'a cream mousse. It was perfect. I made it so I ought to know. It was RIGHT. She was enjoying it.'

Rose was stooping over Mummie. 'Miss Aroon, she's gone.' She crossed herself and started to pray in that loose, easy way Roman Catholics do: 'Holy Mary, pray for us now and in the hour of our death . . . Merciful Jesus . . . '

She seemed too close to Mummie with that peasant gabbling prayer. We should have had the Dean.

'Take the tray away,' I said. I picked Mummie's hand up out of the sick and put it down in a clean place. It was as limp as a dead duck's neck. I wanted to cry out. 'Oh, no—' I wanted to say. I controlled myself. I took three clean tissues out of the cardboard box I had covered in shell-pink brocade and wiped my fingers. When they were clean the truth came to me, an awful new-born monstrosity. I suppose I swayed on my feet. I felt as if I could go on falling for ever. Rose helped me to a chair and I could hear its joints screech as I sat down, although I am not at all heavy, considering my height. I longed to ask somebody to do me a favour, to direct me; to fill out this abyss with some importance – something needful to be done.

'What must I do now?' I was asking myself. Rose had turned her back on me and on the bed. She was opening the window as high as the sash would go – that's one of their superstitions, something to do with letting the spirit go freely. They do it. They don't speak of it. She did the same thing when Papa died.

'You must get the doctor at once, Miss Aroon, and Kathie Cleary to lay her out. There's no time to lose.'

She said it in a gluttonous way. They revel in death ... Keep the Last Rites going ... She can't wait to get her hands on Mummie, to get me out of the way while she helps Mrs Cleary in necessary and nasty rituals. What could I do against them? I had to give over. I couldn't forbid. Or could I?

'I shall get the doctor,' I said, 'and Nurse Quinn. *Not* Mrs Cleary.'

She faced me across the bed, her great blue eyes blazing. 'Miss Aroon, madam hated Nurse Quinn. The one time she gave her a needle she took a weakness. She wouldn't let her in the place again. She wouldn't let her touch her. Kathie Cleary's a dab hand with a corpse – there's nothing missing in Kathie Cleary's methods and madam loved her, she loved a chat with Kathie Cleary.'

I really felt beside myself. Why this scene? Why can't people do what I say? That's all I ask. 'That will do, Rose,' I said. I felt quite strong again. 'I'll telephone to the doctor and ask him to let Nurse know. Just take that tray down and keep the mousse hot for my luncheon.'

Rose lunged towards me, over the bed, across Mummie's still feet. I think if she could have caught me in both her hands she would have done so.

'Your lunch,' she said. 'You can eat your bloody lunch and she lying there stiffening every minute. Rabbit – rabbit chokes her, rabbit sickens her, and rabbit killed her – call it rabbit if you like. Rabbit's a harmless word for it – if it was a smothering you couldn't have done it better. And – another thing – who tricked her out of Temple Alice? Tell me that—'

'Rose, how dare you.' I tried to interrupt her but she stormed on.

'... and brought my lady into this mean little ruin with hungry gulls screeching over it and two old ghosts (God rest their souls) knocking on the floors by night—'

I stayed calm above all the wild nonsense. 'Who else hears the knocking?' I asked her quietly. 'Only you.'

'And I heard the roaring and crying when you parted Mister Hamish from Miss Enid and put the two of them in hospital wards, male and female, to die on their own alone.'

'At the time it was totally necessary.'

'Necessary? That way you could get this house in your own two hands and boss and bully us through the years. Madam's better off the way she is this red raw minute. She's tired from you – tired to death. Death is right. We're all killed from you and it's a pity it's not yourself lying there and your toes cocked for the grave and not a word more about you, God damn you!'

Yes, she stood there across the bed saying these obscene, unbelievable things. Of course she loved Mummie, all servants did. Of course she was overwrought. I know all that – and she is ignorant to a degree, I allow for that too. Although there was a shocking force in what she said to me, it was beyond all sense or reason. It was so entirely and dreadfully false that it could not touch me. I felt as tall as a tree standing above all that passionate flood of words. I was determined to be kind to Rose. And understanding. And generous. I am her employer, I thought. I shall raise her wages quite substantially. She will never be able to resist me then, because she is greedy. I can afford to be kind to Rose. She will learn to lean on me.

There is nobody in the world who needs me now and I must be kind to somebody.

'You're upset,' I said gently. 'Naturally you're upset. You loved Mrs St Charles and I know you didn't mean one word you've just said to me.'

'I did too, Miss Aroon.' She was like a drowning person, coming up for a last choking breath. 'God help you, it's the flaming truth.'

'Don't worry,' I answered. 'I've forgotten . . . I didn't hear . . . I understand. Now we've both got to be practical. We must both be brave. I'll ring up the doctor and you'll take that tray to the kitchen, and put the mousse over a pot of boiling water – it may be hours till lunchtime.'

She took up the tray, tears pouring down her face. Of course I had expected her to obey me, but I won't deny that before she turned away from the bed, the tray, as it should have been, between her hands, I had been aware of a moment of danger. Now, apart from my shock and sorrow about Mummie, a feeling of satisfaction went through me – a kind of ripple that I needed. I needed it and I had it.

I went into the hall and picked up the telephone. While I waited for the exchange (always criminally slow) to answer, I had time to consider how the punctual observance of the usual importances is the only way to behave at such times as these. And I do know how to behave – believe me, because I know. I have always known. All my life so far I have done everything for the best reasons and the most unselfish motives. I have lived for the people dearest to me, and I am at a loss to know why their lives have been at times so perplexingly unhappy. I have given them so much, I have given them everything, all I know how to give – Papa, Hubert,

Richard, Mummie. At fifty-seven my brain is fairly bright, brighter than ever I sometimes think, and I have a cast-iron memory. If I look back beyond any shadow into the uncertainties and glories of our youth, perhaps I shall understand more about what became of us.

CHAPTER TWO

When Hubert and I were children and after we grew up we lived at Temple Alice. Temple Alice had been built by Mummie's ancestor, before he inherited his title and estates. He built the house for his bride, and he gave it her name. Now, the title extinct and the estates entirely dissipated, Temple Alice, after several generations as a dower house, came to Mummie when her mother died. Papa farmed the miserably few hundred acres that remained of the property. Mummie loved gardening. On fine days she would work in the woodland garden, taking the gardener away from his proper duties among the vegetables. On wet days she spent hours of time in the endless, heatless, tumbling-down greenhouses, which had once sheltered peaches and nectarines and stephanotis. One vine survived – she knew how to prune it and thin its grapes, muscatels. Papa loved them.

Her painting was another interest to take the place of the social life she loathed. A pity for herself that she was so withdrawn a character. *Recluse* would be a truer word to describe her. She could have had such a lovely time gadding round with Papa – hunting and race meetings and all those shoots. But she was really frightened of horses, and if she did go to a race-meeting, in Papa's riding days, she would shut her eyes during his race, and once when he was to ride a bad jumper she got drunk in the bar and fell down in the Owners and Trainers. She simply could not endure the anxiety about him.

I don't understand what it was that held them together – they never had much to say to each other. He had no more understanding of her painting or gardening than she had of horses or fishing or shooting – so what can they have had to talk about?

Once she had a show of her pictures in a London gallery. During a whole year she painted for it. No art critic noticed it. Hardly anybody came in to look – one picture was sold. Even that disastrous experience did not stop her painting. She went on with it, making almost anything she painted look preposterous and curiously hideous too. Give her a bunch of roses to paint – lovely June roses with tear-drops of morning rain on their petals – and she reproduced them as angular, airified shapes in a graveyard atmosphere, unimaginably ugly; but in a crude way you could not forget roses as you looked at this picture in speechless dislike. She would laugh and rub her little hands and shiver – it was deathly cold in her studio.

Nowhere was it possible to sit down in her studio, once a stone-flagged storeroom in the depths of the house. Pyramids of cardboard boxes full of old letters, stacks of newspapers and photographs, old hunting boots, leather boxes that might hold hats or again might be full of letters, all hovered to a fall. A stuffed hedgehog, the dust of years solid between its spines, sat on top of a bird's egg cabinet, empty of eggs, its little drawers full only of dented cottonwool and the smell of camphor. Polo sticks hanging in a bunch and obsolete fishing rods in dusty canvas cases, tied with neat, rotten tapes, showed this house to have been lived in by gentlemen of leisure – my mother's family.

Leisure they may have enjoyed but they knew little about comfort. Our water supply was meagre and my grandfather had deflected a considerable quantity of it to a pond on which, in the shelter of a grove of rhododendrons, he loved to row himself about. It was his escape from the land agent and other buzzing tormentors of a leisured life.

I think, now, that Mummie looked at her studio as her escape from responsibility. She had an enormous distaste for housekeeping. The sort of food we ate then owed nothing to the splendid Elizabeth Davids of the present day. I think Papa would have fainted at the very breath of garlic. It was for his sake only that Mummie expended some extreme essence of herself in bullying and inspiring her treasured cook, Mrs Lennon. I have seen her tremble and go green as she faced the slate on the kitchen table and the deadly quietness of the cook who stood so cheerlessly beside her. While longing only to put on her gauntlets, pick up her trug and trowel and get into the garden or into the blessed isolation of her studio, Mummie would penetrate her cook's mind – praising just a little, demanding always more effort, a higher standard of perfection for the Captain.

When we were children the food in the nursery was quite poisonously disgusting. None of the fruit juice and vitamins of today for us – oranges only at Christmastime and porridge every morning, variable porridge slung together by the kitchen maid, followed by white bread and butter and Golden Syrup. Boiled eggs were for Sundays and sausages for birthdays.

I don't think Mummie gave us a thought – she left the ordering of nursery meals to the cook, who sent up whatever came easiest, mostly rabbit stews and custard puddings riddled with holes. No wonder the nannies left in quick succession.

Why do I hate the word 'crusted'? Because I feel with my lips the boiled milk, crusted since the night before, round the rim of the mug out of which I must finish my breakfast milk . . . I am again in the darkness of the nursery, the curtains drawn against the winter morning outside. Nannie is dragging on her corsets under her great nightdress. Baby Hubert is walking up and down his cot in a dirty nightdress. The nursery maid is pouring paraffin on a sulky nursery fire. I fix my eyes on the strip of morning light where wooden rings join curtains to curtain pole and think about my bantams . . . Even then I knew how to ignore things. I knew how to behave.

I don't blame Mummie for all this. She simply did not want to know what was going on in the nursery. She had had us and she longed to forget the horror of it once and for all. She engaged nannie after nannie with excellent references, and if they could not be trusted to look after us, she was even less able to compete. She didn't really like children; she didn't like dogs either, and she had no enjoyment of food, for she ate almost nothing.

She was sincerely shocked and appalled on the day when the housemaid came to tell her that our final nannie was lying on her bed in a drunken stupor with my brother Hubert beside her in another drunken stupor, while I was lighting a fire in the day nursery with the help of a tin of paraffin. The nannie was sacked, but given quite a good reference with no mention of her drinking; that would have been too unkind and unnecessary, since she promised to reform. Her next charge (only a

Dublin baby) almost died of drink, and its mother wrote a very common, hysterical letter, which Mummie naturally put in the fire and forgot about. Exhausted, bored, and disgusted by nannies, she engaged a governess who would begin my education and at the same time keep an eye on the nursery maid who was to be in charge of Hubert's more menial four-year-old necessities.

CHAPTER THREE

The name of our governess was Mrs Brock and we loved her dearly from the start to the finish of her reign. For one thing, the era of luncheon in the diningroom opened for us with Mrs Brock, and with it a world of desire and satisfaction, for we were as greedy as Papa. Although governesses lunched in the diningroom, they supped on trays upstairs – that was the accepted rule, and Mummie must have been thankful for it as these luncheons meant a horrid disintegration of her times of intimacy with Papa. So much of his day was spent away from her. In the winter months he was shooting or hunting, and in the spring there was salmon fishing – all undertaken and excelled in more as a career and a duty than as the pleasures of a leisured life. In the summer months there was a horse, sometimes horses, to be got ready for the Dublin Show, often evening fishing, and always the supervision of haymaking and harvest with their attendant ghastly weather to worry him. So luncheon and dinner were, I suppose, the brightest hours in her day.

Dinnertime was a formal, nearly a sacred, hour – usually

more like two hours. At half past seven they went upstairs to bathe and change into dinner jacket and teagown. During the months of that legendary summer weather, bathwater was too often the problem, for every house was dependent on its own wells, springs, or streams. In the country there was no main supply of water. This was not a problem to defeat people who looked on the bath before dinner as part of the structure of life. There existed, too, an austerity which forbade complaint. It went with loofahs and Brown Windsor soap and large natural sponges draining out the last of the soft water in netted holders hooked to the rim of the bath.

We never came down to dinner of course, but I knew the candles were always lighted on the table, and spoons and forks and plates, salt-cellars and pepper pots were cleared away before dessert. I don't think they ever had a drink in the drawingroom, not even a glass of sherry – that came with the soup – but they always drank wine and port, and often brandy with their coffee.

I came down only once, because Mrs Brock had gone out and I thought Hubert would die, he was so sick. In spite of the desperate importance of my mission, I stood in the doorway for a whole minute, stunned and silenced by the munificent quality of their intimacy.

The window furthest from where they were sitting was open, and a tide of musky, womanly scent from the wet Portugal laurels drifted in, strong against the delicate smells of strawberries and candle smoke and a breath of past roast chicken. They sat at the far end of the long pale table. Her head was bowed and her eyes were lifted towards him, defeating the heavy gesture of her head. She sat on his right hand. Behind him the green luminous gloom of glass within glass retreated inside the doors of a breakfront cabinet that filled one end of the diningroom. Mummie had lined it with grey linen, so that all glass objects floated and were lost in its spaces. It was like water or air at his back, as though the end wall were open to air or water. The austere outdoor look I knew had melted from him into the air, like the glass in the cupboard. Sitting there, he seemed extraordinarily dulled, dulled and happy. Both their glasses were full and his eyes were downwards on her arms, their flesh firm as partridge breasts. He was speaking to her, asking some question I did not hear.

When they saw me in the doorway, when I said, 'I think Hubert's dead,' he raised his eyes from her arms (it seemed a long time, while Hubert and I were shut out) to her shoulders, to her eyes, and then he visibly let her go. If my dressing-gown had been in flames round me it would have taken them just as long to part. Although they weren't near each other I could not have walked, unless they called me, any nearer to that circle they made.

What happened afterwards is less clear to me than that impression of their impervious intimacy. I don't understand it. Even now, as a sophisticated, quite worldly woman. Not when I have to admit his endless strayings with all the other women who longed after him and won him easily through the years.

Mummie said: 'My dear child – what *can* this mean?'

'Only Hubert's been sick in his bed and he has a dreadful pain. I'm frightened.'

'And Mrs Brock?' she asked.

'She's at choir practice.'

'What a good word for it,' Papa said.

'Everybody's out. There's a dance in the gate lodge. Oh, do come quickly, he may be dead now.'

'Extraordinary, people are,' she said.

Papa got up and put his hands under the lace that covered her shoulders and pressed her down in her chair. 'I'll go. You're hopeless about sick. Finish your drink,' he said.

Papa was wonderful. He picked poor Hubert out of his cot and took off his sleeping suit before he wrapped him up in a hot bath towel from the airing cupboard. I loved every minute of it. I rushed about emptying the pots and finding clean sheets.

When at last Mrs Brock appeared – it must have been almost ten o'clock, and she was full of explanations – he didn't listen and he didn't say a cross word to her. Just: 'Sit down and keep him warm. I think I'd better get hold of the doctor.'

Mrs Brock did exactly what he told her. She kept on her lovely hat, covered deep in roses. She sat there under her hat, Hubert on her knees, a hot statue, smelling of armpits and amber scent, till Papa got back with the doctor.

They took Hubert off to Cork that same night, and he had an appendix and tubes and nearly died. I prayed night and day for his recovery and that he might get a reprieve from pain. Constantly with me was the thought of his black hair, peaked on his forehead, smooth on his head as if painted on an egg. As I cleaned out his budgies and his mice his eyes haunted my work – his eyes that never lit and sparkled as blue eyes should, as I knew mine would, if only they were big and blue.

When at last he came home he was a very great disappointment to me. The nuns in the nursing home had spoiled him so that he was really unbearably demanding, sending me in all directions and inventing tasks for me while he lay on a chaise longue under the cedar tree with lemonade constantly at his elbow. In those days thrombosis had not been heard of, and invalids, young and old, were allowed a comfortable rest after their operations. Hubert even had a po in the bushes 'in case.' Another thing those kind nuns had done was to teach him to say 'the toilet' when he meant the po or the lavatory, which was a vulgarity no one seemed able to straighten out. If circumstances forced Mrs Brock to mention it she called it the Place. 'Have you been to the Place, dear?' or 'Have you *been*?' Or else 'Hubert, shouldn't you run along the passage?' when Hubert was fidgeting frighteningly from foot to foot.

When Mrs Brock succeeded our last, drunk nannie I was seven and Hubert was four. With her in the schoolroom there came to us a daily security in happiness, and with it the delightful prospect of such a state continuing into an untimed future – a future when the budgerigar would speak his first word, when Magical Nature would create a family for the newly married mice, when I would sing 'Two Little Girls in Blue, Dears' in perfect tune. And, exceeding in interest even these prospects, were Mrs Brock's stories of her past pupils, their parents and their way of life – stories as graphic and truly coloured as the Caldecott illustrations to John Gilpin.

Even the servants, who had skirmished endlessly with the nannies, loved Mrs Brock and served her willingly, and at any hour, with cups of tea. She was smallish and on the fat side, but neat as a bird. Perhaps she had more of a flowerlike quality, a tidy pink-tipped daisy. Her cheeks were firm and pink, her hair was crisp and more blond than grey, her false teeth gleamed fresh as dew every morning of her life. She was the widow of an organist who had saved very little money before he died at a medium sort of age, leaving her (fortunately childless, though she longed for kiddies of her own) to drag a living from a world out of which she had been cosily embedded in a nice little house with a nice little man who had a nice and not so little job in a large London parish. Mrs Brock was musical too; just how musical I don't know, but she had sung in her husband's choir, and when she came to us the Bechstein upright piano shuddered deeply under the full treatment which she gave the 'Indian Love Lyrics,' with the 'Rustle of Spring' never very far behind.

Her first job after her husband died was that of governess in a bishop's family, where, with the help of Mrs Markham's *History of England* and Gill's *Geography*, she gave every satisfaction until schooldays closed her employment in that family. Her next pupils, Richard, Sholto, and Raymond, were the sons of Papa's great friend Wobbly Massingham, a master of foxhounds and lord of the manor of Stoke Charity. Here Captain Massingham pursued, in a now legendary sort of splendour, a life of hunting, shooting, fishing, cricketing weeks, Epsom, Ascot, Goodwood, Newmarket, and Doncaster – a life which rather depleted the inheritance to be expected by Mrs Brock's three pupils. But at least they were down for Eton, and you can't take Eton away. Mrs Brock's task was to prepare them for their preparatory school. This was not difficult, as Entwhistle's was only too ready to accept the right sort of boy; and if his father and uncles were Old Boys he could be the right sort of moron and welcome. Of Mrs Brock's pupils, Sholto was the most likely to succeed. A child of few words, greedy in a jolly way, and brutally determined with his pony, he would go further with less effort than his elder brother, Richard.

Richard was Mrs Brock's favourite, and years afterwards she was to be my first intimate link with him. His curiosity about her held a privacy as exciting to Hubert and me as the shared tree houses or the secret rude rhymes of childhood. We would piece her together; it was a game in which our memories interlocked or contradicted recollections. He could say oddly unkind things about her, and I could deny her too. But I never told about the mice. What nice girl would?

Richard was a beautiful child and, despite a proper interest in and aptitude for all the importances of outdoor life, there were times when he would lean in silence against Mrs Brock as she played the piano, or even join her in singing 'Speed Bonnie Boat,' 'Yip-i-addy,' or 'Now the Day Is Over.' He preferred Mrs Tiggywinkle to the mildest comic, and liked to dwell on the idea of her transference from the washerwoman to the wild. He liked dressing up, too, but Mrs Brock felt that such games were not quite the thing for little boys. Sometimes she allowed herself to read him her favourite pieces from *The Children's Golden Treasury of Verse*, when they would charge with the Light Brigade, or even lean from the gold bar of heaven with the Blessed Damozel.

Raymond was the youngest of the boys and the least likeable. He was a delicate child, and Nannie's darling. He hated his pony. He kicked the dogs when he could do so without being observed or bitten. There was nothing nice or open about him. He in no way resembled his elder brothers. Although he only touched the fringes of schoolroom life – simple Bible stories and an hour of picture bricks – he usually carried some whining tale back to the nursery, where Nannie sat, brooding and mending the linen – spinning in her tower. Nannie was old enough to have been Lady Grizel

Massingham's nannie and she had never been sympathetically inclined towards governesses.

Mrs Brock conceived a senseless star-struck passion for Lady Grizel. Her eyes and her ears absorbed the sight and sound of this cool, contented lady, whose language differed from Mrs Brock's in being as natural as a peasant's. She looked downwards and spoke rather like a child. Quite simple, grown-up words, such as 'gardening' got lost. Lady Grizel (and now Mrs Brock, of course) would say instead, 'She's diggin' up the garden.' I can't think why Mrs Brock had never ascertained from her the definitive name for W.C.

When Lady Grizel gave Mrs Brock not one, but two grey flannel suits, Nannie made no secret of her disapproval. But Mrs Brock's acceptance of the gifts was simple and delighted. They had been made, she told us, by Busvine – that holy tailoring name in the holy hunting world – made three and five years previously, of course, but classical tailor-mades never go out of fashion. Other kind gifts included a pair of indestructible and eternally right shoes from Peter Yapp. For some unknown reason these shoes, although made on Lady Grizel's own last and all that, were never entirely comfortable, and old Yapp could never improve their fit. They were never entirely comfortable on Mrs Brock's feet either, but she wore them with persistence and courage until at last they became docile friends.

A strange thing about those shoes was the way in which, when she was wearing them, Mrs Brock, who was a heavy treader by nature, planted her feet and walked with the same long steps as Lady Grizel, and stood in the same careless, rather flighty way. A lovely sort of fantasy possessed Mrs Brock as she moved in this new pretty way, this confident way. Part of herself became Lady Grizel – she absorbed Lady Grizel and breathed her out into the air around herself, and the air around was a far less lonely place in consequence.

All that Mrs Brock's grateful heart and tiny brain could contrive in return for these favours was to knit – and for knitting she had true flair and genius. In the schoolroom she would sit alone in a loving glow as frail clouds of wool grew through her clever fingers into wraps and misty bedwear for Lady Grizel's birthday or Christmas presents.

Nannie showed nothing but cold amusement when asked to admire these voluptuous clouds knitted with such speed and skill. She felt Mrs Brock's time would be better employed in organising wholesome outdoor sports for the boys. Nannie herself still bowled to them with a hard ball and had often been heard to shout above any childish uproar: 'Now, now, *do* stop this quarrellin', boys, and let's have a nice talk about huntin'.'

There came a day when every soul in the big house was alerted in the search for a ring which Lady Grizel had lost – her engagement ring – star sapphire and diamonds. But sapphire and diamonds were as nothing compared to its romantic value. No one had stolen it. No one suspected anybody else of stealing it, and everybody longed and burned to find it.

Nobody was more filled with longing and burning than Mrs Brock, and she set about the business of the search with meticulous generalship. She plotted every step Lady Grizel had taken on the day of her loss, living the day vicariously and minute by minute. And on this day more than on any other she projected herself into the absolute life of Lady Grizel.

We too shared in the day's life, and a very long and dull day it was, until the paradisaical moment when, in the evening dusk of the flower room, where, besides doing the flowers, Lady Grizel faithfully composed, from a selection of goodies sent daily from the kitchen, the dogs' dinners, Mrs Brock found the ring hanging, its glitter downwards, its gold unremarkable, on the brass tap of the flower-room sink. Here Lady Grizel – now she remembered – had washed her hands after pinching her way through the Peke's dinner, eliminating the danger from chicken bones. How Lady Grizel loved that dog. 'Oh, Changy, why do your little feet smell of mice?' she would ask him with tears in her eyes.

But to return, as we so often did, to that extraordinary day, that May evening when Mrs Brock made her unexpected appearance in the library. The library was unfamiliar and fearful territory not to be enjoyed by her. It was, as Richard described it to us, an ordinary room of its date and kind, arranged without any feeling that went further than expensive comfort. There was a great dullness about the crowding pictures, as if ignorance of their interest and worth had fogged them. The eighteenth-century gentlemen in their Tailor of Gloucester waistcoats retreated sulking into their century. Only racehorses, of the School of Herring, faithful dogs, and a famous stallion hound were given full importance. Hung where they could be seen and enjoyed, they shared the best light with amusing Spi cartoons. Hepplewhite sofas and loveseats had all been expelled. The present furniture had an assured, comfortable permanence. On club fender and sofas dark red leather was buttoned firmly into place. Low armchairs bulged tidily under their thick, starched covers. Brass-bound tubs of flowers from the greenhouses stood in appropriate spaces, gardeners' prides in plenty, but no exotics. Romantically invading all that was prosaic, the scent from sheaves of lilies of the valley (arranged in silver vases, tulip shaped, by Lady Grizel herself) throbbed and drifted on the after-tea air.

This was the hour when the men had disappeared into the smoking room and the women gossiped and yawned, and the dogs turned and yawned in their baskets. Two of Lady Grizel's best friends, Mrs Gladwyn-Chetwynd and Lady Skendleby, were together on the leather sofa. A haze of frilled blouses rose up from their belted waists to frail high collars, boned to the chin line. They sat in a drowse of consideration over their day's off-course betting, no results known till the next morning's papers. They were a bit uncertain whether or not Mrs Brock was to be introduced to them, so picked up *Racing Form* and the last *Calendar* and went back to Newmarket or Doncaster or Epsom – Mrs Brock was not quite clear on the meeting.

The group could hardly have been further removed from Mrs Brock standing in the doorway. Lady Grizel got up and went towards her, scolding and cuffing the dogs back into their baskets while at the same time agreeing with them that this was something of a surprise, an intrusion.

'Quiet, quiet, *will* you be quiet – heavens, you know Mrs Brock – yes, Mrs Brock?'

A query must have hung visibly on the air, the scented air, the distant air of Lady Grizel's life among her own friends. But Mrs Brock broke through the restraints and skipped the distances. 'I believe you lost something, Lady Grizel' was all she said as she held out the ring.

'Mrs Brock – how divine! How wonderful!' All the dogs barked again. The air rang with excitement. Lady Grizel glowed with gratitude. The diamonds sparkled hugely. The best friends jumped up from the sofa and entered into the drama – 'But how too clever.' 'And what made you look in the dogs' dinners?' they exclaimed, getting the facts wrong at once, and handing the ring to each other without praising it.

Then Mrs Brock had the inspiration that was to be her joy and her undoing. That was when her feet left the ground and she soared into unreality. She ignored all remembrance of her day of exhaustive detective work, the hours she had spent tracing every move Lady Grizel had made, as she answered dreamily: 'I really don't know myself. I just closed my eyes and let a picture float up into my mind.'

'Ha-ha, doggie dindins floatin' about. Too funny.'

'Chang-Chang heard you say "dindins" – didn't you, boy?'

'I say, Mrs Brock, would it work out over racing? Would the winner of the 3.30 tomorrow float up to you?'

'Don't be silly, Violet—'

'It's such an open race – her guess is as good as mine – look – I'll read out the runners – you shut your eyes and float . . . Peeping Thomas . . . '

Peeping Thomas, something told her. And told her correctly, miraculously; for this outsider's win was to remain for ever one of the most mysterious upsets to form, embarrassment to the handicapper and legendary boon to bookmakers, as indeed it was to Lady Grizel, her best friends, most of the domestic staff at Stoke Charity, and many of those employed on the estate. Taken together with the discovery of the ring, this triumph put Mrs Brock in the class of visionaries. Hubert and I would implore her to try out her powers at Limerick Junction or Mallow races. 'No,' she would say firmly, 'not again. That time I heard the drumming hooves. I saw the flash of colours . . . '

'And did you hear the jockeys cursing, Mrs Brock?' we would ask. We wanted to belong to the whole magic of the vision.

'No, dear, I didn't. I just heard the great crowd shouting, "Come on – come on, Peeping Thomas."'

'They don't usually shout so much when an outsider wins.'

'They did that day. In my ear,' Mrs Brock stated firmly. Unfortunately, her selection for that year's Derby finished down the course. Although everybody was most generous and considerate about her failure, there was a sense of disappointment not entirely appeased when she came up with the second in the Oaks, given with a caution on an each-way bet. After this, her questioners and followers tempered her advice with that of their favourite tipster. But with domestic losses the dramas mounted daily. The strangest objects were lost and found, as well as the most ordinary.

'What kind of things?' we always asked, the list was so varied and lively. The dogs' leads: Lady Grizel lost one a day, her plaintive cries of 'Help! Help! Where did I put it down?' echoing often and pleasantly in the schoolroom. The cook's spectacles, the odd pillowcase missing from the laundry list; keys, of course, were high among the losses; earrings even figured when the second footman, Walter, rather a dear boy, came to tell her privately that he had lost one of a pair given him by a friend. After a little talk to put her in touch with the pantry world and a couple of hours' floating, the earring reappeared in a plate of chicken sandwiches Mrs Brock was having for her supper, along with a cup of hot consommé, followed by raspberries and cream. 'Your earring,' she said, quite simply, when Walter came in to take away her tray.

'Oh, Mrs Brock, wherever was it?'

'It came to me' was all she told him.

This was a time when Mrs Brock had the entrée to all sorts of private dramas. Her gift put her in a dreamlike position of importance. Even to herself she did not admit that it was her powers of detection, her valid interest in the lives of other people, which gave her the thread to follow in their losses. Having done her homework thoroughly, she would, as it were, get inside her own infallibility and pull down the blind. 'I don't know yet. I've got one of my feelings coming on . . . '

There were two members of the household who refused to join the circle of excitement and interest created by the exercise of Mrs Brock's strange powers. The more considerable of the unbelievers was Nannie; the lesser was horrid Raymond. Nannie was among the few who had stuck to her own fancy in the 3.30 so had not shared in the Peeping Thomas bonanza. When her fancy finished down the course she simply expressed her own opinion, which was that Mrs Brock's powers of divination were neither natural nor quite nice. But Raymond was the catalyst for disaster. Raymond was a sloven and a malign sloven too.

'Why, Raymond,' Mrs Brock asked him, 'are you using Sholto's hairbrush?'

'Mine's lost.'

'Lost? You haven't been grooming the guinea-pigs again?' Already divination stirred.

'Oh no. Those rotten guineas are hatching again. They eat their young if you groom them.'

'Don't be disgusting, dear.'

'Nannie says so.'

'Perhaps. If it's not with the guineas, when did you use it last?'

'Brushing my own hair.'

'When?'

'Lunchtime. In the bathroom.'

'What about teatime?'

'Nannie brushed my hair in the nursery.'

'Then go and ask Nannie where it is. Nip to it now – be a first-time childy.'

'It's not in the nursery.'

'Nonsense. How can you know if you don't ask?'

'Because I can see it looking at me, that's why. Can't you? Can't you, Mrs Brock?'

Stalwart and solid, usually humane, Richard and Sholto joined in the tease. They didn't know where the hairbrush was themselves, but they jumped up and down, shouting: 'We can see it, we can see it too. Find it, Mrs Brock. Go seek!' they cried as if she were a dog. She was confused and mortified. There was nothing jolly for her about the situation. When Nannie came in, with an enquiry for a torn jersey, the matter worsened. They danced round chanting: 'Mrs Brock can't find the hairbrush – hairbrush – hairbrush!' And Raymond squealed, 'Mister Brock's a badger – smelly old badger!'

'Now, now, steady yourselves.' Nannie spoke, in a moment restoring order and authority, although towards Raymond she suppressed a smile. 'I should leave the whole thing to Mrs Brock. I shouldn't be surprised if one of her feelings isn't coming on. Bedtime, boys, and give her a chance.'

'I've told Raymond to find his own hairbrush.' Mrs Brock's voice was less than steady. 'I don't really have time for such a nursery nit . . . wit,' she added, after taking a breath.

How had the word popped into her mind, or out of her

mouth? It stung Nannie in a vital, secret spot. Once, long ago, there had been just that trouble in her own sacred nursery – caught of course from the gate-lodge children as surely as ringworm came from calves.

'I don't think,' she spoke in her most foxhunting voice, 'that any of us quite heard what's just been said, Mrs Brock. Perhaps you'll think again before you repeat your remark. It's not exactly what we're accustomed to in our nursery.'

That was how the loss of confidence and happiness began. The joking approaches, the laughing asides grew into a mild kind of persecution. Only kind people, Lady Grizel, Julia, the head housemaid, and Walter, still brought her their losses and mislayings. To compensate for her frequent failures in detection and to retain their grateful interest she would knit furiously: a cardigan for Walter, a jersey for Julia, and for Lady Grizel a cloud of purest Shetland wool, light as feathers in a breeze, billowed towards completion. She longed to see Lady Grizel sit up among her pillows, arranged in this pink cloud. But Mrs Brock held no possible entrée to Lady Grizel's bedroom – her place was the schoolroom, 'her schoolroom.' At luncheon in the diningroom, where she had been inspired and eloquent in the family game – inventing conversation, spiced with sharp repartee – between Lady Grizel's precious Chang and the Captain's terriers, Spice, Spider, and Grips, all silent in the tranced discipline of their baskets; where once she had come up with a forgotten cricketing score, and – in the crown of her heyday, such was her euphoric application – had even known the top price at Newmarket sales and the breeding of the yearling that made it, she was silent now.

'If she would apply her mind to geography,' Nannie said in

a holy rather than a foxhunting voice, when Lady Grizel remarked upon this surprising change. 'Only last Thursday Richard had no idea of the capital cities of Europe. And Mr Entwhistle won't be very pleased about that.'

CHAPTER FOUR

The Cambridgeshire came and went and nobody asked Mrs Brock what she thought about it. Perhaps they had grown tired of hearing her say 'a very open race.' Now she sat silent in the diningroom and spent longer hours enclosed in her schoolroom, thudding away at the piano. Sholto, tone deaf, would talk to his hamster or tease a dog, unheeding; but Richard, leaning against the throbbing piano, was secretly affected. This first experience of music delighted him. He found it strangely preferable to the approved outdoor sports.

'She never takes the boys for a decent nature walk these days,' he overheard Nannie report to his mother. 'Remember when you could hardly get into our nursery for acorns sprouting and tadpoles – well it's one of the ways of breaking it to them nicely, at least that's what *I* think, and from there it's just a step on to their rabbits and they can draw their own conclusions. Enough said is quite enough.'

Geography and sex education – perhaps Mrs Brock had failed on both these counts. Such failures were of very little importance in Lady Grizel's simple values. Her boys would grow up as their father and their uncles had done – living and loving the country life, and marrying nice girls with a bit of money. 'So long as they're happy, you old fuss bag,' was her inattentive, affectionate reply as she went on her afternoon way, calling for her dogs.

It was unlucky for Mrs Brock that before Nannie's hints had time to slip quite out of her mind, Lady Grizel should find Richard alone in the boys' tree house, halfway up a Spanish chestnut tree, with what could only be a book – a book, and at three o'clock on a perfect afternoon.

'Doing your prep, old boy?' she called laughingly.

'No. Reading.'

'Reading? Well, stop it. Come and dry the dogs with me . . . did you hear me, darling?' she called again, quite sharply.

'Coming, Mummie.' He delayed a moment before climbing rather hesitantly down the tree and the rope ladder that linked the lowest great branch with the lawn. This upset her, as she liked her boys to do things in the right way, whether they were getting up on their ponies or eating artichokes – there was a right and wrong ritual in doing anything.

'What were you reading?' she asked when no answer came from Richard to quite a funny remark of Grips's about bath-water in his ears.

'Left it in my tree house.'

'What's it called?'

'Just Tree House.'

'No. The book.'

'Oh.' He hesitated. '*Robinson Crusoe*' he brought out triumphantly.

'Haha. Where's your Man Friday – that's what Grips wants to know.'

'My who?'

'Man Friday. I remember he came into it.'

The rims of Richard's ear went very pink. 'Ask Gripsy,' he said. 'Tell us about old Friday, Grips.' Richard and Grips went flying round in circles on the enormous close-woven spaces of the lawn. She laughed, watching them. But, for once, a question stayed at the back of her unruffled brow.

'Perhaps she doesn't give them quite enough to do. You may be right,' she admitted to Nannie that evening. 'I found Richard all by himself, reading.'

'Reading a book?' Nannie asked, incredulous.

'Yes, *Robinson Crusoe*. Quite harmless, really.'

'Harmless? On a lovely afternoon like today?'

Nannie took the matter further. To climb a rope ladder and explore the tree house was beyond her, at her age, but she could persuade Walter to do it for her.

'Oh, Master Richard –' the apology Walter tendered later was heart-felt – 'talk about crafty! ... "You're a proper active young chap, Walter" – oh, she was nice! "You wouldn't take those long legs of yours up the tree-house ladder, would you? Master Richard's left his new blue jersey up there. Fetch down anything else you find – looks like rain tonight." See the cunning of her cleverness? I put my foot straight in, of course, silly me, I know, and handed her down your book ... '

Nannie took the book of poetry straight to Lady Grizel, who talked it over unhappily with the Captain. His response was a genuinely worried one: 'Yes, we'll have to put a stop to this bookworming. No future in that. And he was having a music lesson yesterday when old Sholto was schooling his pony.'

'That's hardly the point, is it? The awful thing is, he told me quite a big fib.'

'That's more natural – it's this poetry that bothers me. What's the book called?'

'*The Children's Golden Treasury of Verse.*'

'Unhealthy-sounding stuff.'

'It's what Nannie says, they don't get enough exercise . . .'

So, I came to understand, went their comments. They are in accord with Mrs Brock's remembered phrases and stories, and true to the intricacies of the rather cruel cult game that, years later, Richard, Hubert, and I were to play at Temple Alice. Richard, creator of the game, enjoyed recalling every level of life at Stoke Charity in that era of childhood when he lost his first love, Mrs Brock. We joined in, despoiling our memories of her with horrid fun. Beyond the decorations and inventions of the game, essential to laughter, behind the lengths and colours of days, or the remembrance of a glance, revealing hidden loves or spites, we taunted the separate childhoods, which had left us the people we were. Richard could look back unforgivingly on his parents' decision: for lying he must take his little flogging, and Mrs Brock, with her music lessons and poetry readings, must go. It was to be hoped that any damage Richard might have suffered from them would be repaired by an early start at Entwhistle's.

'And who is going to sack Mrs Brock?' Lady Grizel would have wanted to know.

'You are, of course.'

'No, my darling, I am not. You are. You thought of it.'

To suit some inescapable duty – judging at a neighbouring hunt's puppy show, most likely – Richard's punishment was postponed until Friday, two days away, and two very dreadful days intervened. Richard, the condemned man, set about his pony in a fiery way, went a great deal to the lavatory, and was sick after breakfast and very sick after tea on Friday.

Sholto reported that he was unable to sleep a wink because Richard was so quiet. Richard didn't know how many people knew he had told a lie and was going to be beaten. He took any kindness or cordiality as an insult. His hair stood up in stiff little dry peaks on his head. He jumped off the garden wall into a seed-bed to prove to himself his manly side. Walter, white to the lips, came to the schoolroom to say the Captain was waiting for Master Richard in the gunroom. Richard, white to the lips too, met the Captain, green about the gills, but prepared to do his duty.

'Why did you lie to your mother, Richard?'

'I don't know.'

'You were ashamed about that rather silly book, I suppose, *and* rightly so.'

'No, I wasn't.'

'But you told a lie. We don't have liars in our family, do we? Anything to say about that?'

'I don't know.'

'Well, bend over this chair.'

'Oh, please, Daddy. Please, Daddy—'

'Look – keep quiet, will you, or I'll have to get Walter to hold you.'

'No. I'll be good. I'll be good.'

'Now, shut up, old boy,' the Captain said kindly, as he put down his leather-covered malacca stick. 'You'll upset Mummie if she hears you. Got to take punishment, haven't we, old son. I've had plenty in my time.' And the Captain laughed heartily, far more from nerves than from any unkindness. 'Cut along to Nannie. She'll look after you.'

But it was to the schoolroom that Richard went, very quietly, almost creeping in. He stood still, lost for a reason, for anything to say, a guilty embarrassed person.

'Forgot to do my history,' he muttered.

'History, Richard? We don't have history this week.' Mrs Brock turned back to the piano, where, when he came in, she had been playing and softly singing 'Abide with Me.' Now her throaty animal voice filled the whole air in the room, as a smell takes over the senses. As the air throbbed round him, all proper rules escaped Richard's control. When Mrs Brock, crying too, twisted her piano-stool round towards him, he forgot all the stiff-upper-lipmanship and threw himself, sobbing wildly, into her arms. Mrs Brock folded him to her breast where he burrowed his head into the dark comfort of that strictly clothed bosom. For ever afterwards he remembered the smell of security in an embrace where Rimmel's toilet vinegar and *papier poudré* fought a losing battle with warm, merciful human flesh. He sobbed on in measureless relief.

It had to be then that Nannie, high priestess of correct behaviour for little boys, made her entrance and stood for a minute, holding on to the door handle for support, as she saw with unaffected horror the pair enlaced on the piano-stool. Speechless for once, she turned away, shutting the door sharply on the scene, and lost not a moment in imparting her triumphantly unhealthy news to Lady Grizel.

So Mrs Brock was next in the gunroom, summoned by a shaking Walter. He had heard Richard's cries and wondered what more could be in store for his schoolroom friends.

'Mrs Brock, do sit down. I asked you to come and have a talk with me because, actually, his mother and I aren't too happy about Richard. Frankly, he's getting a bit, er, well …

first reading poetry when he ought to be getting his pony ready for the Bath and County next Thursday, then lying to his mother – took his beating in a very, well, cowardly way, then, am I right? howling on your, in your, *in the schoolroom*,' the Captain finished desperately.

'Oh, Captain Massingham, the child was so upset. I don't usually cuddle him. Never, in fact.'

'Don't let's discuss it. I'm sure it won't happen again.'

'Oh, no.'

'And another thing I must tell you, Mrs Brock – we've decided that the boys are to start at Entwhistle's this autumn, so I'm afraid we shan't be needing you, much as we're going to miss you.'

'Raymond?' she questioned desperately. The chill of reality circling her, curdling the rich air of the gunroom.

'I suppose Raymond's Nannie's boy for a year or so, don't you think? Only five, after all.'

'I see.' Mrs Brock looked round the room. Foxes' masks (neatly labelled: FOUND —— KILLED —— THE POINT —— THE DATE ——) were grouped, memories of glorious moments, on the walls. Some stood out sharply on their wooden shields, small pricked ears and deathly snarls; others hung down on faked leather couples, ears back, tongues lolling and curling. All the pictures were of foxhunting, foxhounds, or masters of foxhounds. The living terriers, snoozing in their baskets, had their backs turned to her. Everything in the room belonged to a different and more glorious race from Mrs Brock. 'It's hard to believe,' she said. 'I've been so happy—'

'So glad. So glad,' the Captain shut her up at once. 'And another thing, we'd like you to have a cheque for this term's salary, and next, and a little present in token, if that's the word, sounds funny, of our, h'm . . . ' He pushed a thick blue envelope across the writing table. She took it up, overcome by twin floods of regret and gratitude.

'We've put in an excellent what you call a reference, I believe, too.' The Captain's voice was easing into a more usual tone now that the back of the situation was, as it were, broken.

Mrs Brock was stupefied by so much kindness: 'It's not the end of the term for six weeks, Captain Massingham.'

'I know. But we've rather decided to let you go immediately. Seems the best idea.'

'I don't understand—'

'Neither do I, damnit.' The Captain got to his feet, longing to end the whole horrible business. 'Anyway, I'm afraid now I must say goodbye, Mrs Brock, and the very best of luck to you. Have to get the seven-forty-five up to town, and by Jove, I'll hardly make it.' He laughed heavily, as he had after Richard's thrashing. Then he held the door open for her before he went charging across the hall, in the opposite direction from the schoolroom, nursery, and servants' wing, whistling to the dogs and making an enormous racket.

Mrs Brock did not delay. She was in a panic which hurried her through the hall, her heels chattering and muttering alternately as she stepped from whitened flags to spread tiger-skins. How the dogs loved to pee on the latters' heads; generations of dogs, beaten and fed and cloistered in this family; it was just a thought which came to her before she opened and passed through the door dividing the hall and its staircase from the other side of the house.

Mrs Brock went straight to the schoolroom lavatory, where she was overtaken by a violent diarrhoea. When she got off the mahogany seat to lift the D-shaped hand-fitting which swirled out the blue-flowered basin, she sat down again at once 'in case,' that tiny euphemism that covered so much so usefully. The exhaustion of physical necessity calmed her. She washed her hands and blew her nose and decided to follow her usual habit – a cheery goodnight to the boys before Walter brought up her supper.

But at their bedroom door she was met by a brisk Nannie. 'Oh, there you are Mrs Brock. I've just packed those two into their beds. Shouldn't disturb them if I was you. Richard's settled down nicely now and Sholto too – what an imp that boy is.' She stood with her back to the door until Mrs Brock, again defeated, passed on towards the schoolroom. She felt, rightly, that she was betraying Richard. She had not spoken a word to the Captain in defence of *The Children's Golden Treasury of Verse*. The lie involving *Robinson Crusoe* she could neither defend nor understand. She had not attempted any protest or defence of herself either. The whole affair was left in a polite miasma of unspoken suspicions, a net that held her helplessly ignorant and servile. Nothing had been stated, so what charge could she answer in this polite world?

'Oh, Mrs Brock—' Walter fluttered and hovered over her supper tray. 'It's not true you've –' he brought it out with difficulty – 'you're leaving us?'

'Well,' she said with brittle valour, 'the best of friends must part, mustn't they, Walter?'

'But tomorrow—'

'Tomorrow?'

'Yes. Tomorrow – we heard in the hall the Captain had ordered the car for the early train.'

'Yes, yes, of course. I'd forgotten that was the arrangement.

My suitcases will be ready for you by nine o'clock, Walter.' She sat down neatly behind her supper tray: hot soup, a glass of wine, a wing of chicken under a silver lid. Strawberries. Walter still hovered.

'Everything all right, Mrs Brock?'

Oh, if he would only go before he saw her frightened tears. 'Yes, thank you, Walter. Everything. Absolutely perfect, thank you.'

'Thank *you*, Mrs Brock.'

So neither of them cried. No convention was embarrassed. She would eat her supper, keep up her strength before setting into the business of her packing. It would be a struggle to fit in all Lady Grizel's gifts. She decided to wear the bulkier of the Busvine suits; a bit hot perhaps for the time of year, but that other gift, the hat, Tagel straw and roses, would produce quite the right summery effect.

By midnight, all her belongings packed and parcelled up, the anaesthetic busy-ness yielding to the horrid truth of her expulsion, she stood and shivered in the tidied emptied schoolroom. Relief from something near to despair and exhaustion came through her own practical reservation of the glass of wine from her supper tray – port wine too. Walter must have considered the sad occasion merited something more fortifying than the usual glass of hock or Beaujolais.

Mrs Brock sipped, and gradually warming from her stunned and wounded state to a livelier interest in future possibilities, she decided to open the Captain's envelope and assess her financial situation. Counting bank notes is never less than reviving. Captain Massingham and Lady Grizel had been wildly, uncalculatingly generous. But after a recount and another sip or two of port her appeasement and relief were transposed into a new doubt. Perhaps all this overpayment was only compensation for a meagre and demeaning testimonial? She unfolded the thick blue writing paper with its tiny printed heading, and she read avidly: she read how kindly, how adorably kindly, they thought of her ... patient and understanding ... interested in racing ... a strong swimmer ... musical ... tactful ... highly recommend ... leaving us as our sons go to their preparatory school.

Mrs Brock lifted her bowed head and looked radiantly about her. She was back in those days when her schoolroom, besides being a seat of happy and simple learning, had been (warm in its own mystique) a refuge and sorting house for lost and treasured objects, as well as a bureau of inspired racing information. That was before her study of the wretched form book and her reliance on misinformed correspondents had upset her daemon. Unforgettable happy female hours had passed here, while exquisite knitting flew through her busy hands. A pile of Shetland froth and floss still waited, unfinished, for Lady Grizel's birthday. Slightly tipsy now, her gratitude for the encomium and her frenzy for loving and giving decided Mrs Brock to sit up, all night if necessary, to finish this last tribute to Lady Grizel.

It took her three hours to complete her masterwork, then damp and pin it, through sheets of paper, to the carpet, stretched out for the careful, cool spirit-iron. Sighing with pleasure, she left it, airing and floating across the back of a bentwood chair, while she went away to undress.

Wearing her blue flowered kimono and with her hair neatly twisted round steel and elastic curlers, she came back to the schoolroom. Crisp tissue paper and a length of narrow blue ribbon in her hand, she delayed the parcelling while she satisfied her eyes on the faultless beauty of her work. When she had taken off her wedding ring and slipped the shawl effortlessly through it, the elation, the need for praise known to all creators, overcame her. Unshared and without praise such moments can never live entirely; they are an uncompleted act of love. She knew now a raving desire for that moment when Lady Grizel's thanks and delight would overwhelm and satisfy her.

Romantically light-headed and uplifted, Mrs Brock took her terrible decision. Fortified by Walter's inspired glass of port no less than by the glorious written testimony to herself as a teacher, as a tactful personality, even as a strong swimmer, she would go, before these magical certainties escaped her, to Lady Grizel's bedroom. She would carry her offering with her, no wrapping to crush or conceal it, and would fling it, a great cobweb spun of love, over Lady Grizel's feet. So lucky that the Captain had gone up to London; even in her present state of mind she could not picture his reaction under such a cloud.

Nothing stirred in the long distances of the big house as Mrs Brock set out on her adventure. Her slipper soles slapped gently along the black-and-white linoleum tiles of the schoolroom passage before sinking to carpeted silences when she had passed through the heavy door preserving the calm and distance of that other world in Stoke Charity. The house contained different worlds, each designed for its particular occupants: owners, guests, nannies, governesses. To the housekeeper her room, to the butler his pantry, to the servants their hall – a proper setting and place for each and everyone. The least proper place for Mrs Brock – and at four A.M. on a summer's morning – was Lady Grizel's bedroom. This room was a vestry for Lady Grizel's hidden hours. There clothes and under-clothes were laid out with careful ceremony. Corsets were unlaced here and, sighing, thrown aside. It was a place uninvaded except for proper service and for love.

This setting for privilege had ravished Mrs Brock on the few occasions when – in Lady Grizel's absence – Julia had brought her here to stare and exclaim in unjealous appreciation of the loved one's luxuries. 'Everything straight from Waring and Gillow,' Julia had commented as she indicated the great armoury of a wardrobe, allowing generous provision and perfectly appointed spaces for every imaginable garment. Mrs Brock had nodded in agreement – and turned her attention to the grand altar of the dressing-table, so profligate of vast surfaces and small shelves – Malmaison carnations and, in wintertime, violets in christening mugs stood here between tortoiseshell and gold hairbrushes and photographs of the boys as babies – lush cherubs with folds of muslin dropping off eatable shoulders. She had found it difficult to imagine the originals of these pictures growing into replicas of their father. His lightly tinted photograph – jaw set and huntsman's cap well down over his eyes (he had been sincerely immortalised by Keturah Collins) – stood, silver framed and cater-corner, between the pictures of his flowerlike children. Captain Massingham's picture, with its suggestion of coverts full of foxes, kennels full of hounds, and stables full of horses, was in provocative contrast to all the soft and pretty comforts of his wife's bedroom.

Here – Mrs Brock had breathed it in – scent was present in a perpetual warmth. On the chaise longue (to every bedroom its chaise longue) fat cushions in their fresh muslin covers were piled together with smaller head cushions, pale narrow ribbons sometimes threading a sly way through a lace insertion. Neither Julia nor Mrs Brock had looked long at or questioned the validity of the great brass bedstead, unabsolved in ugliness, its springing perfect for love-making or for sleeping. But tonight, the spells of distance and of sanctity broken through, Mrs Brock was to find Lady Grizel sleeping here alone. She would wake her to accept her present, as though to the pleasure of a Christmas stocking.

Lady Grizel was not alone when Mrs Brock, after a discreet knock, came into her room. There were two dogs under the eiderdown of the big bed in which all three were enjoying a delightful night's companionship. She rather liked these lone nights when the Masters of Foxhounds Association or some other great cause took the Captain away. He disapproved of dogs in bed, so only in his absence was she able to give her darlings a treat she enjoyed as much as they did.

At Mrs Brock's knock Lady Grizel stirred on her pillows and murmured. The dogs turned under the eiderdown and growled. Now, unbidden, Mrs Brock came nearer to the bed; she stood, a prim, proper little person in the dawning light, her present in her hands. She might have thrown the pink shawl across the eiderdown, where it would have lain light as a mist. She might have gone away without a word, ever after to remember her beautiful restraint. But the dogs, who only acknowledged people in their proper places, plunged about beneath the eiderdown, barking their heads off and thoroughly waking Lady Grizel, who sat up to cuff them into silence and remained sitting up, frozen in her amazement at the sight of Mrs Brock. Whatever doubts she had felt at her dismissal flew instantly from her mind. Worlds apart, they stared at each other.

'Lady Grizel –' Mrs Brock faltered – 'I wanted to see you alone. Just tell me what I've done – what's happened?'

'Captain Massingham spoke to you and I really can't say any more, can I?'

'Oh, but all the money? The wonderful reference?'

'Yes, I thought we worded it rather nicely.'

Mrs Brock drew nearer to the bed: 'But if that's how you think of me, why do you want me to leave?'

'Oh, do go back to bed, Mrs Brock!' Lady Grizel felt as repelled and alarmed as she might have done at the approaches of an unwelcome lover. She looked beautiful sitting up among her pillows; her pearls (she always wore her pearls at night) tumbling warm from her sleepy flesh, out of her white long-sleeved nightdress.

'But do you know I love you?' Mrs Brock cried out. 'Mrs Brock loves you, Lady Grizel.'

'Mrs Brock – have you gone out of your mind?'

Mrs Brock came nearer: 'I love you,' she said, 'and I'll be with you always wherever I am, whatever happens. I've brought you this – I think it's the very best I ever . . .' Wordless at last, she almost threw the fine shawl across the bed. At its faint impact the dogs started to bark again, while Lady Grizel, outraged, shrank back against her pillows.

'You must be over-tired,' she said, an immense volume of coldness in her voice. 'Please go back to bed at once – now. And please take this thing with you. I simply don't need it.' She scraped up the present and handed it back. 'Try to get some sleep,' she said more kindly. 'I'm sure Julia will call you in time for your train. Julia thinks of everything.'

Mrs Brock stood tearless, wordless, the shawl bunched in a deformed lump under her arm. Lady Grizel said no more. She looked across Mrs Brock to the door and Mrs Brock took the hint.

The day of Mrs Brock's departure was one of the happiest days in Richard's childhood. Nannie called them early to ride out their ponies. With their favourite stable lad as companion, they clowned their way happily through the next hour or so, laughing at his jokes, lazy and unmindful of their horsemanship. There was none of that 'Heels down, please, Master Richard,' or 'Sit well back, Master Sholto,' the only piece of advice offered in those days before pony clubs. Richard came home to a second breakfast, yesterday's pain and shame diminished. The news that Mrs Brock had been called away to London made no grievous impact. Not only were lessons for the day abandoned, but they were to go over to Moribound after luncheon, where Mummie's great friend Lord Lapsely of Derkley had a private zoo, where a mouse deer had just calved and a tiger had bitten a little boy's head off only last week.

A thrilling afternoon and a very good tea over, Richard went bouncingly up to the schoolroom, no thought of poetry in his mind, and faintly embarrassed at the memory of Mrs Brock's lavish comfortings on the previous evening. The room was utterly tidy: all lesson books put away; pencil boxes straight as spirit levels; the piano tightly shut, no open music book stirring its leaves in the empty air. The white mice might have been sugar mice, they stayed so quiet in their night compartments, and the budgies were puffed out sullenly, waiting in their cages for the trilling and the music to set them screaming and raising their wings in ecstasy.

Richard moved about in the hush for a time. He decided to clean out the mice and have them smelling delicious for Mrs

Brock's return; but at the bottom of the corner cupboard, where such things were kept, he could find no newspapers, onto which he usually swept the floors of the cages. An exemplary tidiness pervaded the cupboard; even Mrs Brock's collection of bits of string had gone from their hook. The birdseed had been emptied out of its coloured packages into a glass jar with a stopper. An apprehension, a chill, crept over Richard. He thought of looking into Mrs Brock's bedroom to reassure himself, through her belongings, of her presence and person, but he was afraid now of finding nothing. And afraid Nannie might catch him finding nothing. At any rate he hoped to find Walter in the pantry, get some newspapers from him, and give the old mice a proper doing. He could not admit that Walter might have news for him.

In the pantry, lined to its high ceiling with brown cupboards and slices of green baize, Walter was crying quietly; tears fell on the wine glasses he was polishing for dinner, ruining his work, but he was in that nervous state when the repetition of an occupation meant nothing to him.

'I want some newspapers.' Richard ignored the tears. 'I'm going to clean those filthy mice before Mrs Brock gets back.'

'She's gone for good, Master Richard.' Walter felt a tremor of excitement as he broke the news.

It was no shock to Richard. He had expected this. 'Yes, I know,' he said. 'I'll clean them anyway.'

'She loved those beastly mice,' Walter sobbed.

To see Walter, a grown-up, a servant, with silly tears bouncing down his cheeks, pantry tears, tears decorum forbade in nursery or schoolroom, appeased Richard's shame for his own recent breakage of that earliest rule of life – boys don't cry. There was a gratified superiority in finding himself the big boy of the two, the dry-eyed one, and the one with power to comfort.

'Walter,' he asked, 'would you like me to say one of my poems?' Walter made no affirmation. He was really very upset. 'All right – are you ready? I'll begin: "She is fading down the river –"' Richard paused to get a grip on his audience – '"She is fading down the river" . . .'

'Poor thing,' Walter said brokenly when Richard stopped at last. 'She'll have faded out of Paddington Station hours ago. Poor thing. All those crowds!'

CHAPTER FIVE

Mummie didn't care much about Mrs Brock's singing. 'Never quite on the note,' she would say with chilly tolerance. 'As the children are so unmusical, it doesn't matter really, and the schoolroom is far enough away . . . ' I was surprised and hurt when I heard this, as I had begun to fancy my voice under Mrs Brock's encouragement, and I was learning 'Two Little Girls in Blue, Dears,' with which number I expected to stun the Christmas School Treat. Even if I had owned the truest voice in the world, such an idea would have been discouraged as in the poorest taste.

Mrs Brock found life in Ireland a complete change from any previous schoolroom experience, although, in essentials, her relationship with the family was the same. Mummie ran away from any familiar footing in the schoolroom. There was not even the flimsiest bridge across that distance – not even a dog's lead to be lost or found. Our house stood at the apex of two carriage drives and was quite half a mile from any road; there were no young pheasants to disturb on our bog or river walks, only wild swans or snipe, so our dogs, which were few, did not require leads. Any contact or familiarity with Mummie was as far outside her orbit as were the birds. As in Dorset, the servants loved Mrs Brock. Here they were wild and garrulous, speaking a strange language in which she was disappointed at never hearing the word 'Begorrah,' but she could hear their distant droning of the rosary at bedtime.

She woke to their footsteps early in the morning, when they swept the dust under the sofa in the schoolroom and lit crackling paraffin-smelling fires by eight o'clock. They wore holy medals and scapulars under their cotton dresses, and ate Robin starch from the laundry, partly as a thinning diet and partly because they were hungry. They didn't expect much to eat then, and they certainly didn't get it. Diningroom and servants' halls fed very differently. Mrs Brock would bring them biscuits when she walked with us as far as the village on the river, where two little grocers' shops lurked, dark and low, in a terrace of eighteenth-century houses, and the ruin of a great woollen mill hung above the water.

Hubert and I adored Mrs Brock. We lived again with her the conduct of life at Stoke Charity (years afterwards Richard was to contradict or make explicit much of what she told us), we heard about the boys and their fiery ponies, and thought of their courage with distant awe. In those days we hated our ponies and Mrs Brock encouraged us to get off and lead the dirty little beasts past their favourite spots for seeing ghosts and whipping round for home.

She accepted without comment my grotesque, sentimental fixation on Mummie. She designed handkerchief sachets, matching sachets for holding nightdresses, hotwater-bottle covers, raffia napkin rings, egg cosies shaped like chickens' heads, and countless other objects, at which I would sew while my heart burst with passionate excitement at the prospect of the giving and the gratitude. This manufacture of things was a great happiness to me, and Mrs Brock's practical genius in manipulating scraps from the ragbag into ever more useless trifles held us together in warm accord.

Mummie escaped us all. The tides of her painting and her gardening, and the spring-tides of her whole life with Papa were as the sea between us – no step we took left a print in the sands. After we had toiled (not without pleasure) for hours on end to present her with wild violets: 'Oh, darlings, please don't pick them any more, poor little things. Thank you, yes they *do* smell ravishing, thank you so much,' and she would drop them by her plate, or fill a wine glass with water and drop them into it, to be forgotten. I had seen them afterwards on the dinner tray in the pantry, cleared away with the spoons and forks after luncheon. There they retired into a meaner proportion, as if their scent had been apparent only to ourselves, and their floods of blue had died out in our eyes.

But practical gifts were bound to bring a definite acknowledgement and often a satisfying one. 'Just what I've been wanting. Look, dear –' to Papa – 'a pen-wiper. She knows what a letter-writer I am,' and they would both laugh immoderately. He was the one who patted me and kissed me, lifting me off my feet so that my black-stockinged legs dangled free – he was very easy in the smallest caresses.

Sometimes Mummie would touch Hubert – always in a reserved sort of way. She never tried to paint him. 'My black Bubbles,' she called him. How she disliked that beautiful picture by Sir John Millais! And it bore absolutely no resemblance to Hubert; he was brown as an Italian child, wherever the sun could invade the little boy's clothes of our day – navy blue jerseys and over-long shorts. Even then he used his looks like a shield before making some outrageous remark in a toothless lisping way: 'I theen a terrible thing – I theen a thquirrel laying nuth.' She would laugh with him.

How to please? During the hour after tea when we came down to the drawingroom, I would sit silent in my blue accordion pleats, my christening locket, turquoise and pearl, swinging on its gold chain round my neck, my feet in their bronze dancing sandals crossed tight as in a vice. While Hubert breathed heavily over his Meccano set, constructing a ladder, or perhaps a dog kennel, speechless I sat, my longing to make a good impression twanging and vibrating within. I might try: 'We went for a walk today.'

'Oh, yes.'

'We went across the Horse Park and back along the Ladies' Walk—' She would turn up the blue enamel watch with a diamond bird on its back pinned to her blouse by a diamond bow, and glance hopelessly at its face: 'Yes, and what did my little good-news girl see on her walk?'

By the time I was in bed I could have listed twenty startling pieces of information – from a salmon rising in the river to the rook splashing down his, well, his ... onto Mrs Brock's hat. Now, interrupted in my recital, I could only wait in a blank hiatus before I gabbled out: 'I saw a rabbit.'

'A rabbit? Really? That is interesting. You saw nothing for your flower collection for instance?'

We had never given wild flowers a thought on that happy walk, nor grasses, nor birds' nests, nor frogs' spawn; we had hung on Mrs Brock's arms, transported by her tales to the luxurious and easy atmosphere of Stoke Charity. We were living with Richard and Sholto and Lady Grizel; we could nearly taste the delicious little suppers Walter carried up to the schoolroom. Although these suppers had the Hunker-Munker *Two Bad Mice* quality of false doll's-house food, the breathing life in her telling held us avid as a good rancid gossip about money or love might hold us in later life.

Aching as she did for useful occupation, Mrs Brock found her outlet in the linen cupboard. This enormous, dark, mouse-ridden cavern stretched across the end of a passage; on its back wall a window, firmly laced with ivy, gave a little light to the towering shelves. The linen in our house had been wearing thin, or had been stolen away by generations of housemaids, supposedly its menders and keepers, who had charge of the key. The present housemaid was named Wild Rose; she was bred to be hot, as the stable lads said when ducking her in a tank of water in the yard. Rose, screaming, enjoyed this fun as much as anyone but, not unnaturally, lost the key of the linen cupboard in her struggles.

Mrs Brock's fatal gift came to the rescue. When she heard that a marquess was coming to stay for the Cloneen Shoot and that there were no sheets for his bed because the key was lost, the fatal feeling came over her again, and she was off on her quest, with renewed triumph. From finding the key it was only a step into the linen cupboard with its quiet, ravaged hordes of sheets and pillow cases, tablecloths, napkins, braided curtains, and old printed stuff forgotten for years. 'Rose,' she said, 'we must sort all this out, and *I* shall repair everything.'

'Some wet day we'll be at it,' Rose said.

'It's pouring rain today – we'll start now.'

'Oh, Mrs Brock,' Rose protested, 'and his Lordship's bed not made, and I have ducks to kill for the cook.'

Mrs Brock knew that killing ducks was one of Rose's skills and pleasures, but she held to her point, and kept control of the linen cupboard, discovering in it rare things and rotten things. Sorting and piecing together and darning, her hands never ran out of skill or tired of work.

It was Rose who brought her Papa's favourite pale tweed coat, gone at the elbows, frayed at the cuffs, for which he had an obstinate adoration. Mrs Brock spread the coat on the table, excited by its problem, and presently worked away in the haze of scents impregnating its stuff: turf smoke and burnt heather roots – it had been handwoven in a cottage. Through and beyond this rough base, other smells came faint and vaporous. Egyptian cigarettes stayed the most constant, defeating horses' sweat in the coat-tails and hair oil in the collar. As the coat warmed under her hands and on her knees, a masculine presence enveloped and pervaded her.

Papa noticed the miracle of repair performed on his old favourite. 'So you did remember to have a go at Rose about this old coat, bless you. You know I love it,' he said to Mummie. 'Good old Rose – I knew she had it in her. Never gives her running unless she's under the stick.'

'I don't know what you're talking about,' Mummie said.

'Of course you do – you told me to throw it away.'

'Yes, I wish you had. It's not your colour, really.' She looked into him, through him, lost in consideration.

'Extraordinary.' He lifted his arm, the wing of a jungle cock; he preened with pleasure in his old plumage. 'I shall give her half a sovereign for this job,' he said with firm intention.

It was more than I could bear. 'I know. I know who did it. Shall I tell you? Shall I?'

'Yes, if you like.'

'Mrs Brock. Can I have the half a sovereign for her?'

'No, Aroon – you can't. I can't give Mrs Brock half a sovereign. What can I give her?' he asked, appalled.

'I don't know, a bit embarrassing. Don't ask me.' Mummie drifted away. Her voice coming out of a distance, she said more clearly: 'I wish she was as successful about your French, darling child. That would fill up her time.'

'*Le-chêne-un-jour-dit-au-roseau,*' I started to gabble.

'*Roseau,*' she corrected my accent – Mrs Brock's accent – with a sort of pinching dislike. The word *roseau* sounded much prettier as she spoke it.

I longed to be in the schoolroom, cheering and delighting Mrs Brock with the news of Papa's gratitude and pleasure. But, for a matter of days, I kept it to myself. Somehow the whole affair was now tempered to a chill of silliness by Mummie's attitude towards it – as if Mrs Brock had been giving herself a treat. However, what with my longing for importance, and my heart bursting with love, finally I could not resist the wish to please.

It was on a ravingly glad day by the sea that I told Mrs Brock about Papa's great pleasure. We drove the fat Iceland pony five miles to our nearest sea; the sun shone; the wind twined the long gold sands like feathers on a bird's back. How seldom we got to the sea; how rarely we found so many cowrie shells, fat little wet pigs, scarce as pearls among the pebbles, as we did on that afternoon. Intoxicated, braced with pleasure and the magical change from dark, inland July, I stuffed my dress into my knickers and ran yelling out my freedom like a sea bird. Hubert set off alone into the business of shrimping the rock pools; Mrs Brock did not attend him with help or advice. Nor did she run and yell with me. But she laughed at me, and dug herself a grave in the sand for shelter, after she had put the milk bottle in a rock pool. I knew she was on my side, and less interested in Hubert.

Presently, under capes of striped towelling, we undressed for our swim; Hubert had his cape too, and Mrs Brock her own side of the rock as well.

We screamed and spattered in the breaking waves while Mrs Brock took her real swim. I watched her fat body, a frilled torpedo in the black bathing costume, standing balanced and poised, ridiculous on a rock, before she dived – a joyous plunge into the deep water. Then she struck out into the bay with the strength and buoyancy of a seal; indeed, when the black bathing dress was sleeked by the water onto her body she had all the armoured rotundity of a seal – the same easy glory and enjoyment of an element that frightened me. Soon she returned to our depth and gave us a swimming lesson. I stayed up four strokes longer than Hubert and nobody said, 'Nothing to crow about, is there, Aroon? He's three years younger than you, after all.' While I was drying and dressing I explained my superior technique to him; he chattered his teeth at me so loudly I could hardly hear myself speak.

After tea Mrs Brock yawned and snuggled down into her grave while I played a game of burying her feet in the sand. She did not speak, but when I had them buried and patted over she would poke out a toe, cracking the damp sand. I felt this like a secret joke between us, and in this overwhelming moment of intimacy and love I needed absolutely to give her something. I did: I told her all about Papa's delight in her work on his coat. She listened to me with close attention, sitting upright, her feet still in their mounds of sand. I knew she was tense with pleasure; and, while I glowed in its bestowal, the story was hardly out of my mouth before I knew too that her reception of it was on a different level from mine – a foreign, secret level, leaving me outside, a messenger, not a participant.

Hubert wandered back to us, no shrimps in his bucket. We packed up the picnic mugs and all the bits of paper and tucked the matchbox full of cowries safely away in Mrs Brock's handbag before we walked back to the village, where the pony had been left to shelter from the flies in a tiny stinking cowshed belonging to the fisherman whose lobsters were to cost us two shillings each. 'He's only now gone to lift the pots,' his wife told us. 'Tommy Nangle disappointed him. Wouldn't you drive to Gulls' Cry and see Miss Enid and poor Mister Hamish while you're waiting on them?'

'Oh, no,' we said. 'Please, Mrs Brock, don't let's.' Miss Enid and poor Mister Hamish were our cousins, Mummie's cousins, and they lived in a depleted little manor house looking over the cliffs and the boat cove. They had no money at all; Mummie said they lived on mackerel and sea spinach. We dreaded the hedgehog kiss of Cousin Enid and the drooling silences of Cousin Hamish. So we preferred to wait, sitting on the low wall above the nettles which filled the ditch beneath our feet.

'Any minute now,' the woman repeated every so often. She didn't want us to leave the lobsters behind and unpaid for.

At last the fishermen returned, wet blue lobsters arching their backs as they hung from the men's hands with nippers tied before they were laid on the floor of the pony cart, strong and lively for an early death. Mrs Brock paid. We thanked, and climbed into the round governess cart behind the fat pony, pulling double for home.

Leaving the sea at evening is a death – a parting of worlds. We turned inland, past the Round Tower and the roofless church, where small primitive carvings of apostles were worn by time and sea-winds to blunt thumbs among its stones. In the cove small boats, drawn up on the beach, leaned about awkwardly as swans out of water. Lobster-pots were piled each on each, building into netted castles in the evening; and, plain as cooking on the air, the salty rot of seaweed came with us along the road. Mrs Brock whacked the pony with an ash-plant; the dust flew round us and lay back heavy on the dog roses in the banks as we turned inland.

'My tired,' Hubert said, long before we reached home; this baby talk was always a tiresome sign with him. 'My very tired.'

'Soon home now, chick.' Mrs Brock banged away at the pony while the lobsters clanked and bubbled at our feet. 'What about a biscuit?'

Hubert turned green. 'I wish we were HOME. I wish we hadn't waited for the poor lobsters.'

'Oh, Hubert! And you know Daddy loves lobsters.'

'Papa,' Hubert corrected her faintly.

Three long miles from home we were met by Ollie Reilly, a stable lad who had had his evening with Wild Rose interrupted to go to our rescue. He was driving a leggy, uppish chestnut mare in the shafts of the dog cart; she sidled and fidgeted about as Hubert and I climbed up to sit side by side on the blue buttoned face-cloth seat.

'What kept her?' He nodded back to Mrs Brock in the pony

cart, fumbling along in the dust far behind us. 'The Captain made sure ye'd met an accident.'

'She made us wait for the lobsters.' Hubert, revived now, was full of perky information.

'What about the dirty lobsters at this time of the night?' Ollie Reilly was derisive.

Angrily I answered, 'The boats were late and Mrs Brock' (not 'she') 'knows the Captain loves lobsters.'

He made no reply. He considered what I had said as he sent the mare flying along. Deprived of Rose that night, a popular girl who wouldn't wait for him a second time, his disappointment and irritation were centred on Mrs Brock.

From that time there was a faint note, hardly sounded but evident in Rose's manner, a kind of familiarity towards Mrs Brock. She would flaunt in and out of the schoolroom in her starched pink cotton, crunching starch, leaving behind shirt collars for turning, clocked socks for darning, and pyjama coats with their sleeves out. I felt as if she were feeding Mrs Brock. Shooting stockings were a big meal: Mrs Brock would knit and weave heels for these pale stockings, soon to be trampled again into gaping holes, wet shoes in the snipe bogs dragging them apart – and never too soon for Mrs Brock's eager fingers.

Papa never said an actual thank-you for all this labour. Perhaps during luncheon, if he was wearing a resuscitated old ghost of other days, he might pat himself and give her a look – a look like a ray of light from a distant star, a look that suggested warmth and pleasure.

A day came when, I suppose, he felt these silent looks of understanding gratitude were not enough, and there arrived in the schoolroom a neatly packed parcel with a London postmark.

Chocolates. Exquisite, expensive chocolates. '*The* best,' Mrs Brock intoned happily. 'Charbonnel AND Walker.' Liqueur and coffee creams, powdered truffles, crystallized rose-leaves, crystallized violets, and a fresh mirror-smooth gleam on the row upon row and layer after layer that filled the big box, each chocolate as beautiful as a chocolate could be.

CHAPTER SIX

About this time Papa decided to take our riding seriously – and what an escalation in misery that proved for us. I know he was a perfect horseman with a beautiful seat and hands and a total command of any horse he rode, but as an instructor he was incomprehensible, impatient, and unnerving.

He would look at our whey-pale faces in dismayed irritation as our ponies stolidly refused to jump a small gorse fence we could have hopped over easily on our feet. Out through the wings they crashed willingly enough, and on to scrape us off beneath the low boughs of some tree in the park-like field where these exercises took place.

Refusing defeat, he would make us catch the ponies and, when we had remounted, he would lunge them over the furze bushes on the end of a rope, a stable lad roaring at them to take off. How freely they jumped then, and how freely we flew over their heads; laughter from him followed and tears from us.

Fears fit for a flogging morning or a hangman's measuring session possessed us as he pursued our education and that of our ponies. We adored Papa, and his hopeless disapproval paralysed any scrap of confidence or pleasure we had ever had in ourselves or our ponies.

One terrible day, when I howled and refused to get up after a bone-shaking tumble, he looked at me with bitter disgust and disappointment, and said: 'Don't get up if you don't want to, of course – lead your pony back to the yard.' Humbled and thankful I did so, and on the way met Mrs Brock, who wiped my tears and mopped my bubbling nose, and encouraged me to get up again, leading my pony gently and inexpertly until I regained some contact with him.

'Don't lead him now,' I said grandly. 'Where were you going? I'll come too. *No*, Fairy – get on with you.'

'Fairy knows who's boss,' Mrs Brock said admiringly. Strengthened by her flattery, I drove in my heels and set about beastly Fairy.

Not long after this sad morning Papa, riding a young horse alone (his patience exhausted and dulled by our frequent failures, he had for the time being given up instruction, our cowardice shamed and worried him too much), saw the surprising and, to him, delightful spectacle of Hubert and me racing our ponies into an obstacle without whips singing behind us, or tears pouring down our purple faces.

The fence we faced was not one of those made up of nasty, upright little gorse bushes, but a round-lipped shallow ditch. The ditch ran through a screen of beech-trees and was now full of their dry leaves. On the landing side stood Mrs Brock, in one hand a carrot, a chocolate (Charbonnel AND Walker) in the other. Ponies and children raced each other for their rewards. Papa turned his horse and rode away, shaking his head. He could not understand, nor could he discuss the matter, but Mrs Brock's absurd success in creating our confidence endowed her with an importance which, for him, far exceeded his unspoken gratitude over the restoration of his favourite old clothes.

In those days one did not quite admit the possibility of cowardice even in young children. The tough were the ones who mattered; their courage was fitting and creditable. A cowardly child was a hidden sore, and a child driven to admit hatred of his pony was something of a leper in our society. It appeared to Papa that Mrs Brock had rescued our honour and his credit. Although unspoken, this consideration narrowed the gap between them.

Her part of that autumn was utterly happy. Her influence over us and our ponies was recognised. She was asked to come and persuade us over more formidable fences than the plump-sided ditch. She and Papa walked together across the fields. Sometimes he helped her, with distant carefulness, over a gap or a boggy place. She didn't speak. But the glow she radiated in the pleasure of his company seemed to include him as well. This happy familiarity was begun in innocence and was chaperoned, for a time closely, by our constant presence.

During that September another and larger box from Charbonnel AND Walker was delivered to the schoolroom. Papa came in once or twice to make or alter arrangements about our riding; lesson times were adjusted to the hours when he was free to instruct us; so soon now he would be hunting four days in the week and shooting on the other two – the pressure of time hurrying on towards winter was on us all. A change was coming, and Mrs Brock was at its centre. Her piano playing was soft and coaxing. She wore Lady Grizel's

Busvine daily, as well as on Sundays, and she took the feather out of a felt hat and dragged its brim into a simple country shape to wear on our rides.

One afternoon, when we were ready and waiting for him in the yard, he was late. Then it seemed he had forgotten us; he never came. We were happy in the prospect of a quiet, safe ride with Mrs Brock; nothing spectacular to be asked of us, and time for stories about Stoke Charity as we lagged beside her in the sunshine. But the fun had gone out of Mrs Brock that afternoon. She was abstracted and borne elsewhere beyond our interests. No tales of Richard and Sholto and nasty little Raymond were forthcoming. Hubert and I quarrelled and picked on one another as we rode down the drive between the darknesses of beech and ilex and the spreads of sunshine between them. At the end of the drive, outside the tall iron gates, Papa and Mummie sat in the dog cart waiting for a lodge keeper or a child to come out and open the gates. Side by side they waited without impatience. She was looking up at him, her face pert and elegant under its luncheon-party toque; a light checked dust-rug was over their knees, and he held the reins and the whip in his right hand. His left hand could have been in hers; he was laughing, in total accord with whatever she had to tell him.

No child came out of the lodge to open the gates: 'All at school, I suppose. What a tiresome woman! Thank you so much, would you, Mrs Brock?' Mummie leaned down towards us, as far removed from ourselves as the branch of a tree in a light wind: 'Just tell her we were waiting rather a long time.'

'I think she's having a baby, Mrs St Charles,' Mrs Brock apologised for the lodge keeper.

'Ah, well ... perhaps, *pas devant* ... ' Mummie smiled and

took her ungloved hand from under the rug, briefly to indicate us, and to wave us a pretty goodbye as they drove off.

Papa had not spoken. He concentrated on the flighty mare, playing up in the shafts, over-excited by waiting so near her stable, by flies, and by the presence of our ponies. Under his black-and-white check cap his face looked dark as a rainy morning. Mrs Brock shut the heavy gates and walked on between us; no tales, no jokes. In the silent afternoon I spent myself in avid wonder as to what was going on in the gate lodge, and as to how, in the first place, a baby got into a mother. I had a good idea about how it got out. I put the question at last in a nature study form: 'Of course I do know Mrs Rabbit lays her babies, but how do the babies get in before they get out?'

'They grow.' Mrs Brock spoke in a hushed, special voice, as though her hands were softly touching the keys on her piano.

'Yes. But how do they get *in*?' Curiosity consumed me. 'What puts them there?'

'The dirty old buck rabbit,' Hubert said in his naughtiest voice. I knew he was making it up. Mrs Brock blushed.

'Look, look,' she spoke distractedly, 'I believe I see a squirrel. Look, look, up the beech-tree – a chocky for whoever spots him before he pops down his hole.' Hubert gave her a pitying glance and rode on. Later, when I asked him – for I was intent on pursuing the question – what he meant about buck rabbits, he had nothing more to add. He had heard one of the lads make this remark about someone and he supposed it was a rabbit – bucks and does are rabbits.

That was the evening when I persuaded myself that I had an ugly little pain. It was true, I had a tiny pain, and I petted and exaggerated it into a reason for getting out of bed and going to the schoolroom. I felt under an extreme necessity to see if Mrs Brock was still wearing that look of abstracted disappointment. If the atmosphere, impenetrable to any loving inroad, which had lasted sadly and unusually till our bedtime, was still present, I would comfort her.

But, when I opened the door, drooping and evidently in pain, there was no one there. Mrs Brock, meticulous in tidiness, had gone, leaving her knitting, a blue-grey shooting stocking, in a heap among our lesson books. It was too early in the autumn for a fire, but the balloon-like milk-glass bowl of the lamp was as hot as a stove; moths came in to die about it. In their covered cage the canaries swelled their feathers, their bodies enormous on their threads of feet. The only liveliness in the silence was among the mice. No schoolroom in 1912 was lacking in white mice. Tonight they tore about, squealed minute squeals, flew round on their wheel, and jumped on and off each other's backs. There was a tremendous carry-on, joyous but just a little frightening. It would have cost me something to put my hand into the cage and pick up my own little Minnie. Minnie was romping around, unrecognisable, as though tiger's blood ran in her veins. Hubert's Moses was biting her now. Now he was on top of her. I clapped my hands desperately. 'He'll kill you – he'll kill you,' I shouted; but I was too cowardly to put my hand into the cage and rescue her. The schoolroom door opened and Mrs Brock came in. 'Moses is killing Minnie,' I shouted again.

'Oh, get off it, Moses.' Mrs Brock gave the cage a smart tap. 'Just their play,' she added, as the mice separated, and she pulled the cover over their cage, leaving them to prance away in their familiar dark. 'But what are you doing out of your bed, my darling child?' Her voice was almost gross; she could have been singing a low note at the piano for us to sing after her. She was my darling. I longed for her kind embrace.

'Oh, I had such a pain.'

She sat down and took me on her knee. Only then I noticed that she was wearing her hat; not the riding hat, but the lovely small hat full of flowers and fruit which Lady Grizel had bought in Paris and disliked. She took it off and laid it on the table. The roses, the red-currants were beaded in drops; the fine straw was as wet as if it had lain in wet grass.

'But where have you been?' I asked. I ached to know all her movements.

'Out for a walk.' She laughed deeply. She was as full of happiness and as eager to share it, as she had been desolate and removed all the afternoon. 'Suppose we have a Marie biscuit and a drop of hot milk.' She bustled towards the spirit stove and her tidy milk jug with the bead-weighted muslin cover over its top. Again, as on the evening by the sea, I knew that a space widened between us. I had felt closer to Mrs Brock, she had been nearer to me when I thought she needed my comfort.

CHAPTER SEVEN

In the weeks following the night when happiness had swollen like the canaries' feathers round Mrs Brock, sheltering and conserving her own immense glow, I had the satisfaction of knowing she was less happy, so I was more valuable.

Papa was often away for whole mornings, cub-hunting; or for long days, shooting. It was late September now, so our riding lessons were much less frequent, and we had luncheon with Mummie – dull meals, as she didn't care what the cook gave us if Papa was not there to enjoy it. She took to speaking French with us too – simple tiny phrases requiring only a correct *oui*, or *non*, a *merci*, *Maman*. But with Mrs Brock she would embark on complicated conversations requiring answers far beyond Mrs Brock's limited knowledge of the language. We were aware of this cool play; Mrs Brock's pink cheeks and embarrassed mouthings were not lost on us.

It was in one of the unhappy silences following on such a French exercise that I piped up, a desperate loyalty sustaining my voice: '*Madame Brock tricot très bien*' was what I said, and from there, alas, we reached the stockings. Mummie knew now that Mrs Brock was knitting shooting stockings for Papa, and they became a subject for constant inquiry. Papa was teased about them too, but gently, and not in French. 'Blue too, how *sad* – I hope they'll be ready in time for the Cloneen Shoot ... Cousin Dominick will be amused ...' I heard this between them during one of our after-teatime hours. Papa's half-amused, half-flattered retreat from the teasing seemed to me to put Mrs Brock in the same halfpenny place as Mummie's French did, with the difference that Mummie lifted her eyes and drawled out her little jokes lightly when she was speaking to Papa, in contrast to the vindictive slow repetition of some impossible phrase in French to Mrs Brock.

When I told Mrs Brock what I had heard about the Cloneen Shoot, the grandest of the season as even I knew, she said: 'I'm afraid they won't be ready in time for it.'

'Oh, Mrs Brock, but why?'

'Because I've ripped them,' she said. 'I've ripped them up, Aroon.' She added more quietly, and I knew it was untrue: 'That pattern was all wrong.'

Papa didn't look into the schoolroom any more; and each day that came and went Mrs Brock changed before our eyes. We droned our way through our lessons; our exercise books went uncorrected; she played the piano for hours, and the sounds that came out of it were those of a wild, yearning animal. 'Broken doll – you've left behind a broken doll,' she played; and 'Where your caravan has rested, flowers I leave you on the grass.' On some days she could not face luncheon in the diningroom and had biscuits and milk in the schoolroom. I ached for her, but longed now for the happy Mrs Brock I had known; this creature was fluttering and banging itself about in a world unknown to me. Hubert and I were even driven to enjoy each other's company in preference to the wild gloom which possessed our dear friend's every mood. The birds' cages and the mouse houses began to smell; we were never very meticulous about them, only inspired towards Mrs Brock's ideal – that they ought to smell sweet as a primrose. Now she didn't seem to care, nor about the linen; her mending days were done. 'Rubbish!' she shouted at Wild Rose. 'It's all rotten – tear it up,' and she went zipping and rending through a fine double sheet and laughed at the tatters.

It was the day when Papa came back to the schoolroom that my love for Mrs Brock was, for ever, broken and dispersed. He was a tall man, and I saw him bent over this plump little woman and heard him speaking to her in a patient, reasonable tone of voice. Tears poured over her face, her hands tried to hold on to his coat. He put her hands away from him. 'I'll take a ride with you, children, at three o'clock,' he said. 'I don't think Mrs Brock feels too well. Go and tell Hubert to get ready.'

I was dismissed, but I came back to her when I heard his step going down the wooden schoolroom stairs. 'Are you all right?' I said. She was standing at the mouse cage, looking in. She didn't answer. 'Mrs Brock?'

'Minnie's had her babies,' she said, her voice still thick from crying. 'Look – aren't they disgusting?' They were, squirming and twiddling in their nest. 'You're always asking me how they do it,' Mrs Brock went on. 'Well, I'll tell you. It's that horrible Moses; he sticks that thing of his, you must have seen it – Hubert has one too – into the hole she pees out of, and he sows the seed in her like that.'

'Oh.' I felt myself becoming heated; horrified and excited.

'That's how it happens,' Mrs Brock went on, and she

gripped me by both my arms. 'That's how it happens with people too. It's a thing men do, it's all they want to do, and you won't like it.'

She still held my arms. 'Is it true?' I had to know. 'Papa and Mummie don't. They couldn't . . .'

'Oh, couldn't they?' Mrs Brock laughed and laughed. She was still laughing when I tore my arms away and ran out of the schoolroom. 'Papa's waiting for us,' I excused myself, standing for a moment in the doorway. I knew I was deserting her when she seemed to need me, as I had longed for her to need me, but I felt as frightened of her as I had of Minnie and Moses in their antics on that night when Mrs Brock had been so beflowered by happiness. When I joined Hubert and Papa in the yard I looked at him with quite new eyes. Could he and Mummie really do such a dirty thing? Was it possible? There he sat, elegant and easy on his young horse – but I knew it was true, horribly true. No wonder people kept it so secret.

I did not hear until long afterwards what happened to Mrs Brock when I ran out of the schoolroom, leaving her staring at the new mice. I only felt an odd relief when I came back and found that she had gone. Gone where? Gone for a spin on Wild Rose's bicycle. She said she had an old headache, so she took a loan of the old bike and went for a spin. Then Rose, bringing in the schoolroom tea, found an envelope addressed to herself, and in it a letter: 'Goodbye. Good luck. Don't forget me. You'll find the bike at Fitzy Nangle's.' There was a pound note enclosed. Rose left us with our milk and bread and butter. I could taste the mice through my milk, which had stood for a while in its mug. 'After tea, I'm going to clean them out,' I told Hubert. I needed to do something hygienic and drastic.

'If you do that, Aroon, Moses will eat the babies.'

'Men are such filthy creatures,' I said, and I looked at Hubert with a brooding kind of wonder. Rose came back with slices of chocolate cake from the drawingroom tea. There was a look of delighted excitement about her – an ask-me-not, touch-me-not mystery, longing to be questioned and probed.

'I'm to put ye to bed,' she said, 'and a half hour early if ye don't mind; it's my Thursday evening.'

'And Ollie Reilly waiting in the laurels'; Hubert always knew the latest form in the stable lads' courtships; it was an established joke and Rose screamed with pleasure: 'Oh, Master Hubert, who's the bold unruly boy?'

Far from joining in the fun, I felt a wave of disgust go through me. Heaven knows what they would get up to in the laurels, though not until after they were married, of course.

'Sweethearts, sweethearts, sweethearts,' Hubert chanted.

'Hurry on, now. Wash your dirty mouth out and get down to the drawingroom.'

Papa was drinking tea from a tiny flowered cup. The sandwiches were tiny too, and only our two slices had gone from the new chocolate cake. He got up as we came in.

'I don't like it,' he said.

'I shouldn't worry – just hysteria.'

'But I *am* worried.'

'Then do whatever you think best, my darling, anything you like, I'm only too delighted – *always*.'

He came back from the door. 'Bless you,' he said, and went out again.

'Get out your puzzles, children,' she said, 'and get on with them.'

Even Hubert didn't speak; he breathed heavily over his puzzle and took up pieces he knew and put them back again. My puzzle was full of swans, but I couldn't have fitted a swan's head onto a swan's neck I was so abstracted. Every now and then I stole a look at her, sitting there dressed in pale coffee-cream colour, little rosettes on her bronze house-slippers, a book in her hand. It was impossible. She couldn't have. Mrs Brock invented it.

'*Bedtime*' – the relief in her voice was enormous. Hubert did a funny thing. Going upstairs he took my hand. 'She'll be back, Aroon. It's all right.' I was happy to give his hand a little squeeze. I forgot about the mice and all that stuff. Mrs Brock had frightened me and failed me and now left me alone. Hubert might need me. Wild Rose didn't hurry us to bed. Nobody waited for her in the laurels; Ollie Reilly had driven the dog cart to Lisadore to pick up Mrs Brock. 'And I hope they won't leave my bicycle after them,' Rose said. But there was a darkness behind every joke. Ollie Reilly returned late, with the bicycle which Mrs Brock had left, carefully propped, behind Fitzy Nangle's wall, but without Mrs Brock.

All that night and through the days after, the house was murmuring with prayers: Hail Mary full of grace ... Sweet Jesus have mercy ... Rosary beads were pulled out of apron fronts and churned about in nervous hands. Mrs Brock had gone away, they said. When would she be back? Nobody could say. It was some time before they found her body, swollen almost to bursting the frilled bathing costume. She was a very strong swimmer, and judging from where she was washed up, she must have swum a long way out to sea.

CHAPTER EIGHT

I was sent to school the following year. Hubert went the year after, and in 1914 Papa rejoined his regiment. Mummie stayed at Temple Alice and wrote to him nearly every day. On leaves in London he had a splendid time with all his girls – brief leaves from France, too short for the journey home, and unrecorded in his letters to her. Years afterwards I read his letters, straightforward boring accounts of daily happenings: charmless, passionless, with no relation to the magic quality he possessed. He didn't keep any of her letters, or I have never found them. I don't suppose they would tell me anything I don't know. She was so cold.

Her greatest pleasure and distraction at that time was buying junk furniture. At sales and auction rooms she bought French furniture and Regency, considered both ugly and worthless by her contemporaries; I rather agree with them – give me Chippendale every time. But she brought the pieces home and spent hours cleaning and restoring; it was a holiday from the exhaustion of painting and she liked the biting smells of the varnish removers and oil mixtures she lavished on the objects.

Wild Rose, still unmarried, was her aide and slave. On some days Mummie painted her or drew her in hideous angular poses: long ribs, lean as a greyhound fit for the track, as she worked away at her polishing, crouched over the brass lyres and swans so prolific in the decoration of Regency furniture. Every painting or drawing was half-finished, and full of gaps and holes and unfailingly ugly, while Rose grew better-looking and blazed with more rude confidence every year that passed. She had a snake-like dart of the head, and then the acid tongue spoke. Ollie Reilly had followed Papa to the wars without leaving her the ghost of a hope for a plain ring on her finger, and she only laughed her way through unkindness or pity in the servants' hall.

I wisht I was married
And into bed carried
In the arms of my mother-in-law's son,
That the door would be locked
And the key would be lost
And the night would be seven years long.

She sang it harsh and loud – 'Marriage is horrible anyway, and we've all time enough when we'll be forty, girl. Isn't that right, girl?'

Oh love is pleasing,
Oh love is teasing,
Oh love's pleasure when first 'tis new . . .

When the news came that Ollie Reilly had been killed ('Tell Rose he died instantly; he never knew what got him,'

Papa wrote, and Mummie read her the letter), she was kneeling at the brass harpstrings of some piece of Regency rubbish, and collapsed like a dead frog, Mummie said. 'Such a good thing she wasn't standing up or she'd certainly have fallen on something and broken it, and we'd only just finished washing those Waterford glass rummers. Her howling and screaming made all the glasses ring out.' Mummie laughed. 'Ring out wild bells ...' Heaven knows what she meant by that. She never meant much. She never finished anything. She never completed an act or pursued a serious undertaking. When, soon after the news about Ollie Reilly, a telegram came to say Papa was wounded, she did not think of leaving Temple Alice to go to him. 'There are so many loving friends in London,' she said. 'They'll do far more for him without his wife fussing round. All those women, cherishing and longing. Besides, they're so rich.' She laughed faintly and went back to her painting, or her quiet fun among the Regency pieces.

We burned to rush over to his bedside. All the letters that came about him lay in piles and heaps on the hall table. There were letters from dozens of Wobbly Massinghams and Lady Grizels multiplied over and over into unknown Dorises and Dianas and Gladyses and Enids and a couple of Joyces. Mummie left them there, sticking out of their envelopes unread or half-read, all saying how cheerful he was, and how funny about his leg – so lucky that the amputation was below the knee. Our stomachs turned over when we heard this; but there was a quiet radiance in Mummie's acceptance of his calamity. 'I shan't mind,' she murmured. 'He won't be able to ride again,' we said, facing his nameless, blank future. 'No, perhaps not.' There was a glow within her quietness.

I planned a great welcome home for Papa – Union Jacks

and a wreath of Portugal laurel in the hall, something like that. I would have liked to get in a little piece about Our Hero. WELCOME TO OUR HERO, perhaps. In quite small letters, Hubert suggested. He was against the idea. In any case it came to nothing; Papa returned on leave from his hospital while we were still at our hateful schools.

He was there when we got back for the Easter holidays, reduced in every way: in height; in weight; even his voice was lessened. We kept our eyes off the stump of his leg, with the trouser leg neatly pinned up. He failed entirely to behave like the haloed hero we expected. He repulsed our overtures and Union-Jackish questions, and shunned our riding show-offs, which we had hoped would please him most of all.

This was an interval in his recovery; later in the year he was to have his wooden leg fitted. In the meantime he must rest, he must eat. He did both, and drank as well, growing every day more irritable and rather fatter. He followed Mummie about the garden at first; he even sat in the studio and watched her painting, after he had absorbed the small amount of racing news in the daily papers. All the time he seemed sadly unoccupied, as indeed he was. He couldn't ride. He fell into the river when he went fishing. Long afterwards I knew things that were on his mind then. Reeking, new, they must have been terrible. He had shot Ollie Reilly as he lay mutilated and dying; when he talked to Rose, Ollie's death seemed quite enviable, here and gone, out like a light.

Such things were so near and so apart from the honeyed life in Ireland. Every day was a perfect day that April. The scrawny beauty of our house warmed and melted in the spring light. Through the long screens of beech and ash plantations blackbirds flew low to the ground, calling high and scuttling low about their love affairs. All the blackbirds in the county seemed to be courting and mating in these coverts; with piercing sweetness they screamed, morning and dull eternal hours of evening, for love.

CHAPTER NINE

Papa slept badly. He came down late every morning, white and newly shaved and very cross. Perhaps he went, pegging his way along, down to a field of young horses. Their possibilities and promises of improvement were plain to him, as was the fact that he would have no part in their making.

Mummie suggested that he should drive around in Grandpapa's donkey-chaise. Papa was appalled. 'What do you think I am – some kind of invalid?'

'No darling, an able-bodied gentleman with one leg, *most* unfortunately, who ought to get about his place a bit more.'

'You're always absolutely right.' His patient voice had a savage note in it.

Hubert and I were fired with curiosity about the donkey-chaise. We found it, stored away in a corner of the cartshed; a broody turkey hen had her nest in it. We yoked a stallion ass called Biddy, and with him between the elegant, frail shafts, Hubert leading me in the carriage, we advanced up the drive towards the house where Papa was standing, morose on his crutches, enduring the long, sunny afternoon. The day changed for him when Biddy, taken by some crazy notion, bit Hubert, kicked out the dashboard, whipped round, and bolted back towards the farmyard.

'But he's quite dangerous,' Papa said, with some life in his voice when, much later, he caught up with us at the farmyard gate, where Biddy had stopped, to stand screaming for his wives.

'Get out, Aroon, let me at him.'

'Oh, Papa, should you?'

'Shut up and get out, darling. And give me that stick.' It was the end of our fun for the afternoon. Papa drove about till teatime, master-minding every roguery shown by Biddy, who had any stallion's dangerous temper. So they were pretty well matched. 'I couldn't have the little bastard – sorry, darling – biting and kicking your children, could I?'

'Why not?' She smiled as she added: 'All right – kill yourself. Make a good job of it.' She went back to her painting or her gardening. She could always occupy his absences.

Something from these contests with Biddy lessened Papa's melancholy and revived him. There was a spice in the daily excursions because Biddy would not be tamed. His perversity was indestructible. 'I'd be safer on one of your ponies,' Papa said one day when we rescued him with the chaise upset in a ditch and Biddy on the ground. 'If I had my wooden leg, I'd kick the little bastard to death.' Papa spoke quite crossly as we helped him onto his foot again. 'How am I supposed to get home? Both shafts broken and no crutches.'

'Papa,' Hubert said, 'if you just sat up on Delia, I could lead her, and Aroon could hold you by your leg. Your bad leg.'

He hesitated. Really. He was afraid – we smelt fear. We loved him for it. We waited for him to choose how he would get home. And he chose Delia. It was the start of a new joke. We took him riding every day, and we were the kindest, most understanding instructors. 'Save me, save me,' he would shout when he overbalanced, and, running by his side, we would catch the empty loop of trouser leg below his stump and yank him back into the saddle.

'You're all right, Papa. You're going great. Well done. You're wonderful.' We brought him at last to the dry ditch going into the dry pond. We had all forgotten Mrs Brock; we never gave her a thought in those days – just a dead governess. 'Come on, Papa, you'll do it.'

'I can't, you know.' He looked very unhappy.

'Just let her walk in and out,' Mrs Brock had said to us. 'No nasty jumping.' We said the same to him, and led Delia time and again through the wet beech leaves in the bottom of the ditch and up the plump track out of it, until he found the necessary dash to hit her, one-two, behind the saddle – he couldn't kick without falling off – and jump the ditch in style.

That was the beginning of our friendship with him, and with each other. The glory of this intimacy with Papa was our discovery and adventure. We had originated his recovery. We had changed him. We were even his superiors in the thing that mattered most in his life. Our own fears and nerves were close to us in time and gave us easy understanding of his helpless withdrawal from danger. We loved the same fears that had shamed him in us. We had forgotten Mrs Brock, but it was by her methods that we deceived and defeated fear. We were excitedly happy in our intimacy with him. The charm that was his second self embraced us for the first time. When he did well I wanted to touch him and caress him; so did

Hubert. But we compromised on laughter and long glances. The absolute distance in our childhood, separating children from adults, was bridged. He was dependent, the taker; we the givers.

CHAPTER TEN

This recovery and reinstatement were a way back for him to his separate life, where all his charm and wandering habits found other adventures and intimates to whom Temple Alice was only a distant name, and Mummie a dim legend. The fitting of his wooden leg provided endless occasions for short stays at the Cavalry Club, which meant, as often as not, a night spent not at the Club but with some friend's sleek and willing wife. It was the day of the shingle and straight pailletted dresses and huge pearl chokers; gardenias in velvet boxes; white ladies before dinner; and a night-club afterwards. Dancing was beyond him; but that melancholy uncomplaining stare of his, far into the eyes of his partners, never failed him of his purpose. The wooden leg and the wonder of his recovered horsemanship added interest to the encounters between him and his women.

He would return to Temple Alice battered and exhausted. 'Were your doctors very savage?' Mummie would ask, giving him a look both indulgent and sly, before she went pleading to the cook for some special effort; then back again to her painting until he was recovered by early nights and Mrs Lennon's superb cooking.

Mrs Lennon was middle-aged. She had worked for us for fifteen years, on a wage of £30 a year. She was only Mrs Lennon in token of her office. Now she got cancer and died. Her death made a dreadful change, a real chasm in one of his greatest pleasures, a weakening of one of Mummie's unspoken influences. Mrs Lennon's secrets died along with her, for she despised receipts and the ignorant and mean-minded who cooked by them; she never wrote anything down and, if possible, shut the door against any inquiring kitchen maid while she composed her greatest dishes. No inheritance was left from her years in office. She could not speak the language of her skill (nor did she wish to). 'Partridges Mrs Lennon ...' some friend might say years after her death, and Papa's eyes would drop and his face darken. He would not answer, only sigh.

Her successors came and went; they were more expensive and none of them had a vocation. Mummie's aimless half hints about the Major's pleasures and displeasures carried no weight. She herself could not have told one of them in plain language how to boil an egg, and Mrs Beeton and Mrs Marshall had hardly more effect. At that time the standard of cooking in Irish country houses was lower than abysmal. Mrs Lennon had been a great exception. Papa did not complain, or not out loud. He had his own ways and means of expressing disappointment, even disgust. He would smile apologetically when his uneaten food was carried away, and ask gently for Bath Olivers and milk. Into the milk would go whisky – quantities of it. He grew fatter and his discontent was sad for Mummie to see.

His wooden leg and alterations to its contrivances sent him oftener, and for longer times, to London, where the Dorises and Dianas, Gladyses and Enids, and the two Joyces took their glad toll. All right – confusion was in their numbers. The outings and matings were immaterial, unconfessed, accomplished within a code of manners. Papa's love affairs were run on his own terms. Divorce was something Mummie must never be asked to imagine. She was his escape, his freedom. Temple Alice was an island where a strange swan nested, a swan who never sang the fabled song before her many deaths.

While, as though in duty bound, Papa was hunting, fishing, and shooting in their proper seasons, at Temple Alice money poured quietly away. Our school fees were the guilty party most often accused. Then came rates and income tax and the absurd hesitations of bank managers. Coal merchants and butchers could both be difficult, so days of farm labour were spent felling and cutting up trees – the wood burned up quickly and delightfully in the high fast-draughting Georgian grates. As a corrective to the butcher's bills lambs were slaughtered on the place. Half the meat was eaten while the other half went bad, hanging in the musty ice house without any ice.

Life at Temple Alice went on, well sheltered in the myths of these and other economies. Mummie thought up one which, to her, was as good as putting a big cheque into her dying bank account. I was not to be presented or to have a London season. Papa's efforts were variable and more pleasurable. Every day's hunting improved his ability to ride and thus to sell young horses. The victims of a day's shooting, whether pigeons and rabbits in the demesne, grouse on the mountain, snipe in the bogs, or woodcock by winter springs deep in hazel copses, fed the diningroom. When the servants' hall sickened at the sight of game: 'Then let them eat pig's cheek – delicious. Think of Bath chaps,' said Papa.

During the holidays Hubert and Papa shot together. Papa took a half-hidden delight in Hubert's shooting – improving towards excellence. I think his son's looks were another unadmitted pleasure and satisfaction to him. Lucky Hubert – he never knew the anxiety and disgust of acne. He strode from childhood to youth without pausing in adolescent ugliness. In the fishing season they spent long days and late evenings together on the river. Then the household ate salmon and brown trout until the maids and the stable lads finally struck: 'We're killed from fish,' they said. The cooks, sickened by salmon and exhausted from stoking the Eagle range and its satellite boiler with wood and turf, left, one after another; in those days there was always another to follow, worse if possible than her predecessor.

Wild Rose's transference from housework to cooking was accidental and unpremeditated. One of the undedicated cooks left without warning. 'Gone on the bread van,' Wild Rose reported at dinnertime, 'and it's Teresa's night out so I brought ye a hunting tea – poor Mrs Lennon's poached eggs and rashers.' The eggs were perfect, swelling primly on large slices of buttered toast, the lightest dust of cayenne blown over their well-matched pearls.

'How did you know about my red pepper? It's years since I've seen it,' Papa said sadly, giving Rose one of his embracing looks, distant, grateful, promising.

'I seen herself at it, sir, God rest her soul.'

'God rest her soul,' Papa repeated, and ate his eggs with reluctant enjoyment.

It was after this that Mummie put Rose's wages up by £1 a month and persuaded her to stay in the kitchen. An underling, Breda, took Rose's place as house-parlour maid, rather impeded than helped in her duties by a succession of trainees called between maids. Teresa, a sad, slow-witted character, retained her position as kitchen maid. She cleaned potatoes and other slug-infested vegetables, kitchen sauce pans, and stone-flagged floors. She washed up after the servants' breakfasts, mid-day dinners, and teas, meals which Tommy Fox (the battered ex-steeplechase jockey who was Papa's most valued asset in the stableyard) and his helper (successor to Ollie Reilly) shared with the female staff in the servants' hall.

Rose was young for her senior position in the household. But her plain and careful cooking, her flaring good looks, and her biting tongue kept her underlings and the lads from the yard in order; while her indefeatable will to succeed made her torture Mummie daily for receipts and suggestions suited to the diningroom. Mummie was entirely unable to fulfil either demand, try as she might; at the moment she longed to please and distract Papa, for Goodwood was near, where one of the distant harem had taken a house and invited him to stay for the meeting.

'I don't know what to suggest.' She looked at Rose hopelessly, Rose in her lilac cotton dress, standing in the dull lilac gloom of the kitchen. 'Renoir?' she murmured to herself. 'Not quite. Too hungry looking.' As she looked, a vague idea possessed her, an escape; Goodwood and after defeated, perhaps. 'I don't know what to suggest,' she repeated. 'Why don't you ask the Major?'

Wild Rose went off in a wild peal of laughter: 'Is it ask the

Major, madam? – oh, my God—' She covered her mirth with her hand and bowed her head to her own laughter.

'Only yesterday he said if you could make that sickening chocolate cake you could make a cheese soufflé. Here he is – ask him.'

He was limping down the stone passage towards the rod and gun room, his mind on the Stewards' Cup and a week of luxurious liberties, manifold and unquestioned. 'What's that? Luncheon? Salmon again? Make a Hollandaise sauce and a sorrel purée, why don't you – the haggard's full of sorrel.'

'So it is,' Mummie said, happily relieved, 'and the sauce is sure to be in Mrs Beeton.'

'Spell it for me, write it down for me,' Rose insisted. He wrote on the slate, mysteriously, as if marking a race-card for a chosen woman.

That was how a state of things began that added an interesting dimension to his life. He did go over for Goodwood, but he came back very soon afterwards, bringing with him receipts from his hostess's chef, to whom he had given an enormous tip. The receipts were not easy to follow; their ramifications and the occasional French word involved patient explanations, lengthy sessions. If Mummie sometimes asked: 'Where's Papa? Have you seen him?' the answer to his whereabouts was fairly regularly: 'Ordering dinner' instead of the earlier 'Tying flies' or 'Cleaning his gun.'

I have the most articulate memory of passing the kitchen door one day and seeing Wild Rose suddenly as a person, not as a housemaid or cook. Her hands were on the kitchen table behind her and the curve of her back leaned towards them; her attitude had an easiness, and there was a rough, low tone in her voice. They were speaking of the Eagle range and its awful appetites, of gulls' eggs, and how long to cook them. There were pauses, dragging out the time of giving and taking orders for luncheon; their voices had another world beyond them.

CHAPTER ELEVEN

Although there had been no London season for me, every winter our own and neighbouring hunts held their hunt balls and lesser dances. And every long summer came the nightmare galas of the Dublin Horse Show. Papa, wooden leg and all, was in enormous demand for these routs and parties. His successes with young girls were quite frightening, although he never jeopardised his place in the middle-aged belt to which he belonged – that company of neat, sweet, tough hunting ladies; blue habited and veiled, showing their horses by day; by night richly dressed, sweetly scented, and out for further adventure. I was brought along to the parties; sad boys, often younger than I was, were netted in to partner me. I loved to dance: I suffered in their arms. Or I sat smiling, smiling; or shut for hours in some lavatory; or chattered hysterically with the unwanted, like myself.

Part of my trouble was being a big girl. I have now come to terms with my height; but in those years, when I was nineteen and twenty, I bent my knees; I bowed my shoulders; I strapped in my bosoms till they burst out round my back.

More than a year later Hubert was with me, and Hubert was my friend. He was at Cambridge now, where he had achieved a remote assurance which made our alliance the more surprising and flattering for me. I adored his good looks and I knew he waited for my admiration – it stood for some necessity that he was missing at Temple Alice. He spoke of next year's May balls: 'You'll come – we *will* have a rampage.' He taught me to charleston, a bizarre, pagan exercise, foreign to County West Common. Holding the back of a chair as practice bar I discovered what syncopation meant. 'This way? No, this way? Yes, yes, yes! I've got it. I've got it, Hubert.' It was delicious. Better than my first bicycle on its first day. Surprisingly soon, the pupil excelled the master. But I subdued my genius to his pleasure. He was still capable of that sidelong unkindness I remembered from my childhood. But beyond that a talent for pleasing, for amusing, for softly getting his own way had grown in him. Mummie had to give him £5 to sit for her. It was the first time she had painted him seriously and she put all she knew about angles and ugliness into the portrait. Hubert was neither amused nor pleased. He turned away.

'It's not a photograph, you know; it's a composition.' Mummie sounded faintly apologetic.

'A broken bicycle with two heads and one tiny eye – that's me.' Hubert laughed sourly.

'For a start, you have two enormous eyes and two-inch eyelashes,' I comforted him.

'Yes, Aroon would see you as a box of chocolates.'

Hubert's eyes met mine – met in a past for us alone; 'Charbonnel AND Walker,' he breathed.

'The best,' I answered from the same past. I quite liked leaving Mummie out of our jokes.

Papa loved Hubert, loved him in a silent, vain, satisfied way. Hubert was admirable to him in the deepest sense. He rode beautifully, and with judgement and courage; he was a good shot, and a thoughtful, skilful fisherman. He was all that Papa's friends most approved, and all that Papa wished for in a son. Beyond all these things I think Papa was most grateful for the way Hubert lifted me off his conscience. And I was Hubert's escape and salvation from the girls who besieged him.

That winter when he grew up, I enjoyed myself for the first time. I acquired consequence. To be needed and liked by two such popular characters as Papa and Hubert lent me an interest rather better than second hand. Maybe I was a parasite – but what a happy parasite, happy in their admiration and their kindness, happy in being their new joke. Hubert called me Atom. 'My little sister Atom.' 'Oh, we can't go without Atom,' they said when bidden to some grand junketing, 'Atom keeps us out of trouble. Atom will drive us home, if we're a little tired. We've got to have Atom.' My inclusion became an accepted fact in any invitation; and if I was asked alone they would come too. 'We've got to look after Atom. She'd be up to all sorts of nonsense without us.' They invented a dangerous, glamorous side to me, and took elaborate precautions for my unassaulted chastity.

It was glorious then. There are no beauties now like the beauties of the twenties; theirs was an absolute beauty, and none the worse for being clean and tidy. I worshipped some of those full-page photographs in the *Tatler*. Today I can still feel the grip of a cloche hat over my earphones of hair, and a little later the freedom and sauce of a beret on a shingle. We wore our hats, usually of pale rabbit-coloured felt, when exercising our horses or playing tennis, or for luncheon parties. On our way to the bathroom we wore crêpe-de-chine and lace boudoir caps – what has become of crêpe-de-chine? Or real silk stockings with their transparent clocks, if it comes to that? Or those life-giving white ladies before dinner before the ball? Not that I am actually against martinis, but I want to go back, I want to soak myself in Cointreau, gin, and lemon juice in equal parts.

I was fiercely shy. I would never have got myself to a party without Hubert and Papa. They really worried themselves silly about my success or failure with men. I don't really mean 'failure'; I can't have been one, because, since I had become Papa's and Hubert's joke and invented character, men, real grown-up men, danced with me quite often. Now I never sat out more than two dances running and that can happen to any girl. Of course, I have this wonderful sense of rhythm. My charleston was a poem, and could be the same today if there was any decent dance music.

Dancing with Hubert was the most wonderful experience I shall ever know. Because he was my brother we could do every intricate step and take the wildest positions without embarrassment. Dancing together we were possessed by the music. The band played for us, giving us what we needed. To me it was the absolute. I was resistless in the strength of a river that had no source and reached no sea. With other girls he was not a spectacular dancer. I don't think his girls ever knew when he had stopped dancing and was aiming for the bar and a free drink with Papa. That was not always their destination. I once heard him screaming from a car: 'Help! Help! I'm being *raped*!' He was laughing so much when I got there that all he could say was: 'Atom, she interfered with me.' 'Make up your mind,' the blonde said. 'What *do* you want?' And she went flouncing off. Hubert held my hand. 'I wish I knew,' he said. 'I do wish I knew.' He was still laughing.

It was so marvellous that I should enjoy myself, perhaps I exaggerate the luxurious sensation these times and parties gave me. But the parties happened. I was there, in the heart of things. I see chains of rooms opening one out of another. I didn't discriminate then as to whether they were rooms in grand eighteenth-century houses, or rooms in grand Victorian country houses, or rooms in grand hotels. They are all rather dark to me now, as they were then, banked with evergreens, here and there a gleam from a cold greenhouse – some pallid flower, dim among the mosses and ivies and variegated periwinkle.

The men were the flowers in these mysterious forests, sleek and orchidaceous in their hunt coats, the facings and collars pale, thin gold watch-chains crossing meagre stomachs, white ties as exact as two wings on a small bird's back, long legs black as cypripedium stems, hands sometimes gloved, eyes focused distantly, as if a fox stealing away from its covert was still the thought in mind. They would look over my shoulder and away, and they never listened to a word I said. If they spoke it was about the day's hunting. The theme was always what hounds had done, or what sad stupidity their huntsman had shown in handling them. It was all a stylish performance, never a human side to it; nothing personal, no boastfulness, or only in a very sidelong way, never a heart-warming admission of cowardice, or hatred of a horse. No truth that could betray the myth. When I was twenty, foxhunting was Wholly Holy and everybody was an apostle or a disciple. If you were a doubting disciple, so much the worse for you – keep quiet and show willing. I was neither cowardly nor unwilling, but my great height was an awkward problem for me and for my horse; our groom, Tommy Fox, was always whining away about the state of its back, and encouraging Papa to discourage me from going out.

To be truthful, I rather adored the days when I was horseless and drove our car round after the hounds. The back was stuffed with good things to eat and drink; our car was a famous bar and buffet. The Master would even *speak* to me sometimes, when I handed him a beaker at the end of the day. 'Bless you, darling,' he said once, and the blood drummed in my ears. But before I had wrenched the lid off the box of pheasant sandwiches he had ridden away and his place was taken by the Crowhurst twins.

The Crowhurst sisters were almost identical twins; Nod and Blink were the baby names they still went by, although at that time they were almost thirty, nearing middle age. Everybody was kind to them because they had no money, nothing but Good Old Blood, and deft inventive ways. They did their own horses, and everything for themselves as well. They almost made their own boots. They could not make their bowler hats, which were wide and green and had belonged to their aunts, but their neat double-knitted waistcoats of canary yellow were bright and new and lined with chamois leathers meant for cleaning silver. They rode astride and very well too, one had to admit, and, of course, never gave sore backs. 'Your father told us to have a warming drink,' they said crisply and almost together; it was nearly a challenge to me to offer them soup. 'Port or whisky?' I asked and clapped the lid back on the pheasant sandwiches. The Crowhurst girls were never among my favourites. I cannot understand what Papa saw in them.

When the last covert was drawn and the last sound of the 'Go Home' note had fallen from the air and the hounds, pinch-bellied, thronged the road before their long jog back to kennels, Hubert and Papa would give me their horses to hold while they rummaged in the car for drinks and sandwiches. I can smell the sweat and the leather in the evening air as I waited, talking the horses into quietness, rubbing the itch under their bridles, and doing my all to keep their heads towards the hounds, and their heels turned towards the ditches. Hubert and I would ride home together, so that Papa might rest his bad leg in the car. Then we were in confidence and accord: deciding on how to avoid riding home with the Crowhurst girls, or debating the idea of another drink, when and where we would revive ourselves for the miles that remained of our long hack home.

Once, on a January evening, Hubert delayed so long in the Central Bar (centre of nothing but a bog and a post office) that the horses were getting cold, and so was I. He came out at last, no drink for me in his hand, and the man who owned the Central Bar at his elbow.

'Get him up on his horse,' he said, 'if he's able, and let him keep out of my place; it's not for his sort.'

I was really shocked at his manner. They are usually more than glad to welcome the gentry. After one look at Hubert I could see that he was simply faint from lack of food, so I shot into the bar to buy him a packet of biscuits. A dreadfully naughty-looking boy was standing on a chair and waving to Hubert through a tiny window. He looked as eager as any blonde at a hunt ball. 'Biscuits, please.' I tapped sharply on the counter with half-a-crown. 'Ginger biscuits.'

'We have only Kerry Creams,' he said softly, glancing away

from me and back to the window. I snatched up the packet and hurried out. I didn't like the place.

Then, just as Hubert failed for the second time to get his foot in the stirrup, the Crowhurst twins rode past. He was laughing helplessly, and the horses were all over the road.

'Enjoying yourselves?' the twins said in their sharp way as they rode neatly together into the evening. When they got home they would do their horses and give them chilled drinks and warm, long-prepared mashes, before they had some of that wonderful potted fish (it's their secret still) on toast for their own tea. Good gals, good gals, people said of them. Really keen. They were happy, I suppose, in their exact way. Their days must have been full to exhaustion point, what with their horses to feed and groom and exercise, making all their own clothes, and keeping their dogs as primly perfect as babies with an English nannie; but they never knew, poor things, what happiness meant, as I knew it with Hubert and Papa – and then, Richard.

CHAPTER TWELVE

It was towards the end of the second summer after Hubert had made the happy break and change in my cheerless social round that he brought Richard to stay at Temple Alice. Nothing could have been more pleasing to Papa. His oldest friend Wobbly Massingham's boy, how right that he and Hubert should be friends; how right, and hopeful, that Hubert should bring him along to be my partner and escort for the Horse Show balls.

Although I assumed a great carelessness, I felt hopeful too, and I bicycled early and late to my appointments with the local dressmaker. Mrs Harty was a big heavy woman with a club foot. She had a zest and imagination unsurpassed where clothes were concerned. My height was a challenge to her; there was such a lot of me to be dressed.

'Keep to beige, Miss Aroon,' she would implore, 'and keep it simple.' When I brought her patterns of rose-clouded chiffon: 'We'll only look like an arbour in a garden,' she said sadly. I felt a little cross at this uncalled-for comment but I ignored it, naturally, and ordered ten yards of the rose chiffon.

I was so anxious over the accomplishment of my clothes and so weary from bicycling through hot July afternoons for their fittings that my curiosity about, even my interest in, Richard stayed below the surface. He was a man for the Horse Show and its dances; that was God-given and enough. Hubert did say to me: 'You don't seem much interested in my friend.'

'I am, really.'

'And I've asked him all for you.'

'You know he'll hate me.'

'Why should he? He was dotty about Bronwyn Morbyrd and she has the Burnham legs, poor girl.'

'Oh, don't tease – what *am* I going to talk about?'

'Not horses. He likes a good giggle about Mrs Brock.'

'Mrs Brock? You can't mean it.'

'Yes, I do. She was our first laugh.'

'How weird.' I felt her wild hands on my shoulders; I saw my little Minnie and her squirming mites; I clearly remembered every word spoken then. Not very serviceable as light chat.

'And look what I've found,' Hubert spoke in his most sidelong, jeering voice. He pulled it out of the schoolroom bookshelf, out of a copy of *The Children's Golden Treasury*. It was from Mrs Brock's Stoke Charity gallery, a portrait of Richard, eight years old, sitting on a photographer's balustrading, eyes lifted upwards from the sloped cricket bat in his hands; he wore a white shirt with a deep Byronic cleft to a plump cherub chest.

'Rather silly, isn't it?' Hubert laughed and put the picture back inside *The Children's Golden Treasury* and squeezed the book in between the packed, forgotten song-books and storybooks of our childhood.

I was appalled when I met the present Richard. In him I saw the embodiment of all the young men who had paralysed me into the maintenance of a silence broken only at rare intervals by some vicious platitude. Here he was, and for five days and five nights he would have to endure my company, my size, and my countrified simplicity. I rocked a little on the Louis heels of my strapped lizard shoes as I stole looks at him between the business of marking my catalogue and thinking of anything to say about any horse being judged in Ring 4. Long legs I saw (I had expected that), eyes discriminating and critical as a bird's; small ears; crisp hair; rolled umbrella, swinging stylishly as a sword; he came straight from the middle pages of the *Tatler* and *Bystander*. The right family, the right school, the right regiment had all been his. I was stunned between fear and admiration. He was brown (from Cowes Week), lean and hard (polo at Hurlingham); he had ridden the winner of a Grand Military (Sandown should have been written on his forehead). How could I think of a word worthy of his attention? Leaning on the rails of the judging ring I breathed the exhausted atmosphere of *déjà vu* which he exhaled as he indicated exactly which three horses the judges would pull in first, second, and third. I knew he would move through the show and all its galas in the same mood of exhausted natural disdain. He wore his bowler hat tilted to a distinctive elderly angle, well calculated to emphasise his own glorious youth. As I leaned beside him, the ache of pride and shyness drove me into the farthest depths of silence.

'Don't try,' Hubert said that first night before dinner. I felt his constraint and anxiety. 'Just be your natural self,' he advised. So I was not any more the happy joke he and Papa had invented. Desperation filled me. Right, I thought, I can't talk. But I can eat. I can be the fat woman in the fairground; the man who chews up iron; the pigheaded woman; anything to escape from hopeless me. So, at that first dinner before the first ball, I wolfed down sensational quantities of food. Almost a side of smoked salmon, and I ate a whole lemon and its peel as well; most of a duck; four meringues and four pêches melbas; mushrooms and marrow on toast; even cheese. 'What else can we find for her?' Richard asked Hubert. 'She really is a great doer.' They cheered me quietly. I was a joke again. I was a person. I was something for them to talk about.

He danced with me all night. I longed to exploit the skills Hubert and I had perfected. I ached to show him what I could get up to. But he persisted in his hesitant, intimate night-club shuffle. There was a trick and a style about it too. It retreated from the vulgarity of other people's efforts; it was part of his escape from the usual, a cultivated mannerism such as the old gentleman's tilt to his hat.

The Horse Show proceeded on its traditional five-day course, but how differently from earlier martyrdoms of fixed and smiling loneliness. This time there was no more waiting under the clock for Papa to disengage himself from business or pleasure. Hubert and Richard jostled me kindly between them from breakfast to bedtime. I was so happy, I felt they loved me. It was enough that they shared jokes with me; Richard even invented one of his own: 'Pig-wig,' he called me. And once I heard him say to Hubert: 'Our Pig-wig.' To this living moment I experience a shudder of bliss.

On the last day Richard bought a yearling in the Bloodstock Sales. I sat between him and Hubert on the circular benches, while the yearlings, coming up for auction in the ring below us, were pulling back, kicking, or mincing politely round. I didn't even realise Richard was bidding, his gestures were so quiet and small and knowledgeable. I thank God still that I didn't happen to be talking, just thumbing through the lots in my catalogue. Suddenly I felt Hubert's tension beside me, and I saw Richard's eyes blazing with excitement under the old gentleman's tilt of his hat. Excitement was caged and unspoken in a cool exaggeration of restraint. But, beyond the coolness, as the bidding went on, there was white heat. Outside in the sunlight, on the grass, we looked the colt over.

'Bit plain?'

'That's what I like.'

'And the breeding's right. I think I bought him pretty well.'

For perhaps half an hour he walked round us, and we walked round him. To my surprise he was to be boxed to Temple Alice. I wondered how Papa would like that; he complained the land was horse-sick already. Satiated for the time being, we turned to leave the bloodstock paddock. As he took a last look at the yearling Hubert gave a tingling kind of shudder. 'I think we need a drink,' he said, 'and I'm paying for it.' In the bar they almost forgot to put me between them and, I thought, only just remembered to give me a drink. Of course they were obsessed by that yearling, by Black Friday out of Love Affair by Esperanto.

That was the last day of the Horse Show; we were leaving the spending and the jollity behind us and going home to Temple Alice and the expanding summer. Hubert was just settling into Richard's car for the long drive home when Papa, his face darkening, said, on his sweet complaining note: 'Hubert, dear old boy, I'm a bit anxious about this off-fore tyre. You wouldn't change places with Aroon, just in case? I've had a disgraceful luncheon at the Club.'

'I can change the wheel, Papa,' I said. How often he had let me do so.

'Just stop arguing, would you, and get out.' He spoke so gently only I could hear, but the sweet note was out of his voice.

Richard helped me into his car, wrapped some kind of camel's-hair robe round my knees, offered me an Egyptian cigarette, and, for the eighty-mile drive home, spoke only to ask the way. I was accustomed to miles of silent trance with Papa so Richard's silence seemed natural enough. I cuddled my great body down as kittenishly as my size allowed, and beneath the liberal rug I feigned sleep. Later on, when I got round to reading Michael Arlen, I realised that this was the right sort of car in which to roar through the night at eighty miles an hour before a death crash for Purity's obscure sake.

CHAPTER THIRTEEN

Mummie's reaction to Richard was a question unspoken between us. Our anxiety was ridiculously misplaced. From the first evening, when she found that he actually appreciated Regency furniture, she decided that he was far too intelligent to waste his time on me, and stole his company whenever she could.

I wondered why he need have bothered to please her when everything came his way, even infrequent birds on the mountain. Snipe, too, flung themselves into the pattern of his shot, trout hurried to the fly he cast over them, and horses, good or bad, went beautifully for him. Glamour circling him about, he pitched it to its lowest key. It was as if he deprecated being the tallest in any room, towering silent and repellent of any advance, dressed in clothes which, though they hinted at the Regency buck, were never inappropriate to the occasion. From the disapproving way in which he paused over certain pages of the *Tatler*, I knew he had glamorous friends; royal friends too, though naturally he never mentioned them.

Until now I had been aware of Temple Alice only as our

cold comfortless home – large; full of ill-placed furniture; loud with the echoes of feet on thinly carpeted boards or a chill clatter on black and white tiles; a roof leaking winter, or summer, rain; hard beds; soft, cold bathwater. These were my familiar thoughts about the house, to which I occasionally added an impatient sympathy for Papa's anxieties over rates, leaking valleys in the roof, broken water chutes, as well as his haunting fear and denial of dry rot. But in this eternal August the place took on a sumptuous quality. Every day the lean, deprived face of the house blazed out in the sunlight. Sun poured onto damp-stained wallpaper, through the long windows. It shone on us from when we woke until we changed for dinner.

One morning, from my bed, I heard the sound of horses ridden out early into silence. I sat up, clasping my knees over the blankets, while I watched them, Richard and Hubert, riding out together. Hubert was riding Arch Deacon (Arch Demon, Tommy Fox named him), a difficult young horse that Papa had bought cheap from a hunting parson and given to Hubert to tame and civilise. Now I saw him compelling Arch Deacon to good manners, opening the gate into the near field, insisting quietly on his horse's subservience while Richard rode through. They had not told me they would ride out early. I put away the thought and with it the prospect of exercising my fat hunter alone.

I think it was that day, or the next, that we drove to Kildeclan and Richard bought me a great bottle of scent. He also bought a bottle of Cointreau and a bottle of gin and six lemons, which were stowed away in his bedroom. 'Cocktails at seven tonight,' he said. 'Don't forget, Piggy-wig. Bring your toothglass.'

There was something daring and men-only about that little party. Drenched in Richard's scent and wearing my older flowered crêpe-de-chine, I felt very privileged to be there. I liked to watch the boys as they finished dressing. There was a quick, hard grace about their movements, in the way they put links quickly into the cuffs of evening shirts, such a different tempo from a girl's considered gesture. They wore narrow red braces and their black trousers were taut round waists and bottoms. I seemed to join in the violent act of hairbrushing – each hair into place and no nonsense. I felt easier, more part of them as the minutes passed. How dear they were. Spoilers of girls. Their silences were pregnant with all the things it was bad form to say, so I wonder how it was that we got round to the subject of Mrs Brock. Hubert had said she was a joke with them. I didn't think so. They invented that idea and got behind it. Her name had been buried under silences and unspoken questions for so long that mystery, like the sea, had swallowed her up.

'I wonder why she did it – was it awful old love again?'

'Richard – what do you mean?'

'Well – Nannie found her kissing me and she had this school-girl pash for Mummie too.'

'Our Mummie was absolutely foul to her.'

'Did you like her?'

'Oh, I don't remember. Did you?'

'I don't remember.'

'I don't remember either.' We all denied her.

'Did she find things here?'

'Find things? I don't remember. What things?'

'I never think about her now, crazy old ass,' Hubert said angrily.

'But I want to know,' Richard insisted. 'If you can't remember, invent something. Why did she drown herself?'

That was the start of the Mrs Brock cult. It grew into a game that Richard loved playing. He drew Hubert and me into it. First, remembering things about her; then inventions, sad, funny, intimate details. It was a charade. She had to seem pathetic, ridiculously sentimental, with sly Hogarthian hints on her private behaviour. I didn't understand Richard's avid curiosity. Although, to please him, I fed it for all I was worth, I always kept back what she had told me about the mice, though sometimes I was on the verge. Hubert, when he took wholeheartedly to the game, was a perfect mine of fascinating reminiscence. He remembered how she would sing, and the songs she sang, and how she would twist on the piano-stool, still singing, and draw us close to her for the refrain; and how the faint smell of Mrs Brock beat the faint smell of talcum powder.

'Yes, yes – armpits, armpits.' Richard was enchanted.

'*Papier poudré*, Icilma snow,' I contributed.

They took to dressing and undressing her like a doll, like an effigy. Hubert screamed at some of the disgusting things he thought up. I laughed, not always hearing or quite getting the point, but determined not to be left out, frightened, yet longing to be a party to this violation.

'She made camisoles and she wound the lace insertions onto strips of postcards. "I do like everything to be dainty," she said.'

'Dainty, my foot. She pulled up her skirts and warmed her bottom at the schoolroom fire.'

'Hubert, you know she never did.'

Richard drowned my protest. He laughed so much he lay

back in his chair: 'Split knickers,' he gasped. The game was like a dangerous secret between the boys. They only let me in because I delved so deeply into what I had put away. Everything I remembered was a denial and a betrayal of the other things she was. But between us we almost called her into being. It was such fun sharing in her persecution.

All that month after the show, through the excitement of Richard's presence, we put Papa aside. He had been our darling, but now we formed a charmed circle where the old were uninvited. Until this month of August Hubert and Papa had been interlaced in their interests. They were warm and close in the only things that really counted with them. Now Papa hung back and made excuses over a day's shooting. Hubert and Richard could walk farther and faster without him; he knew it. The harvest was a blessed retreat for him, and an occupation which relieved an inescapable saddened jealousy. He didn't actually work in the fields, but he surveyed and supervised, and banged away at rabbits as his dogs put them out of gold margins. His days were full, but not happy. He had been replaced.

Sometimes the boys drove off after dinner in Richard's great car. I was left out then, because Hubert was learning to drive that dreadful treasure, and I glowed when they said I was too precious to risk. Papa was uneasy if they were very late, thinking perhaps that Hubert had taken the monster onto the roads, although he had asked him to stay on the two long avenues until he knew the car better. One night he was fidgeting miserably, and showed pleasure and relief when I suggested we should walk out the dogs and meet the boys.

'Yes, they're asking for a run, poor chaps.' The importance

was shifted onto the dogs. 'Put on your Wellies, darling, and we'll walk across Long Acres and the Horse Park.'

We went together in the soft night, through the beech groves and beyond them, over the fields where the cattle moved through tall flowers and grasses, or lay side by side in quiet crowns, their great pale bodies bruising the grass to darkness. Volumes of their sweet breath and crushed river mint were on the night air. We found the car standing empty at the open gate into the Horse Park.

'Pretty silly place to leave the thing,' Papa said. 'Young horses in the field might do themselves an injury, kick themselves to bits kicking at it, or eating pieces out of the hood. Can you drive it through the gate?'

'No. Besides, the cows would eat it in the meadow.'

'So they would. You're so bright, darling. Sicken them. Well, can you blow the horn?'

The notes on the horn wavered and echoed into the night, and brought the boys back to us, unhurrying, displeased rather than apologetic when Papa explained the summons.

'The horses were moved to the bog yesterday,' Hubert said. 'There's only my yearling and a donkey here now.'

'Your yearling?'

'Richard's yearling. The Black Friday yearling. We went down to look at him.'

'I see.'

There was silence. And the night air that had been so sweet was charged and tense with unformulated, unspoken mistrust. Suddenly, rain fell – the first rain in the month. Papa and I and the dogs bundled into the car with Richard. Hubert shut the iron gate behind us, and we left him with rain pouring on his dark head. When we got to the house Richard kept the engine running, revving it loudly as Papa got out, awkwardly and slowly with his wooden leg.

'Aren't you coming in?' Papa said, standing in the headlights.

'No. I'm going to pick up Hubert.' Richard swept the big car backwards and round and roared down the drive again.

'Bloody nonsense; the rain won't hurt him,' Papa was shouting. But Richard was gone far out of ear-shot. Papa stood another moment in the rain, looking after the car helplessly. I understood. He wasn't first with Hubert any more. It was a lonely business.

'Let's dry the dogs,' I said.

'Yes,' Papa said, hopping up the steps. 'Yes, yes. First things first.'

It was coming to the end of August, and Richard was still with us. Our intimacy grew in value as the days passed. In the mornings we rode out fat, bright horses that had to be exercised, and Hubert's unruly brute that had to be schooled and civilised. There were the evenings when we danced in the nearly dark drawingroom, one oil lamp poised in a Negro's hand near the wind-up gramophone, His Master's Voice, with the alert white dog on the black lifted lid.

Here, to my delight, Hubert and Richard danced with me in turn. I almost preferred dancing with Hubert, because I loved showing off to Richard. I loved those moments when he seemed compelled to lift his head from the *Field* or the *Tatler* and watch us as we charlestoned our exuberant rhythmic way through the spaces between the rugs on the floor. Hubert's dancing with me had an inspired quality; it was more exciting than I had ever known it, very different from Richard's cool understatement of the rhythm. Richard would put an iron hand between my shoulders and compel me to a change of style, looking over and across the top of my head while we danced, and my disturbed heart hurried and turned as it never did in the most exciting dance with Hubert – although I adored Hubert then as much as I did Richard. In turn I was fulfilled by them. I felt complete. There was no more to ask.

CHAPTER FOURTEEN

Soon he must go. I would face the bright autumn without him and without Hubert. I forbade myself to count the few days left before Hubert went back to Cambridge and Richard to his regiment. I hated to lose a minute of our time together. That evening I was in a haze of melancholy which was to find its climax in one of those pains I had been taught to disregard as slight monthly discomforts, not to be over-rated; to take them seriously was to be guilty of a social nuisance. This time I had the remedy near. At last I knew what gin could do for me. Toothglass in hand, I knocked at Richard's door.

'Come in,' he called, not quite at once. He seemed immense and almost lowering, shrouded in his dark dressing-gown, lighting a cigarette, glaring at himself in the square mahogany-framed looking-glass. Hubert was sitting on the edge of the bed, wrapped in one of those great rough bath towels, sampler-stitched in red, which must have been fifty years old even then. He stretched out a bare arm for Richard's cigarette case. Neither of them offered one to me. After a moment Richard said: 'Did you want a drink?'

'Yes. I'm feeling rather awful.'

Hubert didn't speak. He maintained the sly, withdrawn silence I remembered when, as a little boy, he was Mummie's favourite and I perched out in the cold. Before I had grown to love him.

Richard belted up his dressing-gown with exacting discretion and took the bottles out of the clothes basket. 'No lemon, I'm afraid,' he said, as he sloshed the gin and dribbled the Cointreau into my toothglass and, as he said it, my unbelieving eyes saw a lemon on the dressing-table, waiting for their drinks, not for mine. I think Hubert knew that I saw it, and knew that he was too late when he crossed from bed to dressing-table to brush his hair with Richard's hairbrushes. He sat there, his bare shoulders sloped towards their reflection. Richard gave me back my glass and turned away. I think he looked at his wrist for a watch he wasn't wearing yet.

'Perhaps we ought to dress,' he said.

'Yes, you'll be late,' I managed, although I knew they had hours of time till dinner, 'I'll let you get dressed.' I put down my glass. No doubt I could come back. In the mirror Hubert saw what I was doing.

'Take it with you, sweetie,' he said gently.

I stood outside the door with the dreadful brimming glass in my hand. Inside the room I heard them begin to laugh, relieved giggling laughter, and when they supposed I had gone, shouts of laughter followed me – laughter that expressed their relief from some tension and left me an outsider. Puzzled and anxious I sat on in my bedroom, sipping at the disgustingly powerful gin without gaining from it any lift or exuberance. I waited for the minutes to pass, minutes that I had so carelessly expected to spend in their company. Soon the gin overcame my pain, but not my mistrust in happiness, or certainty in happiness.

The boys had a lot to say to Papa that night. They stayed a long time in the diningroom while Mummie and I sat in the library, each near a silver lamp, and stitched away, I at my camisole, apricot crêpe-de-chine and écru lace, she with her tapestry, green tulips on a white ground.

'It's rather sad they'll be gone on Thursday,' she murmured, as Papa and the boys delayed longer and longer in the diningroom. She put away her tapestry and took up her patience board, as though to mark how time was going. I felt dry, set for ever in my place as daughter of the house, unmarried daughter.

Papa came in and sat in his winged armchair. 'They're in the gunroom writing up the game book,' he said to me, certainly supposing that I would want to join them.

'Oh, yes, are they?' My voice came out cold and stifled, as changed as tonight was from last night. I felt him give me a look, but he had the new *Horse and Hound* to read. Politely occupied we sat on, our thoughts our own, incommunicable. And then, coming faintly from the drawingroom, we heard music: '*Wien, Wien, nur du allein* . . .' Last night I had swooped round to it, swayed about in its plunging and soaring melodies, sharing all the romance, and the regret.

For a minute or two Papa didn't turn or rustle a page of *Horse and Hound*. He stirred round in his chair as though he couldn't find a comfortable position for his wooden leg. Then, as if it were a new idea, he said: 'They're playing the gramophone.' Then, after a pause: 'I expect they're waiting for you in there.'

I couldn't answer. Mummie said, turning a tiny card: 'Well, they know where she is, don't they?'

Papa rustled and bunched up *Horse and Hound* and threw a dog down from his knees as if to hush or drown what she was saying. Then he was on his feet. 'Come on,' he said. 'I need some exercise. May I have this one? Shall we dance, darling, shall we dance?'

I was mortified for us both. They didn't want Papa, he knew it, and they didn't want me, not this evening or ever again perhaps, and I knew it. Yet here we were, two unwanted children determined to ignore our ostracism. Papa caught my hand and pulled me with him as he hobbled down the hall, a nannie towing a reluctant child to a party.

'*Wien, mein lieber Wien*' came to us, shamelessly sweet through the shut mahogany door of the drawingroom. I hung back, despairing.

Richard and Hubert seemed not to hear Papa opening the door; the room was so filled with music. Hubert was sitting, a dog on his knees, below the Negro's shaded lamp. The light on his bent head shone his hair to a blue-black, and the forward turn of his neck, between hair and white shirt collar, was as dark a brown as his hands on the white dog. Richard, standing behind the tall wing chair, stooped his extraordinary height over Hubert and the little dog. His eyes, when he raised his head towards us, held a look of anger and loss as if he suffered some unkind deprivation – something quite serious, like getting left in a hunt.

'Not dancing tonight?' Papa said.

Hubert didn't even look up. 'Fleaing Tarquin.' He pinched the nail of his forefinger with his thumb, destroying a flea.

'I'm keeping the score.' Richard sounded grave. 'That's five and two ticks.'

'Bad light for that work, isn't it?' Papa said. No one answered.

Towering in the doorway, I only longed to turn and go. But Papa pushed me forwards into the room. 'I've brought you a partner.' The words sounded affectedly forced and silly. In my embarrassment I could feel the clumsiness of my hands as I clenched them, of my height as I shrank it together, ashamed of being me, ashamed to be there. A moment more and I was rescued from myself. I was changed, because Richard broke from the group by the Negro lamp and came across the room – his grace, his strength, his intention all towards me. I was their object. I was to be their host.

'Shall we dance a little?' As he put a hand on my back, the music sobbed and died. He kept his arm round me while Hubert wound up the gramophone and changed the record. 'Whispering . . .' it croaked, 'Whispering while you . . .'

'Let's dance a little more'; the invitation was meagre. His voice always deprived any intention of its worth or warmth. Acceptance should be on the same level. 'Oh, if you like,' I said, glowing in his strict embrace. He bent his height over my height. He held me nearer than he had ever done before, as we danced away from Papa. Across my blinding happiness I heard Papa saying: 'That's right, that's it. Keep tambourine a-rolling.' He hobbled back to the hall – a boy let out of school.

I was shuffling happily through the heap of records for my next favourite when I knew that Richard was saying something urgently to Hubert. Urgent and low, it did not concern me. I was out of the trough of that terrible wave in which I had suffered and endured. I turned to dance with Hubert, when Richard caught me in his arms again; strange, because it was always dance and dance about.

'Where's Hubert going?'

'Walking the dogs with your father – I think that's what he said.'

We moved away together. With Richard, with the music, with the pallor in the windows and the darkness in the room, my happiness was restored to me, sounder, more assured than it had been in the morning. I took it with me to bed. Next morning, when I woke, I could almost look at it, it was so real.

In those last days the boys kept me with them continually. Each day of early September was more perfect than the last. Grapes were ripe in the battered vinery – those muscatels Mummie knew how to thin and prune. Butterflies – fritillaries, peacocks – spread their wings on scabious, sedum, and buddleia, waiting heavily, happily for death to come. We sat among them, eating grapes, the sun on our backs.

CHAPTER FIFTEEN

Our sea picnic was on an afternoon more encompassed by summer than any summer's day. The haze between water and land carried the one into the other. Cornfields, dry sand, rocks, sea merged in some sort of embrace, denying the summer's end. And we denied the idea that we should ever part. We swam. I felt a kind of abandon in the water and I showed it by letting my hair flow out in the sea. Richard ascertained Mrs Brock's rock and dived off it, turning about in somersaults and clasping his knees under the sea. Hubert swam out, and away.

'Call him back,' I said. 'The tide's going out.'

'Come back!' we called. 'Come back, you fool!' Richard sounded angry and anxious.

Hubert was slow in returning and sat down on a rock with a towel, laughing and gasping, rather pleased by our anxiety. 'Terrific current,' he admitted unwillingly, but anxious that we should know. My hair pouring great gouts of water onto my shoulders, I stooped, crawling on the sands to find cowrie shells at the feet of the rocks among wet shoaling pebbles, shells so small they were only just not sand.

'Come on, old Sea Cow, unpack the tea.' Hubert broke my picture of a sea-creature with wet hair. Was I only useful? Before I found time to be hurt Richard was on his feet and caught me by the hands. When he pulled me up from the sand and towards himself, I shall always be sure that his lips touched the sandy, salty crook of my arm.

'You're cold,' he said. 'Let's run.' We ran barefoot together with all our strength, far along the bare wet sands; the indecipherable waves drew faintly back from our footsteps to the sea. I felt light as an antelope; I ignored my bosoms, shuddering and swaying, inseparable from my life.

When we came back, Hubert had unpacked the tea. He had made a long hole in the sand and was sitting in it with all the mugs and jam-pots and packets of food spread within his reach. He was being Mrs Brock. After tea I buried his feet in sand, and we remembered something: Mrs Brock's toes coming up through the sand like huge pearls; like young pigs. I sanded his feet up again and patted them down.

'You're tickling my feet for burial,' Hubert said. When Richard shivered and said he must walk and run again, Hubert caught my hand this time and said: 'Stay with me.' He didn't really seem to need me, only to stop my going with Richard. 'I want to talk to you, Aroon.' He was lying back in his hole, games over. 'I want quite a serious talk. You're a big girl now.'

'Yes – well?' I had to admit it.

'Sit down. Stop looking like a swan.' A swan – my favourite bird. 'A swan on dry land,' he took it all back.

'All right. I know. I don't care.' Again I felt my bosoms impeding my true progress; I couldn't forget them as when I thought I was an antelope. Swans had great bosoms too. But off the water, of course, they look terrible.

'The place for your bosoms,' Hubert was reading my thoughts, 'is bed.'

'Bed?'

'I've seen you looking glorious in bed, in that white satin nightdress.'

'The one cut on the cross? Nobody ever sees me in bed.'

'Shall I tell you something? Richard wants to.'

'I'll put my chest-of-drawers against the door,' I said, delight filling me.

'Don't rupture yourself, dear,' he said crossly. Now I was displeasing. I felt the tide running out from me.

'What could I talk about?' I was giving way, little by little.

'About me, if you can't think of anything else.' Hubert's eyes were full of amusement.

'And if Papa hears us chattering on about you? It's past my door to his dressingroom.'

'Papa won't interrupt.' He gave me a longish look. 'I promise.' It came back to me, Mrs Brock: 'It's a thing men do. You won't like it.' Those awful mice.

'I don't want to do it, Hubert.'

'Oh, and you were to have a share in the Black Friday colt.'

To share with them. We were a trinity. Hubert put his hand over mine. 'Don't give it another thought,' he said, 'just an idea. I'll tell Richard to forget it.'

'Hubert,' I said, 'don't tell him.' We looked at each other deeply. We shared a tremor. But we had neither confessed one another nor told our purpose. The air came between us, chill off the sea and wet sands. I stretched down my long arms and pulled him out of his nest in Mrs Brock's grave. 'There's a boat coming in,' I said, escaping into occupations. 'Let's go to the quay for lobsters.'

'When Richard's back.' He gave a sweet yodelling cry that echoed off the water as stones skip over a quiet surface; it was a gift he had, but he used it very seldom.

'Did you hear?' I asked Richard when he came back.

'Hear what? I didn't hear anything.' Hubert smiled.

Low under the quay boats were coming in to their moorings. From its cliff top our cousins' little house, Gulls' Cry, seemed to lean and look downwards, calculating the catches or disappointments below its windows. The two old lives up there were as distant from our own as sand martins in a sandbank.

When lobsters were handed up to the quayside Hubert and I laughed and bargained with the fishermen we knew. Richard left us and wandered off down the quay to where a young fellow – a gigantic, sullen blond – had just climbed up the ladder from his boat. They stood together talking, and were still talking when the other men walked back in threes and pairs to the village.

Hubert and I waited, impatient to get our lobsters home in time for dinner. The same frustration and delay had happened here before on the same sort of day; I remembered it now: with Mrs Brock when we were children – the recollection stood far behind me.

'You call him, Aroon.' I wondered why Hubert had not sent out that bird-call of a yodel; neither would I shrill and call. I walked down the quay to where they stood together, matched in their similar height. I saw Richard give the boy (he came from a rotten family, drunks and Fenians all) a pound note. In exchange he took from him a fish-scaled box with three crabs in it. I was silenced by his absurd extravagance.

'We're to take these crabs up to your cousins,' his explanation for delay somehow faintly apologetic. 'He says the old fellow dying up there has a great fancy for a dressed crab.'

'So have I. Let's go home.' Hubert sounded spoilt and tense.

I was entirely on Hubert's side. I didn't want Richard to meet our old relations, bearded Cousin Enid and drooling Cousin Hamish hobbling round their dingy little house. Snob, of course I am not, but they would defile the end of such a day. Now there was a division between us three, nervous and unspoken.

Richard didn't argue. He turned the car and drove away from the sea and up the hill to our cousins' house as though he had been that way before.

A woman who looked neither a servant nor a friend opened the door: 'Miss Enid's above in the bed playing a game of snap with Mister Hamish. I don't know would she come down. She's not so well herself.' She turned away discouragingly.

With his unquestioning acceptance of being welcome anywhere Richard followed her into the house. 'Oh, go and ask them if they want these crabs.' He spoke as if to a servant of his own and she succumbed, almost pleasantly, to his authority. He looked back, compelling us to join him.

Hubert and I knew the room where we waited too well for curiosity. We were familiar with its splitting marquetry, its dusty famille rose and verte, its blistered Chinese wallpaper, since miserable childish hours. The window that hung out like a great tongue above the boat quay had been our only entertainment and reprieve from games with an incomplete set of ivory dominoes when we waited for Mummie. Mummie kept hold of a tenuous connection and cousinship as she conned and considered the ever more damaged and neglected pieces and prints. Cousin Enid would never sell – but she might bequeath.

This evening Richard walked across to the window, staring down, absorbed and pleased, into the quiet empty boats as though he saw an open box full of toys.

The woman came back: 'Miss Enid can't come down. Mister Hamish is losing and he mustn't be upset. I'm to take the crabs, dirty things – I hate crabs.'

Crabs, the Cancer sign, I thought, no luck about them. Endless work, picking out the live-boiled flesh from the dead men's fingers.

As we turned, all three together, from the window breast, a sound above checked and held us waiting. It was a knocking, a stick knocking on floorboards, gentle, querulous, then louder, doubling taps, hammer strokes on coffin lids – or do they screw down the dead? If we had been children we might have held hands, squeezing out fear, not running away.

The woman turned back to us as if she sensed some unreasonable questioning: 'Ah, don't mind that noise at all – she must have beat him in the finish. He'll kill her someday with that old stick if she won't give up winning.' She laughed at the absurdity of her joke. I hesitated before I echoed her laugh, and the boys waited before they echoed mine.

We fled the house to sit close together in the big car. Our youth commanded its powers; our youth was immeasurable, we knew; but for a passing moment a shiver had left us defenceless.

'Drinks soon … come to the bar,' they said, as we hurried apart to change for dinner. My gold dress dipped to the floor at the back. A palmful of Richard's scent behind my ears, yes, and the insides of my arms. I smiled alone, and laid my cheek to them before I picked up my toothglass and tore along the corridor. In Richard's room they filled my glass to the top with champagne.

'Steady,' Hubert said, when Richard filled it again, 'we don't want the girl unconscious.'

'Don't we?' Richard answered gently. And I thought, in a second of delight, how he might watch me sleeping.

After dinner, sitting together in the library, I felt in my new distance of happiness that Mummie had grown smaller, meaner, of no account. When we heard the men leaving the diningroom I rose to my feet – light as a bird, I felt young as the morning.

'Must you look so majestic, darling?' She sighed, considering the word and her tapestry as she cuddled her little body closer into her little chair. I must have heard, or I shouldn't remember, but at that moment she could have called me a wardress and spoiled nothing for me. Soon I would be dancing. Again my feet would skim the floor. Earlier in the day they had scarcely printed their bare soles on the sand. I was so glad now, levitating in happiness, that my breath alone could have held me off the ground.

We danced, much as usual. Oddly a sort of restraint was on me; it suited with his night-club shuffle, and his hooded, unspeaking look. It was a prelude to a meeting. Were we both afraid? Afraid together? It was beyond delight.

When they went out on a last rat-hunt with Papa and the dogs, I ran upstairs so fast that the flame of my candle rushed backwards in the wind of my going. Every summer night smelt like Christmas when you put a hand behind the candle flame and blew it out. Safety matches always on the po cupboard beside your bed. How often had I struck a match and lit a candle to sit up and read a good detective story, refusing all impious thoughts. Not tonight.

Alone now I unhooked my gold dress and let it fall sumptuously round my feet. I unhooked my deep bust bodice too, and my bosoms puffed out at me as though filled with proven yeast, alas. No matter. Flat in bed, I would be more like a swan on water. Leaning towards my glorified eyes in the mirror I could have kissed my image. No curlers. No face cream. My nightdress, all on the bias, clung to me like scales to a fish, to a mermaid. Quite literally, my appearance took my own breath away.

I got into bed; I spread my hands on the sheets, I arranged and rearranged myself on the pillows; a nesting swan is beautiful too. Moths pelted against the window panes. Tiny flies met and dispersed and met again at the candle flame. As no man likes an over-eager girl, I had a book with a finger between the pages for a pretence at reading when the door should open.

I heard the dogs and Papa and the boys come back into the house – vague affectionate voices talking to the dogs, not to each other. Pauses. Were they lighting candles? Steps on the stairs. My heart turned over. They passed my door. My heart turned back again. I debated whether or not to blow out my candle. No. Better leave it – how could I be reading in darkness? I would put the book down, finger still between the pages. 'Richard?' Whispering, I rehearsed the inflexion for my voice. I must not expect him too soon. Hardly before Papa went to bed. Would Papa ever go to bed? He could be so late. Not tonight, for once; please God, let him go to bed early.

The whole night bloomed for me as the door handle was turning. In the moment before he came in I owned the world. The moment after he came in, a kind of practical reality subdued my mood. He came across to my bed and sat down, near my feet. 'What are you reading?' He spoke in quite a loud voice.

'Shs.' I leaned towards him and put my hand across his mouth. When I did so I got an odd feeling that he was nearly laughing. It didn't seem right to me.

'Oh, don't put it out,' he said quickly, when I blew at the candle.

'Papa,' I whispered.

'Perhaps you're right.'

There was a longish pause while he took off his dressing-gown. He got into bed beside me as coolly as if he were stepping into a boat. Then he gave a childish kind of bounce, setting the springs screaming and vibrating. He pulled a pillow away from me and stirred about and settled down as if for a good night's sleep. I longed for something to say. He spoke first.

'You have such enormous bosoms.' His voice came from a distance in place and time, but still far too loud. 'Shall I lay my head on one of them just to see what it's like?'

Why did I have to think then of the Mrs Brock game? I denied the thought.

'Yes, you may.' I felt the weight of his head, and I saw the line of his cheek and neck. A ravishing content flooded me. I wanted this. I lay still beside him.

'It's a bit hot,' he said after a minute. I turned towards him.

He must guess. 'I really must NOT touch you,' he said quickly. 'We'd regret it always, wouldn't we, Piglet? Wouldn't we?'

I could hardly endure the thought that through his chivalry, not through my own faultless behaviour, I had made a lucky escape. I felt cherished and defrauded. 'Yes. We'd hate ourselves.'

'Let's talk about something else now,' he said, back on his pillow.

'What about?'

'Oh, anything – Hubert, for instance.'

Perhaps Hubert was the closest thing in both our lives, but now I would rather have talked about Richard and me – and why not? Here he was in my bed, the bed I still sleep in.

'What do you like about him?'

I turned on my other side. I didn't flounce. I just turned over.

'You're such a big girl,' he complained. 'Why do you have to flounce about like that? Every time you move you tilt the bed over.'

'What about getting back to your own room?' I strangled back the hurt in my voice. It was growing more and more like games some girls played in Number Six Dorm.

'Can't. Not till the Major's gone to bed, can I? He *is* late.' Plaintive was how he sounded now.

That was when I heard Papa. He was so dextrous with his wooden leg, but on the stairs you couldn't help knowing about it. He had a way of throwing his weight onto his good leg, and pausing a moment.

'Does he ever come in to say goodnight?' Richard asked much too loudly in one of the pauses. I think he wanted everything to be more frightening. Again I put my hand across his mouth. He sat up in bed, making the springs scream. I could feel him swing his feet out to the floor, and the bed sag back to me as he left it. 'Can't find these slippers.' He struck a match, even before Papa had passed the door. I was so tense I could hear myself creak. 'It's all right now.' He was listening. I heard Papa shut the door of his dressingroom. When I looked round Richard was standing over me. His dressing-gown was belted like a vice round his waist, but it was open from the neck to a long narrow nakedness of dark, faraway skin. I didn't understand how or why he should look so malign and light-hearted. And so friendly. He bent down and kissed me on both eyelids. 'Sleep well,' he whispered.

'And you,' I managed.

My anger and anxiety at the appalling noise he made getting back to his room suffocated and choked down a different sense in me: one of absolute loss. But we had both known how to behave. We had behaved beautifully. No pain lasts. And another thing: I can never look on myself as a deprived, inexperienced girl. I've had a man in my bed. I suppose I could say I've had a lover. I like to call it that. I do call it that.

CHAPTER SIXTEEN

The next morning, with Mummie and Papa, I stood about in floods of sunlight on the steps, or wandered back to the dark hall while maids carried down suitcases and coats and parcels and armfuls of forgotten unpacked possessions for Richard and Hubert to stow in the car. At last the car was packed. There was a pause while they put on their camel's-hair coats.

'Good sort of coat,' Papa commented. 'Where did you get it?'

'From kind Mrs Jaeger.' Hubert's little joke sounded confidential; just for Papa. Their good manners sustained them; they showed no impatience to be off. The engine throbbed its great heart out, splendidly ready for the journey; still they delayed, although we had no more goodbyes to exchange. Nobody kissed. Nobody shook hands. At last they were gone. We looked after them for a minute as they went down the drive. Eleven o'clock in the morning, and no shadows on the grass. The trees stood up shadowless, neat and clear as tin trees in a child's zoo. Horses moved between them. We were thrown out of balance by the leave-taking. We were late for anything we had to do; we had nothing to do, nothing to catch up on. Mummie was making for the studio, but without vigour, when Breda came back to say the young gentlemen had left parcels for us in the library.

'PIG' was written on mine. Inside was a Jaeger coat like theirs – outsize. Love and trust repossessed me. A case of Heidsieck for Papa. 'What a dear boy,' he said, when he had ascertained the year. A huge illustrated gardening book for Mummie. 'How *very* sweet. I'm afraid quite useless.' Presents always disgusted her a little.

I carried my coat away, upstairs to my bedroom, and there on my dressing-table, a square, squat, tremendously tidy little parcel waited for me. 'Pig. Pig-wig. Piglet' written on it. A jewel? A ring perhaps? I could hardly breathe. It was rose geranium for the bath, strong and fragrant and straight from Floris. But four times that morning he had written my name.

By the next day I had established in my own mind a sober, blessed state of hope. The day they had left had been, after all, quite endurable. Then I fattened out my least memories, slyly building up a future. And why not? I thought on the following afternoon as I bicycled powerfully along towards the dressmaker to have my new coat let out, before Mummie could tell me it was straining at the armholes. The dear dressmaker's interest and admiration were comforting and unrestrained. But the size of the alteration required depressed me a little. Only when alone could I feel a small cherished person.

I held on to this minuscule vision of myself as I pedalled homewards, past pale rushy fields and gold fields empty of their corn stooks. The further time and distance separated me from the actual Richard, the more certainly I could hold his image in my mind. I trembled and leaned yearningly over my handlebars, thinking how sometime again I would run with him on the sand, and another time he would come into my bed, and another time …

I was utterly possessed by happiness when I left my bicycle in the yard and went into the house by the back door, passing the warm cavernous kitchen and going along the flagged passages to the swing door and the front of the house. I know I have never breathed in the same way since that evening, since I went through that door, walking on a full sweet breath of happiness, its volume contained within me.

At the distant end of the hall the door stood open to the steps and the quiet evening. Papa and Mummie stood together in the wide doorway. She had the handle of a flat basket over her arm. With the secateurs in her other hand she snipped, meticulously splitting up the stems of late roses. I hoped to get up the stairs before she saw me. I had the humour of love to preserve. But Papa called me over.

'Pretty awful bit of news, I'm afraid,' he said. He had a telegram in his hand, and he started to read it in a perfectly ordinary voice. Then he changed his mind and said with embarrassed importance: 'There's been an accident.' My heart stopped. 'Hubert's been killed.' My heart went on again. Papa handed me the telegram.

REGRET TERRIBLE NEWS STOP CAR ACCIDENT STOP HUBERT KILLED STOP WIRE TIME ARRIVAL STOP MEET YOU BATH WOBBLY

Mummie looked up from snipping at her roses. She looked at me then and through me to what I really am. She knew what I was thinking, and she laughed. She went on laughing hysterically.

'Darling,' Papa said. 'Please.' Tears were pouring down his face. He took her hand and led her back into the house.

In the stillness of my shock there was only one reality: Richard was alive. A shiver of expectation went exuberantly through me: Hubert's death must link us more closely.

Papa brought Hubert home to be buried. He didn't come back to the house. They brought him from the station to Temple Alice church. The stark little Protestant church at our gates, endowed long ago by the family, was visited only for funerals and christenings and weddings. I would be married there, naturally. It was chill and stuffy, and dead birds usually lay about in the aisle. Someone had swept the place up for Hubert's funeral, and it was all flowers. Everybody sent large homemade wreaths and crosses and sprays. The only beautiful wreath came from the Crowhurst girls, who did such things to perfection.

Every friend we had came to the church; it was full to the last notch in the last pew. The hunt servants came too, and all the men on the place. They stood round the graveyard gossiping in whispers about cub-hunting and racing, honey bees, or the price of oats. They couldn't concentrate for a whole hour on the tragic circumstances, and as they were Roman Catholics they couldn't come into the church. Four lively young stable lads carried Hubert carefully out into the sunlight. His grave was lined with bright moss, pinned to the sides of the stark hole by long, strong hairpins.

Papa and Mummie stood together, as close as possible without actually touching each other. In the warm air I smelt brandy on their breaths. They had not thought of offering me any. A deep gust of lonely privation blew through me as I stood there, towering over them both, until it was time to shovel in the earth. Then Papa turned her round and took her by the elbow to lead her away. But she walked on composedly, and looking wonderfully distant from it all. Her fine black felt hat would have been as suitable for a race-meeting (where she never went) as for a funeral; it was exquisitely right and becoming, like the long wrinkling wrists of her gloves.

Three men were going backwards and forwards, carrying flowers from the church to the grave. The wild bent grass and briars in the tangled churchyard were overcome by flowers and the scent of flowers. Everything was determinedly beautiful; Mummie pausing at the right moment to say: 'Thank you. How lovely your flowers are. Please come back to the house. A cup of tea – you've come such a long way. How kind. How kind . . .'

And Papa saying: 'Thanks. So good of you. Come up for a drink.'

'Thanks, old man,' they said. 'Tragic,' they muttered. 'Great boy. Must get back.'

Papa saw the Crowhurst girls standing together. 'Bless you, sweethearts, your wreath a real winner. Come up to the house and have a drink.' They swayed towards him just a little, and remained quite silent. But they came, and so did all the friends.

When the last speechless hand-grip was completed, Papa, Mummie, and I were left in the hall, with the empty glasses and the empty plates; funerals are hungry work. We exchanged cool, warning looks – which of us could behave best: which of us could be least embarrassing to the others, the most ordinary in a choice of occupation? I tried first.

'I might ride out the Arch Deacon.' I didn't say 'Hubert's horse.' Papa said it for me, and no nonsense.

'Ah, that brute of Hubert's. Watchit, sweetie – pull the bit through his teeth and set into him before he sets into you.'

I shuddered – not really pleasantly. Mummie said: 'I'll get out of these ghastly clothes. I must finish dividing my blue primroses.'

Papa had his usual escape. 'Those poor little miseries, shut up in the gunroom since lunch, they must be bursting.'

'You can't go out in those absurd clothes,' Mummie reminded him.

So when we met each other again we had something to talk about ... The right bit for Hubert's horse. I couldn't begin to hold him in a plain snaffle ... Which of the dogs had made a huge mess in the gunroom ... Why Mummie would have to dig up all the blue primroses and replant ... How wrong she had been to imagine they would like her first choice of situation. She was considerate towards all weakness and eccentricity in plant life.

CHAPTER SEVENTEEN

For me, the September days held a prospect of hope only before the morning post came in. Each day I expected a letter from Richard, and each day I delayed longer before looking through the letters on the hall table, dreading that sickening moment before I could find my excuses for him: I must remind myself he had a bad concussion and broken ribs; Papa had mentioned them coldly. Who was driving? Hubert. Where I had expected an onslaught, Papa had added nothing to this. Now how I wished it had been not Richard's ribs but a broken arm, preferably his right arm, so that I need not rack my brains to excuse him. Later in the month Mummie had a short letter from him. Little words, miserably polite and inadequate, squeezed together on a huge sheet of writing paper. She gave it to me to read. It didn't cross her mind to say: Answer it for me, would you?

Then Papa heard from his old friend Wobbly. They were sending Richard to South Africa on a safari. It might help him a bit. 'He's taken this whole ghastly business terribly hard, poor boy,' Wobbly wrote. Again Papa was wordless.

Our good behaviour went on and on, endless as the days. No one spoke of the pain we were sharing. Our discretion was almost complete. Although they feared to speak, Papa and Mummie spent more time together; but, far from comforting, they seemed to freeze each other deeper in misery.

I stood outside in a black frost of my own. It was less hard for me because my loss of Richard was so eating out my heart I had no strength left for the other desolation.

Papa oiled Hubert's gun and put it away very much as a matter of course, shouting at his dogs as he oiled and clicked and put the pieces neatly in their leather case. His rods went into long canvas shrouds and were hung up by little loops on brass hooks. There was to be no sentimentality. It was the worst kind of bad manners to mourn and grovel in grief. They avoided his name when possible, but if necessary to speak it, they did so in over-ordinary tones of voice. Mummie, more than Papa, seemed drained of resolution.

One morning, on my way to the stable yard where I faced the terrible menace of Hubert's horse, I saw her. She had left the gardeners at work behind her, hacking down Pontican rhododendron, and now she broke away into the open through an untrimmed thicket of Portugal laurel. Her face was an old dryad's, crowned by, and drifting through, shining pointed leaves; her body was hidden still among the dark thornless branches of her grove. She didn't see me, or care what I was doing. I knew she was only greedy to find Papa, to cling silently to his company, to keep him all her own in this time of unspoken mourning. She absolutely required his presence.

I think her need told on him and drained away his power of recovery and forgetfulness. Every day he expected that she would lose and satisfy herself in her painting, going, as she used to, quickly and determinedly to her studio, not lagging uncertainly past the kitchen door where he was having his cheerful ambiguous morning talk with Rose – talk of food inspiring them both with thoughts of the necessary pleasures.

In this hour with Rose his cheeky balance was restored to him. Later in the morning, when Mummie pursued him to the fields, he was pulled back into the dull trough of their grief. He appeared to walk lamer when she was beside him; he was doubly infected by her silent requirement of his presence and company.

I saw her again on the same morning when she had appeared to me like a dryad. She was standing with Papa on the sunny side of a corn stack. They were watching the dogs fiddling about for mice in the bottom of the stack. I felt jealous towards them both. They had each other. And they were on their feet in a different world from mine.

My world, as I rode Hubert's horse, was a fearful place. I could ride him, but every day that he was in and fed and exercised he grew more devious and abominable. I was afraid and knew it, shamed by my fear and hating the Arch Deacon. Soon I would have to take him out with the hounds. Last season, with Hubert riding him, he had been a brilliant four-year-old. I faced the coming season – each falling leaf brought winter nearer – with a weakened stomach. My only thought was to keep my secret, to smile across my shame. Now, as I felt him tighten under me, preparing to shy and swerve away from the group round the corn stack, I was ready to deal with this circumstance and to send him past them with a show of ease and determination.

I was not ready for the foxhound puppy which, bitten by a

jealous terrier, galloped howling under my horse's tail. It was his opportunity of the morning, providing all that I had ever feared in him and guessed that he could do.

I shall never know how I survived his swinging plunge sideways before he took off across the stubble field. My hopeless hands were low on his neck in my first pretence of going with him, of sharing in his fun. The field was wide, so somehow I turned him before we faced the fence at its further end. There was no chance of stopping him. The muscles in his neck stared out at me as we thundered past the group round the corn stack.

'Good girl!' Papa shouted. 'Take it easy. He'll come back to you.' But as he called he was running and hobbling and stumbling towards the iron gate out of the field nearest to the stable yard. He was standing there when, after a third appalling circuit, we charged down towards its iron height. I was sobbing, my nose was pouring, I was in an extremity of fear. My enemy, the horse, knew it all. I was within his terrible strength and will. He would kill me.

Papa brought it to an end. Standing there against the gate, waiting to be ridden into the ground, his friendly, powerful voice, his assertion and assurance, reached through all temper and delirium. Crazy, black with sweat, Hubert's horse dropped into a wild kind of trot and let Papa catch him.

'Bit much for you, sweetie.' He laughed. 'You weren't nervous, were you?' 'Nervous' was Papa's word for terror. I laughed too. Laughing took the horror out of what had been happening. 'Here –' he called to Mummie, who was coming towards us over the sunny field – 'keep these dogs out of the way, would you?' She waved a careless acquiescence and wandered from us without hurrying, whistling to the terriers. In spite of our laughter I felt he knew how shocked I was. He was panting and sweating too from his run across the field. 'Nip off and nip back to the yard and tell Tommy to nip up on this bastard and give him whobeganit. Tommy'll love that.'

Tommy Fox was smiling in genuine calm pleasure; tucking his ashplant under his arm, he tightened the girths and shortened my stirrup leathers before he jumped up and settled himself with neat ease in the saddle. As he walked him, jogged him, and rode him in circles and figures of eight the horse answered to his strong approach and complacent dexterity with the same good manners he had used to show with Hubert.

My new fear was that Papa, gay executioner for my own good, would put me up on the horse again, just to steady my nerve. Fear repossessed me entirely. My stomach turned. Again, as Tommy rode back to us, I felt the sweat in my squeezed hands.

'Ah, only gay in himself is all he is,' he said. I could have struck him for those words. 'Canter him down there slowly,' Papa said. My reprieve. I loosened my hands. I prayed that he might take off and hop it with Tommy as he had with me. As we watched, it happened. No blundering hound puppy to give him a motive, only out of his wicked will he lengthened his stride, he set his cheek against the bit, and he was off. I remembered his neck, a pillar of fire against my hands, and a consuming gladness went through me, nearly a pleasure in Tommy's danger.

'The so-and-so –' Papa was laughing again – 'No brakes. No brakes.'

How warm the hour became, how human and relaxed I was, standing there apart from the terror I had known so lately. Now they see he can do it. Tommy can't hold him either. Can he turn him? Yes, just. They thundered over the stubbles past us, round again and back down the field. Tommy dropping his hands, smiling, pretending confidence as he passed us again. They might have gone six times round the big field before he tired. Tommy was driving him on now, up the slope, stopping him, and kicking him on again, dispossessing his memory of that power he had to take total charge, bringing him back to the habit of obedience; riding up to Papa and waiting for further orders.

'A steady hack canter was what I ordered.' Papa spoke lightly.

So did Tommy. 'Ah, that's the lad, Major.' He jumped off in his spry way, turned the reins over the monster's head, put his stirrups up and loosened the girths. Hubert's horse leaned down his sweating, itching head with a kind of innocence. A shudder ran through his whole dark frame, a haze trembled in the air over him and round him; he reached out a mild foreleg on which to rub his cheek while Tommy pulled his ears and waited, giggling, for Papa's next orders.

'That's about enough for one morning,' Papa said. 'Walk him round till he cools off.' He turned to Tommy again after we had started on our way back to the house. 'Ask Rose to give you a Guinness when you come in.' He looked at me. 'He may need something to steady him. I do. What about you, sweetie? Let's have one together, shall we? Just one.' It was a cheerful idea. His pace quickened as we crossed the stable yard. On the level flags inside the back door he shouted for Rose in the empty kitchen. Her presence was in the beautiful smell of hot bread, swathed in a cloth and leaning against the low wooden tower of a sieve. 'Where were you?' He looked through her when she came in, gloriously strong and clean.

'Killing the kitchen maid,' she answered. Then, meeting his look: 'Was there anything you wanted, sir?'

'Give Tommy a bottle of Guinness when you see him. He's had a bit of a doings with Mr Hubert's horse.'

'Is it pamper that little sauceboat?'

'Lucky he's not hurt.' Papa spoke reprovingly. 'And that goes for Miss Aroon too – come along, sweetie.' Rose was excluded. She had her place.

In the diningroom, quiet and orderly and sombre between breakfast and lunchtime, its silver shining down again into all the polished wood, Papa dived into the sideboard and brought out the meek sherry decanter with its silver label neatly hanging. He thought for a minute, and shook his head. 'Better idea. Port and brandy.' He sat down to pour out the drinks; on his legs he was a bit off balance. I sat down too and watched him pour the glasses, just not full. His hands were shaking. All on my account? Or on account of Hubert's horse? We drank together.

'And if I may say so, here's to you, darling girl, and bloody well you rode him.' It was nothing so vulgar as a toast, but I felt lauded and elated. We drank, and we looked at each other in confidence. Were we being rather naughty, rather in secret? Papa filled his glass again, and put another drop into mine, which was still three-quarters full. It was a show of affection and concern.

Presently Mummie came in. She stood a moment in the doorway while the dogs flew across the room to Papa. '*Well*,' she said, 'rather early for it?' It was more of an acceptance than a question.

'Not a bit.' Papa was restored now. There was no shake in

his hands as he measured out a glass for her. She sat down on his right hand and looked at him, deeply amused. A whole relationship was in her eyes. It expelled me from any secrecy with Papa.

'I think I'll go and change,' I said.

'Yes, you must be hot – you *were* a funny sight – scampering round that field.'

I stood for a moment waiting for Papa to say a word in my praise or favour. I stood there stupidly, betrayed in his silence. I saw her looking up at him, with something else to say. I saw her hand folded mouselike on the table's edge. It was the paw of a small animal. He gave it a look that as much as covered it with his own hand. I turned away, my loneliness walking with me, taller than my own height as a shadow is tall – and irremediable as my height was.

Back in my bedroom I knew myself suffered and accepted among my own possessions and habits. Here I was isolated from denial or dismissal. Possibility was actual. After all there they were, Richard's presents, undeniable – the scent, the bath essence, the bird's-eye scarf. Soon it would be cold enough to wear the Jaeger coat. And what did they tell me? All these expensive objects told me plainly that I was loved although still untouched by that thing men do. Untouched, because no doubt he had held me too dear. Out of the charged memories of disappointment, I flowered to myself, a desired, a forbidden, an enchanted creature. I took the cold scent bottle between my hands and kissed it.

The moment went past, and I still faced the afternoon. While I reconsidered the long hours to come, the scent bottle warmed in my hands.

CHAPTER EIGHTEEN

At luncheon Papa decided for me. He said: 'Got to go to the Wine Cellars. And the car's not her burning best either. Care to come along in case she stops with me? We'll get her sharpened up while we're busy in the Cellars.'

'So long as we don't have to go to tea with the Crowhurst girls.'

The girls lived near the Wine Cellars and he had often been known to call in and bask for an hour in their acidulated adoration. I can only suppose the girls and their lives were like a comic strip to Papa. He followed their activities, some of them rather shady; it was a game, laughing at their contrivances. Their bitter, nipped tongues kept him guessing at what they might say next. He liked to nose out their small scandalous escapades – nothing like love affairs, poor things, of course not, more likely a sharpish bit of horse dealing. One of their pleasures was not telling. It put an edge on everything they did or said. Poor unhappy things. Much as I pitied and faintly despised them, they had the knack of making me feel

I was lolling helplessly through an objectless, boring life. I never wanted to see them, or listen to them, or even to eat any of the delightful food they produced from air, or sea, or garden.

Papa, I knew, felt very differently about their ways of overriding poverty, rejecting its limitations. He was fascinated by all they had taught themselves about horses, and never tired of analysing the curious theories they accepted from that wild tinker fellow they employed as a part-time groom. He could charm warts, or go up to any horse, where another dare not lay his hand. Besides being so knowledgeable on horses and horse lore, they knew the cures for all the diseases from which dogs could suffer. They despised vets. Even when one of their viperous miniature dachshunds was in hideous whelping difficulties, they used their own clever fingers, and an hour after achieving a safe delivery for their darling they would be sitting on a sofa at their petit-point, their hands as elegantly and carefully employed as those of any ancestress. They were very well born and never forgot it.

Today I could sense Papa making his way wordlessly towards a cup of tea with Nod and Blink; it was a delayed action. At the garage he ordered work on the car which must take hours to accomplish. At the Wine Cellars we stayed a long time ordering good things in the dark drift of smells in the grocery department. After that came the real matter of the visit, wines and their years and qualities, their prices unimportant when compared with the delights Papa was accumulating.

When, at half past four, I heard him ask for a bottle of Gordon's gin, a bottle of Noilly Prat, 'and, of course, a lemon,' I knew we were bound for tea with the Crowhurst girls, bringing a little present with us. 'Calling for this lot later,' he indicated his purchases.

The elder of the two gentlemanly old gnomes who owned the Wine Cellars was ushering us out. 'And if it would be convenient, Major,' he said, laughing a little, 'we were wondering could you let us have something on account.'

'Of course, of course – what a terrible pair you are. Why haven't you sent it in long ago?'

'We did, Major. Excuse us, but we have it furnished a few little times now.' It was an extreme apology and he accepted it, royally.

'That's right.' He hobbled away, very lame, still talking. 'Times are awful, always are awful, send it in again *at once*, do you hear me? Don't delay, never delay, and I'll let you have a cheque by return of post.'

Out in the sunny street he was soon walking more soundly, heading for the Crowhursts without any unnecessary explanations to me. I went along beside him, the gin under one arm, the vermouth under the other, the lemon in my handbag.

'Can you manage, darling, bless you? Poor things, they do need it so.' He put me on his own level, while they sank to the position of being simply pitiable.

I was less able to pity them as we clicked open the neat iron gate, painted by themselves, and walked towards the house, past groupings of electric blue hydrangeas. 'How do they do it?' Papa paused to admire. 'And they won't tell a soul.' His admiration of the cruel electric blue and the girls' secrecy was equal. Round the corner of the little Regency house, a blazing autumn border caught his eye. 'Good girls, good girls,' he murmured, 'redhot pokers – my favourites.'

Blink opened their door to us. She was close-lipped and

elegant and nearly thirty. I thought the twins hopelessly aged. 'How awfully kind,' she said to Papa, taking the gin away from me. Then: 'Oh, Aroon,' as if she only now saw I was there.

The hall, where we delayed, was that of a small country gentleman. Leather-covered sticks and hunting whips lay on an oak chest. A series of good prints hung on the walls. A water dish marked DOG and a trug of clean garden tools and powerful secateurs stood together in a corner.

In the drawingroom, where dachshunds lay like a nest of serpents in a round, well-cushioned basket, tea was laid for four. The position of the teatray commanded a splendid view of the blazing border, where huge, meaty dahlias (fit flesh for cannibals I always think) were divided, and given added value, by fish-shaped drifts of Michaelmas daisies, and grey-blue pools of agapanthus lilies. Blink looked away from her border with affected indifference, giving Papa time to admire and wonder at its perfection. Presently Nod (Papa's favourite one) came in with a trayful of beautiful food.

'We heard you were in the Wine Cellars,' she said unaffectedly, 'so we hoped you would come to tea.'

'You made all these sandwiches just on the chance?' Papa said gratefully. 'Just for us? Good girls.'

'Well, Blink and I could have finished them for dinner –' they never talked about supper – 'the more we eat, the thinner we grow.' She looked at me as if she were going to apologise for an unfortunate remark, and under her veiled glance I felt my bosoms and bottom swelling up through my head. I was so conscious of their size and presence they could have toppled me off my legs.

We had China tea out of thin, shallow cups, and I found the fish pâté sandwiches irresistible. The dachshunds crawled out of their basket to join in the pickings, and one of them almost took my hand off when I gave her a tiny piece of buttered scone.

'*Please* don't feed the brutes,' Nod said gently. Then with chill command: 'Basket, girls, to your basket.' They slunk away, remorseful and vindictive. 'The postman won't come here any more,' she told Papa with great amusement. 'They've bitten him twice now and one bite festered. Blink's making a letter-box for the gate.'

'Big enough to take garden catalogues and the *Times*.' Blink spoke seriously of her project. 'They gave me a lovely old brass slit or slot at the post office, and I picked up a beautiful piece of teak on the beach – just the thing.'

'You'll make a job of it,' Papa said, approvingly. 'You should use copper nails.'

Now and then they spoke to me politely and handed me plates of food or filled up my tiny cup. But I knew their joint unjealous interest focused entirely on Papa. Tea over, Papa provided us each with a cigarette from his never-empty case. 'I knew I meant to ask you something,' he said to Nod. 'How's Fred Astaire's leg?'

'I'm afraid he's finished,' she said.

'Oh, that's a great pity. Best hunter in the country. Shall I go and put my hand on it?'. There was nothing he liked more than fiddling round lame horses. Now there would be an hour of suggestion and counter-suggestion. When I got up to follow them out of the room Blink spoke unhurriedly from behind the teatray.

'You've seen darling Fred often enough, dear fellow, wouldn't you rather look at Heidi's puppies? They're very sweet.'

'Shouldn't we call Papa?' I said, after a lingering examination of Heidi's litter. 'The garage will be shut soon.'

'Oh yes, if you must. Nod's so upset about Fred Astaire, let's give them a few minutes while I get hold of some glasses.'

Blink took another ten minutes to find and polish the right glasses, and the only knife suitable for paring zest from a lemon. In the drawingroom, where we carried the tray of drinks, she said: 'Oh, wouldn't it be nice if we cleared away tea? Could you feed Heidi while I tidy it up?'

'No,' I said, 'you feed Heidi, let me do this.'

'You can't really be afraid of her; she's so gentle.' She left me blushing with rage as I piled up the doll-size cups and plates.

'Oh,' Nod said, coming in with Papa, 'that awful Blink – she always finds someone else to do her work.' She spoke with indulgent approval.

'You want to watch it,' Papa said. 'Aroon's champion cup smasher.' Nod took the tray from me immediately and carried it away. 'I don't know about you, sweetheart,' Papa said, when she had gone, 'but I need a drink. Martinis for us all – sort of – no ice.' When the girls came back he was paring lemon peel. 'Perfect blade,' he said, 'worth anything.' He pinched the peel into their glasses and handed them with grave concern that the drinks should be absolutely as they liked them. They might have been glamorous women. He was far too kind, I thought. After two powerful martinis Papa roused himself out of a pleasant lull to say to Blink: 'I haven't seen your letter-box yet, have I?'

'Oh, *Papa.*' Kindness was one thing, but this was silly. 'The garage will be shut. We can't walk home.'

'No,' he agreed, 'of course not. The old leg, you know.

Look – you nip down to the garage, child, and bring the car up here, if you'll be so sweet. I'll be waiting at the gate.' 'I'll be waiting at the gate' – the words had a dying fall, a promise to me alone, the chosen companion.

At the garage, the owner was ready to tell me that nothing whatever had been done about the car. It was more than one afternoon's work and an expensive job. Would the Major call at his convenience to discuss it, and would I remind him about the account?

'The Major will call on his way home,' I said. 'Will you be here?'

'I will, if there's any chance he'll call.' He sounded as though he doubted the likelihood. I felt he ought to have said 'the Major,' not 'he.'

Of course there was no one waiting at the gate. I had hardly expected it. Papa wasn't in the drawingroom either. Nod was snuggled down on the sofa with five dachshunds and her petit-point. She glanced up as I came in. 'I expect they'll be here soon,' she said, settling down again.

Presently they came, walking slowly together over the perfect grass, almost more brilliant than the awful border around which it curved, neat and level as water. Papa stopped and stooped (always a job for him) to pick something out of the grass. 'Look what I've found,' he said when they came in, as unhurriedly as though it had been three o'clock. 'Plantain in the lawn. It's disgraceful. I am shocked.'

They did not deny the plantain. 'Have a drink,' they suggested amiably.

'I'm not sure if Aroon will allow it.' He looked at me remorsefully. 'And what about the car, pet? All right?'

'Not all right,' I said. 'He's done exactly nothing and he

wants you to call and see him this evening.' All the ease and pleasure went from Papa's face and attitude. Suddenly he was a tired, middle-aged, worried gentleman, with bags under his eyes, licking his lips uncertainly. A gentleman on a stick, gaiety spent, his son dead – a thought to be escaped: Hubert's horrible death never confronted.

'I'm awfully tired,' he said. 'Take me home. We're going to be late for dinner and I ordered a soufflé. Why did I? Let's be off, darling. No, I don't *want* it,' he refused the offered drink rather crossly, then picked up the glass. 'Oh, you *are* naughty,' he said to the girl who gave it to him.

On the path to the gate the girls' pigeons were carrying on as if it were Trafalgar Square. 'You forgot their feed,' Nod accused Blink. 'How could you?' Fantails and birds with heads like Pekinese dogs circled them, cuddling into their shoulders, toppling over red feet on the path. It was a Walter Crane picture – a picture of two lives of innocent content and industry, full of birds and flowers and dogs, not to mention dear old horses and minute tapestry works.

'Well, we made their day,' Papa said. 'I suppose that's something. You drive. Why are you turning round?'

'The garage,' I reminded him. 'The wine.'

'No, no, no. Not tonight. First things first. Let's get home to dinner.'

CHAPTER NINETEEN

It was after seven o'clock as we drove past the crouching church at the gates of Temple Alice. The church, throughout my life a sight as familiar to me as my breakfast, had adopted a fresh importance now – a grief we must ignore or it would suffuse our lives always.

'Which reminds me,' Papa avoided looking towards the church, 'I've made quite a useful plan about the Arch Deacon horse.'

'Oh, good. What?'

'The girls want to take him on.'

'Papa,' I said, appalled, 'he'd kill them.'

'You couldn't kill them, or tire them.' Papa spoke crossly. 'And they're wizards with a difficult animal – magical.'

His respect for them was like a bad taste in my mouth. This certainty was with me: where I had succumbed and failed, they would succeed and prosper. They would win a lightweight class with him next summer most likely. And I would have to stand at the ringside and echo congratulations and smile approval. In every way I was lessened and abandoned.

The morning's happenings, even my fear and my relief, were losing their truth.

'Why don't you see what Tommy can do with him?' I offered.

'But Tommy's such a useful lad,' Papa said, without thinking. I took in his meaning. It was a ruthless double convenience, and after my horrible afternoon I was less than shocked. I felt a thin kind of connivance. 'I gave them the true picture, naturally,' Papa said in his simplest voice.

'What did you tell them?'

'Just told them you couldn't begin to ride him.' He gave a snort or a chuckle. 'That clinched it. I knew you'd understand. After all, it's not a very kind thing to send Hubert's horse to the kennels. Mummie would be dreadfully upset.'

In my anguish and jealousy even protest was numbed in me. So lately, only this morning, he had been my companion and saviour. I could see him still, stumbling and running, pitching about on his wooden leg, to get to the field gate before another circuit brought me near it again. And in the calm of the diningroom I could hear 'if I may say so ... darling ... ' but after that I had been lessened and left in the cold, undefended from Mummie's faint amusement. Tears of misery hurtled down my cheeks. How could he treat his poor girl so? Papa put his hand on my knee. 'You're the one I mind about. You know that, bless you, don't you know that, sweetheart?'

He had used me and pulled me down, tumbling something truer than my vanity, and at a soft word I could forgive him. My dependence on him had nothing to do with sense or reason.

When we had changed for dinner we met again in the library.

'Well,' Mummie said, lifting up her glass of sherry, but not drinking, 'then you didn't get the car fixed, so how did you pass the time away, my darling?' A cunning light of indulgence was in her eyes: 'Sparkling before the girls, I suppose.'

'A bit of that,' he admitted. I broke into a recital of the endless chain of delays created by the girls, their underground industries, their horses' legs, their letter-boxes, and his patience through all their nonsense.

She usually enjoyed a story against them, but tonight she only said: 'If they gave him the smallest amusement, Aroon, I'm only too delighted,' looking beyond me to him as she spoke. Perhaps she was thinking: anything to take his mind off Hubert. But it was not that. Separate as she stood from him, in the light warm clothes that seemed air-borne on her, wearing jewellery as carelessly as beads, her pale face, her powdery hair, and light eyes were all parts of an immense reserve of power. A power which she might reserve through any self-crucifixion.

There was, as I remember, not the smallest irregularity to enliven that evening. Its hours passed and it was time for Papa to let out the dogs. Then time for Mummie to take her candlestick from him. Leaning up to Papa, as she took the candlestick, she said: 'Not *too* long?' It was partly a question and far less than a suggestion of any obligation on him.

'I have to tuck up the dogs and write a few letters.' There was a hurried inventiveness in his voice. 'If I'm very late, I'll sleep in my dressingroom.'

'Yes,' she agreed with him, 'you do that.'

Beyond the small busy-ness, I felt there was something else he was longing to get on with; his good manners hardly hid his impatience to be alone. He lit my candle and kissed me.

'You've had quite a day, haven't you? Bless you, sleepy-well,' and I was set off on my way to bed.

The staircase at Temple Alice parted right and left under a high window; from there two separate flights took one upwards on light, shallow steps. They embraced the hollow to the hall below them. A single flight went on to the next storey of the house, and above that was the glazed bell of the dome. I took the left stair upwards, and Mummie took the right, so when we got to the bedroom corridor there would be no need to speak or kiss. She wafted up her side, and I trudged up mine.

'Goodnight,' we said, 'goodnight,' and we turned gratefully away from each other.

Papa was right, I was tired. I was so tired that I could not sleep. All the day had done to me was imperishably clear, bright and certain. Fear seized on me, relief sobbed through me again. Praise elated me, grief was a spasm ... 'Now the Day Is Over' ... the hymn I had chosen for Hubert's funeral, Mrs Brock's hymn ... 'With thy tender blessing may our eyelids close' ... Hubert's eyelids would have been burnt: forbid all that. Forbid the private ecstasy in the thought of Richard – he was no more than a great retreating symbol of happiness – a longing now far distanced from reality. No fetish, as when I held his present in my hand, could give him back to me. I was as much alone as the curlew I heard crying briefly from a far-away bog.

Hours passed while I lay, filled with my fuming despairs, alertly, indissolubly wakeful. It was only after I had taken the decision, last resource of the sleepless, of getting out of bed and going to the lavatory that I remembered Papa had not yet come upstairs to his dressingroom. My watch said one o'clock.

He was seldom as late as this, but he could not have passed my door on his way to bed without my hearing his lame step. I delayed and hesitated; we would feel shy of each other, meeting on my way to or from the lavatory. After a time the delay had me in an aching fidget. I opened and shut my door and went, without my candle, down the passage towards the one upstairs lavatory. To reach it I must go round the balustraded circle at the stairhead.

Light bloomed below me, welling up and failing in the hollow heights reaching to the dome. The last lamp left burning in the house, a cut-glass bowl on a long silver stem, waited for Papa's bedtime and its extinction. Before I had passed the stairhead the library door opened and I stopped, hesitating whether to hurry on or to hurry back to my room.

In that paralysis of indecision I watched Papa, dwarfed by my height above him, come out of the library door and stand staring at his bedroom candlestick, placed as usual beside the lamp on the narrow side-table. Instead of following his usual custom – bedding the dogs and a last visit to the downstairs lavatory – he stood by the lamp and his unlighted candle as though he had lost his way through the small ceremonies of bedtime. Finally he picked up the large silver-encased box of safety matches and struck three or more of them before his candle was alight. Next, he set about the business of putting out the lamp. Here again, a dignified patient awkwardness impeded him. He turned the wick up, he turned it down, he blew round the glass chimney top. What was the matter with him? It was all so simple; you turned the wick down and clicked a small lever on the brass burner. Why this puffing and blowing?

I longed to call down directions but, as I hesitated, I saw

him put a hand on the table as though to steady himself and, with his other hand, pick up the heavy lamp and lean it nearer to the strength of his breath and blowing.

'Papa,' I screamed, 'wait, let me do it.' Did I scream or did I whisper? He can't have heard me, for a last gigantic puff sent the flame flaring up into his face. Still holding on to the lamp, as in a dream one clings to instabilities, he let go of the table's edge, took a staggering step forwards before – like a tree rocking and going from its roots – he fell. The lamp, flung out of his hand, crashed and splintered and splayed out oil over the floor where he lay. Crazy with fear I hurtled down the long flight, ready to burn with him, and welcome, if it had to be.

Before my moment came, it had gone. The door at the back of the hall opened wide and quietly. It was Rose. I watched her hurrying down the long hall to him; she had no apron on and no shoes. She ran light as a child on her stockinged soles. I could feel she was both tender and angry as she stooped, pulling and lifting him on to his foot.

'Rose, dear girl,' I heard him say, 'where were you all this time?'

'Playing cards with the lads.' Her answer was somehow both coarse and playful. 'Drunk again?' she said. 'Well, aren't you very naughty?'

Drunk? Papa? How dared she speak to him like that? I turned away and crept up the stairs, at one step denying, at the next accepting the shocking possibility; only thankful, if it was true, that I saw no recoil in Rose. She put an arm round him and went on his legless side as they climbed the stairs. She was a good servant, and strong as a horse, of course. He groped for the bannister rail, and paused and clung to her. Once they laughed together.

I padded away from them on my heavy feet. In the dark wood-panelled lavatory I waited, trembling as the minutes passed. His dressingroom was at the end of the long corridor; I must give them time to get there. When I felt it safe to venture back to my room, only the night sky bent to the dome's shape held some pallor above the dark and quietness.

CHAPTER TWENTY

Things happened in our house which, afterwards, seem only to have happened in my mind. Except that I remember them perfectly, they become extinct. This was so the next morning when Papa came into the diningroom, his elegance restored. His skin was newly shaved and brown as a chestnut. His hair smelt delicious. His old tweed suit and his striped flannel shirt were clean as a baby's clothes. There he sat, eating a big breakfast, making plans for the day: he must drive in to town to see that fool his solicitor and that shark the bank manager. Soon he was trotting briskly round to the yard, shouting at the dogs, calling out orders to the lads, getting into the car, blowing the horn for Mummie, and muttering more about seeing off those sharks and fools. 'You coming, darling? No? Quite right, quite right.'

Contradicting this restoration to the usual was my remembrance of what I had seen from my window earlier in the morning: his velvet dinner jacket and trousers swinging from the high clothes line in the laundry yard. No doubt Rose had dealt successfully with any whiff of paraffin. When I went down to breakfast, the hall smelt exceptionally airy – no hint of paraffin oil here, either, nor a splinter of glass on the floor. Only the morning currents of furniture polish, methylated spirit from the hot plate in the diningroom, and late roses wavered together on the morning of a new day. I was hypnotised, I was bemused. I was deprived of my certainty that Papa had been terribly drunk and that in Rose's approach to him there had been something easy and practised which I could not name.

That morning was fresher than any day in spring. This last heat of summer had none of the exhaustion of spring. I had nothing but this abyss of beautiful days. Perhaps I would wash the dogs. Papa would be pleased. He loved to fondle a clean little dog. The very thought of pleasing helped me to distance him from what he had done to me, and from what I had seen.

In the hall, in its usual place on the long side-table, the day's post was lying. Lately I would hardly cross over to look at it, knowing quite well the fall to disappointment that waited, and happened, and passed. So it was not until another hour had gone, and the dogs were bathed and dried and bustling for a walk, that I came back through the hall and saw, separate from a pile of business letters and bills for Papa, a letter for me, from Richard.

I picked it up and held it unopened because I expected this agony of happiness could not last. I went into the drawingroom to read it. Nobody ever came in there. The blinds were down. The air dead but well preserved. I shut the door and crossed over to one of the long windows and pulled up the blind to let in a great wealth of sunshine. The dogs pushed and shoved me into a corner of the window seat, so that they could warm their damp backs in the sun, and I opened my love letter.

It came from Kenya, and there were at least four pages for me to read. I took a great breath to steady my delight, and I read . . . I read a page totalling the heads and horns of the game he had shot, measurements complete. I read that there was quite a variety of fish in the rivers; that one lights a huge fire at night and fishes for bottle-nose fish, well supplied with cold beer (the fisher I supposed, not the fish). I read of an old bull elephant who came to drink just opposite to where he was fishing. Then I read of the hospitality in the nearly stately homes of the settlers, cousins and cousins of cousins, and friends of old so-and-so's, who had all been terribly kind. And in all the letter there was not a word to link him with me. Not a word about Hubert, only this total recall of heads and horns and fish and birds and buffalo and draft foxhounds that hunted lynx. 'Yours ever, Richard,' it ended.

I thrust the clean dogs away from me and moved out of the sun because I was sweating. I was in a rage of disappointment. I would read the letter again, and slowly. There had to be something I had missed. Between the lines there was some word I could feed on. Religiously, methodically I again devoured the Wild Life of Africa. As I reread hope flickered and grew. I smelt out hints towards the past. Why describe night time and rivers and moonlight – all right, bonfire light – if not to convey that he was alone and that he missed me? And why the catalogue of trophies, if he was not sure of my interest? Was that it? Yes, that was it. We were so sure of each other, it was needless to put it in words. Perhaps there were no words for it. Then I felt it dawning on me: now I could write to him. Of course this letter asked for an answer. I would write easily about the horses (nothing about Hubert's dreadful Arch Deacon, of course), the dogs, our yearling, hunting, when the season opened. Later I would match woodcock to buffalo, and never a word of love. He would answer and I would write again and he would answer.

I was folding up the sheets of the letter when I saw across the back of the last page the very words which I could translate into glory: 'I want you to know, Aroon' (he had written Aroon), 'the Black Friday yearling is all yours, my share and Hubert's. Richard.' All our names together. My happiness appalled me. For the whole morning I was in a state of energy and delight. I would not read the letter again. I did not want to know it so well that familiarity could dissolve my assurance. I had breathed my own truth between the lines – it was the breath of hope, to shelter and harbour and keep secret.

They were very late coming back to luncheon. 'Did you take the car to the garage?' I asked Mummie.

Cool, and still hatted and gloved, she stood by the hall table disgustedly turning over the bills. She opened the drawer, swept the lot inside, and shut it again. 'No more worries till after luncheon.' She moved away from me, pulling off her gloves by the finger-tips. 'No. That ghastly solicitor kept Papa there for hours, worrying him dreadfully too.'

'And did you collect the drink?'

'Was there drink to collect? Perhaps he forgot. Shall we go in to luncheon?'

The dogs followed us. Papa followed the dogs. He didn't seem to notice that they had had a bath. 'No post?' he said to the maid, who was waiting, rather sullenly, to serve us.

'I left the letters in the hall as usual, sir.' Luncheon was appallingly late, Breda's own dinner would be cold, washing up would make her late for the garden fête at the rectory, and now she was being found fault with by implication and unfairly. 'Didn't you get your letter, Miss Aroon?' she asked me defensively. I felt a terrible blush begin behind my ears and spread its way from my hair's edge to below the cleavage of my shirt.

'Yes. Actually,' I said. I felt them all three averting their eyes from me and wondering about my blush.

'Well, where are mine? That's all I want to know. That shark Kiely told me there would be some form from some other shark and he had to have it at once.'

'Now, listen,' Mummie sounded inspired, '*could* I have swept it into the drawer with a load of other old rubbish? – If I have I *am* sorry.'

Breda went out and returned with a stack of manilla envelopes on a salver.

'Oh, good girl, Breda. Thank you.' Papa groaned miserably through the pile.

'Don't open it,' Mummie said as he picked out one envelope and sat staring at it uncertainly, 'or you won't eat any luncheon.'

'You're so right. First things first.' He proceeded to eat an enormous amount of luncheon. After that he was more like himself and able to ignore the offending letter. But it was not forgotten. 'Tell you what we must do,' he said to Breda when she came in with the coffee. 'I hear you're all booked for this jolly at the rectory. Tommy had better drive you there. Go by the village and post this for me.' He shuddered as he looked at the letter. 'I shan't open it,' he said to Mummie. 'I don't know what I pay Kiely for. I suppose I must re-address the thing.' He set off for the library, as no gentleman carried a pen about in his pocket.

'Is everybody going to the rectory?' Mummie asked Breda. 'Who will bring our tea? Perhaps Rose—?'

'It's Rose's afternoon today, madam.' Breda looked longingly at the coffee cups before she walked off with the cheese plates.

'They're all so Bolshie, these days.' Mummie sighed.

Through all this, having recovered from my blush, I had floated unheeding in the happiness which I would not tell. Held within like this it transcended grief or jealousy. I felt as nearly as could be back in the moment when I had run along the wet sand, when he had touched the inside of my salty arm. Linked with this was the other afternoon when I had first learned to swim, when the sea water had borne me up and Mrs Brock's delight in my achievement had shone from her to me, joining us blissfully, keeping Hubert out. He was out of this too. I denied the thought, lapping it up in proper grief for him.

Papa joined me on the steps where I was brushing the clean dogs. 'They do look lovely,' he said. 'You make a wonderful job of them, don't you?' He didn't say 'thank you.' 'Shall we go on a rampage? What about the rectory fête?' He laughed at his own immoderate joke. 'Coming for a walk? The dogs are longing.'

'I was going to have a look at the Black Friday yearling.'

'All right.' He started off faster than his leg could carry him, always his pace when annoyed. 'If we must we must. I suppose we've got to. *I* wanted to go and see the horses in the Fairy Bog. I'll have to get some of them out. Can't keep them eating their heads off all winter.'

'They won't eat much in the bog,' I suggested comfortingly.

'They can't stand and stiffen on the bog.' His face was quite red with annoyance. 'You ought to know that much. They have to be fed. Up to its eyes the whole place is. Have you any idea about the wage bill?'

'No.' I felt dreamy and inattentive to his irritation, far off, and smoothly optimistic.

'I don't suppose you have. I hadn't, till this morning. That piddling niggler Kiely – he's upset me terribly.'

We walked out from under the beech-trees into the sunlight. 'I shouldn't worry,' I said, blessed by the sun. He took off his hat and mopped at his forehead with a dark red silk handkerchief – Papa, who never sweated.

'I feel hot,' he said. 'That damn curry, I expect. God knows what Rose puts in it. Food bills too,' he said. 'They're all pirates. The butcher – he's not the worst robber, mind you. I'm quite simply just about in the bankruptcy courts. Kiely says so. Looked into his office for a moment to see about a little something when he opened up on me. Frightened me to death, dearest. Rightly in the soup we are, financially. Everything going out. Nothing coming in. Now, take that—' We had stopped and were looking over to where the yearling and his donkey stood together, making, for me, a perfect picture in the low brilliant light across the grass. 'I don't even own that fellow, and he'll have to be done like a king all winter.'

'He's come on a lot, hasn't he?' A sense of possession filled me warmly.

'Yes, and there's a lot of improvement in him,' Papa admitted grudgingly. 'Just the same, he's going. Why should I feed him? I'm writing to my old friend Wobbly tonight to remove him. That'll be a start anyway. That'll show Kiely I'm serious.'

'Papa, you don't mean it?'

'Yes, I do mean it. Things are drastic. We have to cut down somewhere.'

My eyes filled with tears. 'But he's *mine*,' I whined. 'I own him.'

'You own the little thief?'

'He's not little at all. You can't call him small. Richard gave him to me. His share and Hubert's share.'

'You might have told me, sweetheart,' Papa said reproachfully, as though I had been keeping a secret from him. I had. I felt a longing rush through me to share it with him now. 'I had a letter from Richard today.' I was blushing cruelly again. This time Papa didn't take his eyes off my blush. His eyes were eating into me, eager for more.

'Richard *gave* him to you?' All the nervous irritation had left his voice. He leaned towards me without saying any more, waiting, pleading for some certainty. What should I tell him? How put into words all that only I could trace behind his big-game catalogue of a letter?

'Well,' Papa said at last. He lit a cigarette, his hand was shaking. 'One for you?' he asked, and I nodded. He gave me his, always a gesture of affection with him, and lit another. I knew he was giving me time. At last he helped me: 'Did he say when he'd come back to us?' He put all expression out of his voice. I found his portentous tactfulness, his extreme wish to establish my happiness, beyond my powers to resist. I felt I must please him in return. I must be the person to raise his temperature, to excite him.

'He's coming back in the spring.' The lie came jumping out of my mouth. My thumping heart delivered it like a great frog – a monster to torment me as soon as I was sane again. But for the moment I enjoyed the lie, and I felt a hot importance in Papa's thoughts of me. Pleasurable, that was what it actually was, before the doubts could crowd in. So little was enough to convey so much between us. But I knew he wanted to hear more than this from me. His face was crumpled in anxiety and shyness as, leaning on the fence and looking away from me on the ground, he muttered: 'That night, darling girl, before they left, don't tell me if you don't want to . . .'

'Yes,' I said, looking steadfastly over at the colt and the donkey.

'The lot?' Papa said.

'The lot,' I answered firmly.

'Well, thank God,' Papa said quite loudly. And then, moderately: 'Thanks, sweetheart . . . You can't think how worried I've been, dreadfully unfair of me. Impossible, of course, I realise now, preposterous. Looked ugly though. Looked funny. Didn't like it. All clear now. I *am* grateful.'

All this time what had he been thinking? That I might be having a baby? That Richard might have left me for always – so that a hideous interview was before him with his old friend Wobbly? He had endured Hubert's death and burial, Mummie's grief, his own grief, deadly anxiety about me – and not a word spoken. To crown it all, today's morning of stress and worry with that solicitor. No wonder if he was drinking. No wonder if his morning sessions with Rose stood, for a brief moment, between his own suffering and Mummie's sad possessiveness. And only now I understood the anxiety eating him for me. Darling Papa. I leaned sideways against the fence and put my hand for a second over his: 'I'm all right, Papa. I promise.'

'Oh yes,' he came back from far away, 'yes, bless you, you have been a help. Look –' he said, absently apologetic, 'I think if you don't mind, I'll go on by myself. You take the dogs with you. They'll be kicked to pieces in the bog.'

I stood discarded, watching him bundle off down the drive. When he had gone out of sight the implications in my lie to him over Richard's promise to return set me worrying and biting my nails. When spring came round, where should I be? Each day the post would be quietly observed, and a deadly tactful silence maintained. Of course he would discuss the matter with Mummie, as he would discuss Hubert's horse with her, and his progress with the girls. Her cold pity would extend itself further over me.

In the hall Mummie was standing, planned and prepared for some exercise. Not gardening, I thought, because she carried her slight hazel walking stick, a gleam of gold about its handle. A doll-size garden trug sat on the side-table among the letters and whips and hats, and in it a little bunch of cyclamen lay, firmly tied among their spotted leaves. Perhaps she was going to paint them. Sometimes she painted flowers, the completed pictures looking like ghosts of wire and tin.

'Back again?' she said, commenting on another of my little failures. 'Why aren't the dogs with Papa?'

'Because he didn't want to take them among the young horses in the bog.'

'Ah,' she said with satisfaction. She looked suddenly sure of some adventure. Her afternoon was to be far more vivid than mine. Of course – idiot me – I had told where to go and meet him. She had got it out of me without even a direct question. As she picked up the little basket of flowers and turned away I saw how languorous was the turning of her felt hat against her cheek; like everything else she wore, it became her in a way that was her own mystery.

CHAPTER TWENTY-ONE

When she had gone, the silence of the house consumed the afternoon. Not even a murmur or sound of servants – all at the rectory fête. The smell of past hours was in the library: flowers, cigars, polish on wood. Newspapers lay baking in the sun.

Everything was in a trance of the usual. My bedroom waited for me, impassive.

Looking at my bed, I knew I was no unwanted grotesque: a man had lain there with me. I knew what Papa believed, and his belief encompassed me and made a reality of my hopes and longings. Richard's letter was an absolute reality.

I read it again to find all that was there – unwritten. For instance: the river, the moonlight, the old bull elephant – and me. That was what he indicated of course, of course. Anything that brought me to his mind was welcome, but the idea of the old bull elephant and its bulk in the moonlight seemed too much in focus with my own big body. An echo whispered: You're such a big girl . . . then he had been lying in my arms. No – only in my tilted bed. No. It must have been in my arms. It was in my arms. All the same, I wished it had been a gazelle, or a herd of gazelles, drinking in the moonlight. Then I would have known he remembered our running on the sands and that he had kissed my salty arm. Had he? Once, said the echo. And once was enough, I answered myself, enough to tell me. I don't need to have everything spelled out. I know how to build the truth.

Breaking into the void and silence of the afternoon house, a voice came calling distantly, then nearer. 'Rose,' it called, 'Rose, Rose!' Mummie, of course, forgetting that the servants had gone out; that was quite like her. So she rang the library bell. So nobody answered the library bell. So she called, distractedly demanding. Let her call, I thought as I opened my bedroom door; let her go on calling. Then, as I reached the staircase, I could hear panic, high and faint, in her voice. What a fuss. What nonsense. I proceeded in a calm, sane way downstairs, my hand on the rail, my head still high among the African stars. I was detached from this absurd flurry.

Then I saw her, pattering and running, stripped of her poise, awkward as an animal in clothing. I was back with terrifying Mrs Tiggywinkle turning into the wild, running from me as she had in the story, elemental before my eyes. And this was Mummie, always so cool, so balanced, here she was, her hair flying loose out of that hat, its pretty tilt ridiculous, her mouth grimacing.

'Rose,' she called. 'Rose!' Then, when she saw me, 'Oh, it's YOU.' Her passionate disappointment infuriated me and kept me outside her terror. 'Find somebody,' she said. 'Find somebody. He's dying!' She tottered and ran on towards the swing door, away from me. She didn't have to say it. I knew it was Papa.

'Where is he?' I went after her. But she didn't tell me where to find him, only ran before me, following her hands, her feet fumbling on the flagstones, calling, 'Rose!' into the dark pantry door, and the lamp room, and the boot room, and 'Rose, Rose,' into the hot empty kitchen. I stood in the doorway before she could escape me. I caught her by the shoulders – something impossible I had never done. I shouted at her: 'Where is he?'

'He's terribly ill; he can't get up. Find Rose, oh you fool, find Rose.'

'You know they've all gone to the rectory. Mummie, where is he?'

'I had the cyclamen for Hubert. He's there – he can't speak.'

'He's in the graveyard?'

'Oh, can't you listen, how often must I tell you? Get the boys, get someone to carry him, get the doctor.'

If it's like last night, I thought, must they all know? I had to take this on myself. Nurses faint at operations. The thought sustained me. If they can steady themselves, so can I. I was a young nurse.

'Put hotwater-bottles in his bed,' I ordered sharply, and turned away.

'Where do they keep hotwater-bottles? How am I to boil the kettle? Don't leave me like this. How am I to do it alone?' she cried after me as I ran away from her, down the last passage to the stable yard, out through the stable arch and on to the driveway.

He was not dying, I knew. He was drunk like last night. I wasn't going to say it to her; I wouldn't tell her. Last night I turned away from him, I left him to Rose – Rose, tough as a proper nurse, strong as a man, had brought him up to his bed.

What must I do, I thought, running down the drive, how to

get him home? The car had gone, taking the maids to the rectory. If I pulled him up on his feet I could link his arm and walk him back to the house. I must hurry. I must be the first. No one else shall help him – I'm the one.

In the dog-shaped shadow cast by the stolid little church on grass and graves, I found him. Rose was sitting on the grass, her knees spread, holding him in her arms. His head was lolled back absurdly against her breast and shoulder. Her blouse was ripped out at the armpit from dragging and holding him. The coat of her navy-blue suit was across his foot. There was a brooding look about her, melancholy and wild. Her flowered hat was lying on the grass. There was a mushroom dew on it and on the graves. I remembered Mrs Brock's hat, dripping from the wet grass, one silly hat recalled the other, clear and meaningless, conjuring together that night with this evening.

'Rose,' I said, 'what are we going to do? He's drunk.' We would have to admit it to each other. She just sat there, nursing him in her arms. 'We must get him back to bed,' I said. Bed was the proper place. Bed and concealment.

'He's not drunk,' Rose said violently, and held him nearer. 'It's a seizure – he can't speak. Look—' She tilted his head as if he were a sick baby, and I saw the fixed drop of his mouth and his loose hand. 'Go get the doctor – he could be at the fête – take my cycle, against the church door. Tell them at the lodge to bring me blankets and send for the lads and a gate to carry him home.'

She gave all these orders in an imperative, hot rush of words. It was impossible to argue against her sense, or to suggest any alternative. There she would sit, spreading her bottom on the wet ground, holding Papa away from its chill, until the gate and the blankets and the doctor were brought to him. It was a distillation of the strength and passion that she put into her cooking. She would have it this way and no other. I was in second place again.

But as I tore down the road on Rose's bicycle, beyond the grief and fear and the shock of seeing only an effigy, a bad imitation of Papa, a fearful feeling of ease and relief came over me, linked to something Rose had said: 'He can't speak.' That was it. He might never speak again. God forbid. God forbid. And I pedalled furiously on towards the doctor. Leaning over the handlebars of Rose's bicycle, yearning for more speed, driving down on the pedals with all my weight, I escaped from my terrible wish.

CHAPTER TWENTY-TWO

Extensive brain damage, that was what they called it. His bedroom became like a nursery with a new baby in it. Every morning Rose helped the nurse from Dublin to lift him in bed. From on and off his bedpan he made great sad eyes of apology at them. The hour was strict and they kept to it with strict enjoyment.

Rose brought up the ironed and aired pyjama coat, the warmed towels, the new hotwater-bottle, the clean pillowcase, and they made his bed and dressed him up like a clean favourite doll, a doll with no legs, for one was dead and the other was put away in a cupboard. They propped him against the pillows and put the hotwater-bottle in its flannel bag at his foot. 'Hot or cold, that foot won't feel it,' the nurse said.

'His foot feels cold to me.' Rose was definite, and held Papa's foot for a moment in her hand.

Mummie and I came in to see him then. The odd thing was that she seemed to want me to go in with her. She was afraid. She wanted to pretend things were quite ordinary. She would bring the dogs in too. They were something to talk about.

'Go on. Can't you say something?' she whispered to me when, in a silence, Papa shifted miserably. I was not confounded.

'Perhaps he wants his you know bottle?'

'Call the nurse.' She jumped distractedly to her feet. 'Don't touch the thing. What's she here for? Nurse! Nurse!'

Nurse came quickly from her bedroom. She was the embodiment of starched calm. 'I think he wants to do something,' Mummie whispered so that Papa shouldn't hear. Papa looked satisfied. I thought he gave my hand a tiny pressure. I felt agony for a moment, wondering how much went on in his mind.

Everybody in the country made pilgrimages to Temple Alice to ask about Papa; they usually came about six o'clock, and they usually accepted a drink, talking in sad lowered voices becoming to the misery of it all. An evening came when there was only half a bottle of whisky left in the drink cupboard and none in the cellar. The next day Mummie sent an order to the Wine Cellars for six bottles of Scotch whisky. They sent out three bottles and their account. It was for two hundred and thirty-seven pounds.

'Quite impossible,' Mummie said, and stuffed it into the drawer with all the other bills.

The dogs felt the change in their lives. They became turgidly bored and unattractive, looking backwards sullenly when asked to leave their baskets and follow with me in the tracks of Papa's routines and habits – for instance, the stable yard after breakfast. There they moved peevishly around while I had a word with Tommy.

Tommy was grooming Hubert's horse. Strength seemed to spurt out of his resistant but pleasured body as Tommy wisped away and shouted warnings and growled and purred as he worked. He stood away from his horse like a groom in a print. 'I wonder what do the Major intend doing about him?'

I felt my blood quicken a little. 'Did he mention anything to you, Tommy, before he, before ...'

Tommy came to my rescue. It was so difficult to say that Papa was speechless. 'Before his little turn, miss? No, miss – only to slacken the oats to him was all he said.'

Now I knew, a warm tide coming slowly into my mind, that Papa had said nothing to him about his gift or loan to the Crowhurst girls. I felt in power. I must think for Papa. After all ... extensive brain damage ...

'Will he ever speak again, Dr Coffey?' – 'Well, it's a question. Sometimes these cases do recover. We must be optimistic.' – 'How much does he understand? Does he remember?' – 'Perhaps. It's a question ... it's hard to tell ...' So it went, whispering on in my mind, a sort of contentment.

That was the evening when the Crowhurst girls bicycled over to enquire for Papa. I could hear them taking off their coats – coats beautifully made by themselves out of rust-coloured sailcloth, a kind of poor man's Burberry; then light footsteps crossing the hall to the library.

Breda, our cross parlour maid, met me, a duck and a bunch of gentians in her hands. 'It's the Miss Crowhursts to ask for the Major, and all they brought, you'd think we had nothing here.' Lightly derisive and disloyal, she went on her way through the swing door, saying: 'Madam's up the garden.' So I was to have them to myself. I wondered if I should ignore their underground trafficking, messages in flowers and ducklings going to Papa.

They were sitting comfortably reading the gardening articles in the last two *Fields*. I poured out two glasses of sherry, denying the thought of Papa pinching lemon zest into martinis. Actually his martinis were quite ordinary, apart from a lot of gin; their magic was only in his manner.

'Thank you,' they said, keeping their fingers in the *Fields*, so as to find the gardening pages again. 'And the Major?' Blink asked sadly. Polite and incurious, specifying nothing much. It might have been a bit of a cold. They had beautiful manners.

'Not much difference,' I said. That didn't tell them a lot.

'We weren't thinking of seeing him.' Nod opened the *Field* again.

'No,' I said. 'Naturally not.'

'You might tell him,' Nod spoke decidedly, 'that we've come for the horse.'

'I don't understand.'

'Hubert's horse, the Arch Deacon. The Major thought we might be able to do something with him.'

'You know he thought he was a bit much.' Blink left it at that.

'I really don't quite follow you. Tommy has him going beautifully. You might like a day on him. After Christmas, perhaps.'

'Actually, we thought Maxie Riley might ride him home this evening.' Maxie Riley was their tinker groom. Their calm and conviction were absolute.

'Look,' I said, 'I'm awfully sorry, but don't you think we must wait till Papa can tell us about this himself?'

'He *has* told us,' they insisted politely, but their long elegant faces flushed. They were more eager and less polite than before.

'I wonder if he said anything to Tommy about it? Not to

me. The moment he does I'll let you know. Till then, perhaps . . .'

'Can't he speak at all?' Gently as they asked the question, the coarse practical demand was evident in it. I was choked by my resistance towards them and my anger at their curiosity.

'No – he can't speak at all.'

'If he could,' Nod said, as she and Blink got on their feet in one clocklike motion, 'I wonder what he'd say to you?'

I was no more ready than usual with a quick answer. Perhaps they saw the tears I would not shed.

Inside the archway of the stable yard Maxie Riley sat on the corner step of the granite mounting block. The grey seeding flowers of traveller's joy drooped and sprawled above his red tinker's head.

'Tommy,' I said, after I had nodded a surprised 'good evening' towards the tinker, 'did the Major give you any instructions about Mr Hubert's horse?'

'No, miss. The first I heard, this man came in here saying he should ride him home for the Miss Crowhursts.'

'Maxie,' they said reprovingly, 'didn't we tell you to wait in the road?' I know they exchanged a look. It passed round the three of them like the shoe in a game of hunt the slipper. Then, graceful as lone birds, they mounted their bicycles and drifted away, a wind behind them and their tinker running by their side.

While their awful courage and effrontery really appalled me, I did begin to wonder what Papa would say if he could speak. I was afraid he might be only too pleased with them. Of all their talents, their talent to amuse was the one I felt most repellent.

Rascally as they were, their duck was perfection. Papa could only manage a small piece, Nurse said, and Mummie never eats a thing, so I had two delicious helpings; there's not very much on a duck really. I enjoyed this one more than anything I had eaten since Papa's illness. I could feel my pleasure in good things coming back to me, surreptitious but lively.

'At least one thing doesn't change,' Mummie said, getting up without impatience, because the evening was motiveless, 'and that's your appetite, dear girl.'

I didn't feel humiliated. My mind went straight back to the Horse Show, and to Hubert showing off my eating paces to Richard, and Richard's riveted attention and amusement. Everything she didn't know about me was a strength. Thank God, I had secrets to keep. Now Papa would keep them too, I was safe.

CHAPTER TWENTY-THREE

It was the middle of October and Papa showed little change. Sometimes he tried to speak, but the words were sadly unintelligible. We accepted disappointment in his progress as we accepted the shortening days. His pretty nurse dropped some of her antiseptically challenging ways. Her polish dulled and she and Rose were not now the best friends they had been in September. I heard Rose one morning insisting that the Major's sheets were to be changed.

'Ah, they'll do,' said Nurse. 'We were a good boy last night.'

And Rose's answer: 'Pull that sheet out your side before I hit you,' spoken with frightening authority. He would look from one to the other, making obedient small noises, ready to please. Four-thirty was Mummie's hour.

She came in with the China tea and a tin of very special biscuits from Fortnum's which some friend had sent, and they never ate. Pity. She would bring a sprig of verbena and rub a leaf of it in her ringers and sniff at them before bending over him to murmur a greeting. I don't know what she said after Nurse left them alone together with the silver teapot and the blue Worcester cups. She never stayed very long in his room. I would hear her calling unhappily for Nurse or Rose before I was halfway through the scones and sandwiches in the library.

One evening she left him sooner than usual and came into the library wearing a lost and injured air. 'That nurse –' she said exasperatedly – 'She *is* a bore. She's complaining about her "elevenses." What *are* "elevenses"?'

'Oh, it's a thing they do,' I said. 'It's quite harmless.'

'She says Rose has sent her up cold tea and soft Marie biscuits on three mornings running. She says do I expect her to clean her own shoes. What do I know about her shoes?'

'Or care.'

'Exactly. What's more, she wants to be paid. Now.'

'She's been here more than six weeks. Haven't you paid her yet?'

'Of course not. I leave that kind of thing to Mr Kiely. Anyway she does almost nothing for Papa. Rose does all the real things. It's like having a guest in the house. An expensive guest. And a boring guest.'

'Papa does need her.'

'Rose thinks she's not as careful about Papa as she ought to be. Rose thought,' Mummie hesitated, 'he might have bedsores – Papa.' She gave the faintest scream of dismay or disgust. 'And another thing, Rose thinks she's rather dishing out the sleeping pills.'

'Let's talk to Dr Coffey about it all.'

'Yes, I must.' She spoke wearily, longing to put it all aside. 'And I shall have to see that ghastly little man Kiely. I haven't any money.'

*

A few days after this I drove her into Kildeclan to see Mr Kiely. I sat in the car outside his office waiting for her while rain drove onto the windscreen and trickled on me, small and icy through a tear in the hood between canvas and talc.

Little Mr Kiely came out of his office holding his umbrella over Mummie. He had a face far too handsome for his height. It made him into a grotesque, just as his clothes, faithful imitations of the kind of clothes Papa wore, seemed to be characters on their own account, as foreign to his body as if they had never left the shop.

'Thank you so much,' Mummie said, giving him the straight tips of her gloved fingers while she shivered her body back from the rain. He held on to the glove-tips for a moment more, leaning his handsome face, with the great darkness of the umbrella behind it, into the car. He smiled, a glitter against the blackness.

'No more worrying,' he said. 'That cheque should steady things for the moment, and I'll be over next week to look at the bullocks.'

'Oh, you *are* kind.' She retreated near me, almost to my shoulder. 'Drive *on*, Aroon, please.'

'I think,' she said as we drove down the street – every house in it, pretty or ugly, black-faced and similar in the rain – 'I think we might have a cup of tea with the Crowhurst girls.'

'Oh, Mummie, no! Must we?'

'You've no idea what I've been through,' she said. 'I know they must invent all these things; one can't pay too much attention; everything will be all right. But just now I do need a cup of tea. *Dreadfully*.' She dredged the last word up with infinite delicacy and certainty.

In spite of my victory in our last encounter, I felt cold and sick and shy as Mummie pushed open their door and called out their names with plaintive authority: 'Girls,' she called, 'girls, girls, Nod, Blink! Tea, please, tea!'

Nod came out of the diningroom to meet us. She seemed less well arranged than usual – her hair not so crisply set, her jersey and cardigan not twins, or not identical twins. 'How nice of you to come,' she said in her disparaging way, 'and on such an appalling day.'

'Oh,' said Mummie, throwing back her coat, as if it were sables, 'business, horrible business. Otherwise we shouldn't be here.'

'Do forgive me an instant.' Nod backed away from us. 'I'm mending china and my cement's just setting.' Mummie followed her into the diningroom. 'Oh, that lovely piece,' I heard her say, 'I've always loved it. It's perfect.' I knew she didn't mean the broken china. It was the Regency side-table she had envied and sighed after ever since the girls had bought it for some trifling and never told sum in some poor, never named house.

I put my head round the drawingroom door and saw Blink sitting among a lot of knitting, and wearing a lot of knitting, but not actually knitting. Never before had I seen her without some sharp purpose.

'Have you been out in the rain?'

She did not bite back as usual on the nervous stupidity of my question. Sitting there in her wet Wellies she seemed unaware that I was waiting, defensive, for a sharp answer. There was an unhappy languor about her. I dimly recognised some sort of patient desperation clouding her habitual smart vigour. It was as though she had a secret to carry.

'We've been for a long walk. Do sit down. I'll make some

tea.' She spoke to the air as if I were not there, or, if I was, I counted for nothing. 'China or Indian?'

'Mummie likes China.'

'Oh, is she here too? Fancy.' She got up from the sofa as if the effort were almost beyond her – an odd change from her usual whiplash certainty in word and movement.

When Blink had gone I sat rather quietly on the sofa, hoping that the dogs, stirring aggrievedly in their basket, would forget about me. Knitting billowed round me. I counted the makings of at least five cardigans, not yet stitched together. The industry they represented was a little desperate.

I realised, as the minutes passed, a change in the room since that day when Papa and I had visited the girls. Then the room was bright and dignified. It had a gleam in its eye. Today a sticky dust of cold wood-ash hovered on the tables. The fire was not only cold and dead, it had the look of a fire not cleaned out or set or lighted for days. Flower arrangements had died in their vases, poised to the last dead leaf. The dogs, on that previous day neat and sweet and dangerous, now steamed and smelt in a tousled basket. A glass sat on a book, near to where Blink had sat among the knitting. I smelt that, too. Gin. Gin and what? I dipped in a finger. Just gin. All the small shapeliness and delicate contrivances in the room were overlaid by this new sluttish ambiance. I didn't enjoy sitting there alone.

At last Nod and Mummie came in with tea. (Only tea. Indian tea, too.) No Blink.

'Where's Blink?' Mummie asked.

Nod looked at her watch. 'It's her bath-time,' she said. Then, noticing that I glanced unbelievingly at my own watch, she added firmly: 'Nothing like a hot bath if you're silly enough to have a frightful cold, walk six miles, and get soaking wet all on the same day.'

'Oh, I see,' I said. 'It just seems funny to have a bath in the afternoon, except after hunting.'

'With one lame horse between us,' Nod said acidly, 'we shan't do much hunting.'

'You'll get a lot more *knitting* done,' Mummie comforted. She pulled a piece of violet cardigan round her shoulder, and sipped, shivering, at her Indian tea.

'Yes, that *is* your colour.' Nod at once assumed that Mummie was trying on the cardigan. 'We could let you have it cheap. It's a small size for most people.'

'It's a wonderful colour.' Mummie took off the piece of cardigan. 'Wanda primroses. But no. Alas, I mustn't spend any more money. No lovely new clothes.'

'Perhaps you could afford a few double pink primroses?' Nod suggested.

'Well, perhaps.' I felt Nod's fury to sell was having a cumulative effect on Mummie's resistance.

I looked through the streaming window panes, out to the terrible dahlias, lately so flaming with life and colour; they were sodden and rotting now, their flowers jelly, their leaves gross and blackening.

'You haven't lifted the dahlias yet.' I couldn't think of anything else to say.

'More tea?' Nod lifted up the teapot. She put it down neatly and decisively before she said: 'No. We'll have to get that done before we start for England.'

'England?' Mummie and I, for once, spoke together. For once disbelieved the same thing at the same moment. Since leaving school the girls had kept away from England. They avoided their quite grand English cousins, never had them (or anybody else if they could help it) to stay, and certainly never accepted invitations to the courts and halls and manor houses of their family, although we all knew these invitations were issued often and kindly to the two poor relations – who were also almost professional gardeners, inspired knitters and stitchers, and, I will be fair, superb horsewomen.

'We're faintly in a pickle,' Nod said. 'I mean we have to catch up on the bills a bit.'

'Oh, don't,' Mummie implored her. 'We all know about that. *Monstrous*, shop people are. How do you think England's going to help you?' she asked enviously.

'Cousin Imogen has had to move to the dower house at Husband's Budsworth, and she wants us to design the garden – it's been a wilderness for years.'

'Chair covers too, I suppose.' Mummie envisaged the situation at once. 'Then you'll be away for months.'

'Yes, I'm afraid so. Six or eight months, I don't quite know.'

So they were going away. I felt quite warmly towards them now. Things must have come to a pass for the girls to leave their whole life – garden, pigeons, ducks, horses (well, horse) – behind and take off into the world of Gloucestershire.

'The dogs?' I asked.

'Oh,' said Nod snubbingly, 'they'll be all right. We'll make some plan.' I thought she looked as if reality had drawn back, to strike her fully.

'I think if you've quite finished tea –' Mummie looked at me as if I had been eating an ox – 'we really ought to get home to Papa.' She pushed back the sleeve of her coat to find her tiny watch. 'If I might – may I go to your bathroom? It's been such a long awful afternoon.'

'I'm afraid you can't. Blink's in her bath.'

'Not still in her bath? She can't be. It's more than half an hour.'

'Yes,' Nod said firmly, 'she is. She needs a good soak. You'll have to try the downstairs. I'll just turn out the cats. They love it on a wet day.' I could imagine them there, crouched between the loo and the croquet mallets and the Wellington boots and the weed killer. While we waited for Nod to banish the cats, Mummie nipped into the diningroom. She reappeared with a look of pious gratification about her.

'It's much earlier than she thinks it is.'

'It's after five now.'

'Oh, time?' she said. 'I mean my side-table. It's that serpentine front. They could have stuck on the ram's head later.' She had always been obsessed by the girls' side-table.

On the road home, thinking of that lilac, bell heather, or Wanda cardigan, I asked: 'What about my dress allowance?'

She withdrew a little further to her own side of the seat. I could feel her wrapping herself closer, protectively, in the loose coat. 'Oh,' she answered, 'yes – it was to have come out of that miserable little cheque.'

'How do you mean, Mummie, "was"?' A wave of anxiety swelled in me.

'I've had quite a little coup,' Mummie said contentedly. 'Do you know – Nod sold me the side-table.'

'How much?'

'Do you mind –' Mummie spoke with polite restraint – 'I think that's rather my own affair. I gave her quite enough.'

There was gratification in the way she settled back in her seat as she spoke. 'More than enough.'

'Are they in a bad mess?'

'Yes. I think they are.' She sounded mercilessly amused.

CHAPTER TWENTY-FOUR

I could see and hear Nurse become every day brisker and at the same time more sullen in her handling of Papa. Fewer happy jokes were cracked as she went about her duties. She was mannerless in her indifference to his jumbled baby talk. Single words that he now struggled to pronounce he achieved only by an exhausting concentration of effort.

Rose watched her. 'I wonder does he get his rights,' she said darkly. 'She choked my fish down him in five minutes, that way she wouldn't miss the post with her letter . . . his foot was stiff with the cold and she wouldn't go to the kettle for a hot jar . . . would he have bed-sores, I wonder? . . . Do you get a heavy smell from him ever? You should speak to the doctor, Miss Aroon.'

Dr Coffey came to see Papa every Thursday, and sometimes more often. He told him about hunting and how many snipe were in the bogs. I caught him hurrying through the hall one morning. In his leisurely patience with Papa one felt he had no other calls on his time, or none so important.

'How is he today, Dr Coffey?'

'We can't expect much change yet. Just carry on the way we are.'

'That's it,' I said. 'We can't. Nurse doesn't seem at all happy.'

'Yes,' he said, 'that's our problem. It's a pity. She's a capable girl. The trouble is – my dear child – she wants her money.' He started at once to hurry away from the problem and towards the hall door. I fastened on him.

'What if she goes, Dr Coffey?'

'Rose is very competent. Tommy in the yard could help her lift him.'

'Rose is the *cook*.'

'Yes.' He spoke in an odd, reserved way. 'Yes. But perhaps she might be the answer.' So nothing was resolved. There was nothing for me but a powerless doubtful refusal to despair over Papa. I remembered especially what Rose had said about a heavy smell when I watched Mummie bruising and pinching sheaves of frosted verbena leaves as she bent over him at teatime. When she had gone I put medlar jelly on buttered scraps of scones and fed them to Papa in little pieces, and ate them whole myself (Rose's tiny scones). He looked at me with terrible discontent and made impatient sounds, rabid for something I could not supply. Oh, dear, if it was his bedpan?

'Do you want Nurse?'

'No-no-no,' he could mouth that much. 'NO-NO,' I could feel him shouting.

'Rose will be here for the tray soon,' I said loudly, and he collapsed back on the pillows in a sad impatience. I managed to finish the scones and a slice of cherry cake before she came in. I had longed for her, and now I resisted her strength and assurance.

'Her ladyship got a drive into town and not back yet.' She spoke as though the nurse's outing were a licentious indulgence. 'I suppose he's perished.' She moved the tea table away from his bedside to turn back the blankets and put her hand on his foot. 'It's ice, all right,' she said, satisfied at the neglect, 'and his hot bottle dead cold. I bet it wasn't filled since morning. I'll rub a bit of life into it for you, Major,' she said, gently kneeling by the bed so as to reach his foot more comfortably. 'Could you take the bottle down to Teresa, Miss Aroon, and tell her to boil the kettle – maybe you'd bring it up here to us again – she has my pheasant to pluck yet.' I left her, bent with wonderful pliancy over the bed; his cold foot in her hands, she was talking to him easily, as if she were part of the drift of his mind.

There was nobody in the kitchen. A glorious pheasant lay unplucked on the table. Dark alcoves yawned back into the walls. High, huge, and Gothic, a framed text hung above the loaded dresser, I AM THE BREAD OF LIFE. The capital letters were blue and red and gold, under years of smoke and dust and grease. I put my hand on the pheasant's breast, a stone under the fiery feathers. I looked out of the windows to the stars. Tomorrow there would be a letter for me. Or perhaps not. He was moving round Africa. He had never had my letter about Papa. I saw a native running on to nowhere with my letter in the cleft of a forked stick, or it might be his letter to me. The idea cheered me.

Before I picked up the hotwater-bottle I heard laughter in the servants' hall; someone came out on the laugh, as on an exit line. It was Nurse, neat and lively in her town clothes.

'Thank God for one hot cup of tea today,' she said, a sort of bold excuse for enjoying herself in the servants' hall. 'Am I seeing things, or is that my patient's hotwater-bottle you have there, Miss St Charles?'

'Yes,' I said, 'I've just filled it for him.' I felt I should have apologised, and I was right.

'If I may say so, we consider it important that a case like the Major's should find its own body heat, at its own level.' The professional tone was far removed from the friendly giggling of the past, or the sulky efficiency of present days.

'All the same,' I maintained, 'his feet were cold.'

'There's no sensation whatever in that foot,' she said coarsely emphasising the singular, as if I didn't know about Papa's leg.

'I wasn't the only one who thought so – Rose thought so too.'

'And sent you down for the bottle, I suppose, thank you very much, and please understand that no one comes between me and my patient only excepting the doctor on the case. I'll take that bottle from you now, please, and that, I hope, will be IT.'

I was cowed by her stunning authority, and gave up the rubber bottle which I had been holding against my chest. I walked away from the beastly girl to the swing door, the benignity of my sense of usefulness falling from me with every step I took towards the library.

Mummie was stitching away at her great summery piece of tapestry, lilies and grey leaves tumbling over her knee.

'You've forgotten the fire, Mummie.'

'I rang.'

'I suppose nobody heard the bell.'

'I suppose nobody listened.' She went on stitching with blue fingers. There was a haze of damp air round the globes of the lamps. 'Ring again,' she said, her eyes on her work.

I was bending over the fire when the door burst open and Nurse, young and strong and furious, flounced across the room towards Mummie, crouching among her lilies and leaves, to pour out a flood of words, accusing Rose – of what? She screamed about getting her money, about leaving in the morning, about a hand under the bedclothes. Mummie was listening too patiently. I was appalled. I had to speak.

'He was cold – whatever you say, Nurse. He was so cold.'

'Cold?' she repeated on a rising note, 'when the heat of herself would scorch him!'

'But I was there. His hotwater-bottle was cold. Rose was rubbing his foot.'

'Foot?' she screamed. 'What I have to tell you is what I'll tell my priest and my matron and my doctor—'

'If it gave him the smallest pleasure, Nurse, I am only too delighted.' Mummie interrupted in a cool small voice, and Nurse stared back at her, somehow defeated of her object. She subsided into a sort of sulky acquiescence.

'You understand, Mrs St Charles, I require my salary and I leave in the morning.'

'Such a pity it can't be tonight.' Mummie went on stitching at her leaves.

When Nurse had gone she stopped stitching. She pushed away the tapestry as if its weight were too much. She got up from her little chair. She went to the writing table and shuffled about among the papers on it, as if she must find something useful in its confusion. 'It's no use,' she said, 'there simply isn't any money.' She left the writing table and went from chair to chair touching their backs, straightening a cushion, marshalling some resource.

‘But what about Mr Kiely’s money?’ I wanted her to see sense. I wanted to distress her.

‘No, no. I gave it to the girls.’

‘Not all of it? You can’t have.’

‘It was necessary.’ She spoke in the cool tired voice in which she had repelled the nurse. ‘They needed it.’

‘And you needed the side-table?’

‘So you may think,’ she said, and went on walking from chair to chair.

CHAPTER TWENTY-FIVE

The next morning, after breakfast, I opened the hall door as usual to let out the dogs. I was waiting for the postman, too. When he came I took the letters from him – four manilla envelopes and another, larger one, marked PRIVATE.

Mummie was coming downstairs as I put the letters on the side-table. She was wearing her old fur coat, so I knew she was going to paint. I felt the long boards in the hall chill under my feet as I waited, and a chill under my heart from which I had to make some escape. I had to find my way into something that mattered.

'The post is here.'

'Oh, letters. There'll be nothing but nasties. Nasty upsetting things.'

'Have you thought any more about Nurse?' I brought out, a blunt rush of words from nowhere.

She picked up her letters and put them down again without curiosity. She pushed the bills into the drawer where they always went and brushed her palms, lightly crossing them against each other. 'Oh, do we have to think about her? I expect everything will have simmered down by now.'

'But, Mummie, you know it won't have simmered down. She was so angry. And Rose doesn't think she's looking after Papa. And Dr Coffey thinks she wants her money, and she won't leave without it.'

'My dear girl, must you create such a drama out of everything? Why don't you go and exercise the Arch Deacon?' She stood for a moment in the circle of winter light under the dome, gathering herself back into isolation. Then she walked away, elegant as if on stilts above all the trouble beneath her feet. Even the old fur coat with its cracked skins had a cloudy airiness as she wore it.

So she guessed I was afraid of Hubert's horse, and grateful that my own old hunter was lame. What to do? I looked at my watch. Three long hours till luncheon. As I stood, undecided on any occupation, I heard feet running down the back staircase, behind the wall which divided the servants' stairs from ours, which – except to clean – of course they did not use. The padded door burst softly open and Rose, hot and raging in her thin, cotton dress, came bursting through it. 'She's giving the Major a bedbath and the fire not going yet and he crying with the cold.'

I felt as if Papa were being murdered, and I could only stand aside.

'How can I stop her? What can I do?'

'He's crying,' Rose repeated. She turned away from me. She was crying too. She accepted my uselessness. She went back quietly through the service door, leaving me to myself in the cold. I sat down on the swollen woollen roses on the huge Victorian sociable that stood in the hall, under the gallery and the dome; and on that seat, decorated superbly by a great-aunt, a despairing resentment invaded my acceptance of my powerless status as daughter at home – a child of the house living in the grace and favour of unexplored obedience. I was still sitting, dumb on all those roses, when Breda came past me on her way to answer the hall door bell, which had been ringing, unheard by me, far away in the pantry passage. It was a man's voice at the door, asking for Mummie, and not the kind of voice for which she would suffer an interruption of her painting.

'Would you wait inside a minute, sir . . .' Breda knew her mission would be fruitless. One could hear that in the flat, hesitant politeness of her tone. She opened the door wider, and a warm gust of outdoors welled indoors. Compost, black-currant leaves, horses' urine and bullocks' breath lived and wavered momentarily before expiring on the suffocating chill within.

Then I saw who it was, coming down the hall towards me, although Breda had indicated a wooden chair, near the door. He was wearing a Jaeger coat, the twin of ours, a rakish high-necked jersey, and whipcord trousers. He carried a brown felt hat with a very broad ribbon, which made all the rest look false. It was Mr Kiely, and I could have told him now that his visit was born to failure. Papa's name for him, 'that piddling niggler,' flitted into my mind, and reproduced itself in my tepid greeting.

'I thought I'd save Mrs St Charles a journey,' he said. 'I have some rather urgent papers for her signature.'

'Oh, I don't really know where she is.' I felt he ought to be prepared for the rebuff which was certainly on its way to him.

Breda brought it, a minute later: 'Madam is out,' she said

with ominous uncertainty. 'Would you care to leave a message, sir?'

Through and beyond my dislike of common little men, a feeling of embarrassment and sympathy came over me; Mummie was behaving towards him as she did towards me. 'I'm so sorry.' I looked down at him. 'I suppose I can't be of any use?'

He sat down on the sociable and sorted some papers out of his briefcase. 'If you'd ask her to sign these where I've pencilled in the signature, and post them to me today. Things are a bit sticky at the moment. Of course, circumstances . . . but banks have very little patience these days. Mrs St Charles mentioned there were a few little accounts pressing.'

A few – opportunity was clear to me. I opened the drawer of the side-table. Let the rabbit see the dog, I thought, matching it up with Papa's piddling niggler.

'I expect they're mostly duplicates,' he said calmly, taking on himself some of my phobia about that stuffed drawer.

'These came today.' I handed him the pile and he opened the envelope marked PRIVATE, screwing up his mouth as he read it.

'Not very nice. It's the garage. Cash on all future transactions. And that includes petrol.'

'But cars won't go,' I said, stupefied, 'without petrol.'

'Well, yes. It's one of the facts.' The drawer was hanging outwards, its full mouth open. I was petrified in my dismay. 'Put the lot in a sack, and send them in to my office, I'll see what can be done.'

'I'll have to ask Mummie.'

'I don't think that will get you far. She's not, if I may say so, a very businesslike lady.'

'I know.'

'And financially we are in a bit of a mess at the moment, or I wouldn't have come out of my way this morning, on my road to Leopardstown races too.' That explained his clothes, and a kind of gay financial security in the air about him.

'I know,' I said again. The cold bit into me. I could feel Papa crying in his bedroom in the hands of that vindictive nurse. I sat down. I bowed my head. 'I suppose you couldn't let me have any money out of the farm account or something . . . Mummie hasn't been able to settle anybody's wages.'

'I gave her—'

'I know.'

He looked at me. He knew too. 'The bank's owed too much,' he said.

I felt a suffocating band of despair tightening round inside my head. Now, like Dr Coffey, he was hurrying away from my problems, leaving me to agonise alone. We got to our feet together. 'Couldn't we sell something?' An idea came to me: 'That horse of my brother's?'

'Are you talking about a brown five-year-old? By Great Moments out of a half-bred mare?'

'He's a brilliant hunter,' I said. That was true enough of Arch Deacon when Hubert rode him.

'All the same, there's a kink in all these Great Moments horses and he hasn't a very nice reputation.' He looked at me. It was a penetration. 'He hops it, doesn't he?'

'Oh, I wouldn't call it that.'

'Well,' he said, 'I don't know how the story got around.'

'My father was talking of selling him.'

'Talking is as far as we'll get. Now,' he looked away before his eyes came back to me, 'as it's a question of urgency – that's one great yearling out there. He's saleable all right.'

'Yes. I own him.' I felt pleasurably inflated by the simple statement.

'There's something you could turn into ready money.'

'I'm not thinking of selling him.' The value of my present from Richard grew immeasurably real to me. What if he did bite or kick me and do nasty things to the donkey, he was there, a solid testimony to my love, our love, growing more cheeky and better-looking every week. He would be there when Richard came back. We would walk up to him together.

'It's just an idea,' Mr Kiely said. 'Two hundred pounds – perhaps I'm foolish … you could have it in notes.' He paused. 'I'm meeting an English fellow today; he's a spotter for one of the big trainers; I could have interested him. However –' he sighed and gave up the idea. 'If I'm to see the first race,' he said, 'I must be off.'

A door upstairs banged, clapping shut; the bedrooms were too far off for any voice, even a child's cry, to reach the civilisation of the hall where we stood, but the angry sound recalled Papa's circumstance too clearly. I reeled towards a decision: my present, my all. It was the death of my heart. Mr Kiely was edging away. I would lose my only way out. 'Make it three hundred,' my voice was saying, 'and I'll put the brown horse in the deal.'

'Right, and not a word to Mother, isn't that it?'

I resented the degree of familiarity. Why should he know whether or not I kept the matter my own secret? But, as we sat together on the vast round of the sociable and bank notes fell between us among the woolwork roses and petunias, I felt rather less intolerance towards him. I had never seen so much money. I rustled my hand through it, like feet in autumn leaves.

'I must be off,' he said. 'Do you ever have a bet?'

'Oh yes, sometimes.' I never did.

He picked up one of my many five-pound notes. 'There's a good thing in the fourth race. I'll put you on a fiver, if you like.'

How could I tell him five shillings would be my limit? I didn't care for his gesture. Win or lose, it would be another link.

'That's all just between our two selves.' He was smiling as he shook my hand (quite unnecessarily) before he went skipping down the steps as fast as a child, out into the morning and away from Temple Alice. I wished I need never see him again.

I hurried back to the sociable, eager for the comfort and security the money in my hands must give me. No comfort came to me. I sat among the bank notes and the roses, great fat tears bouncing off my fat cheeks. I had sold my only true love-token. The shudders going through me were as deep as my loss.

Tears are such rotten behaviour, but a disgraceful warmth and ease followed them for me, and I knew a purpose, and a power to fulfil it, actually belonging to me and to nobody else. I was someone. I felt respect for myself and a sense of authority. I would dismiss Nurse, and I would have her out of the house and on the train to Dublin before Mummie left her studio. But I owed myself some ceremony in the act. I rang the bell and sent Breda to summons Nurse to the library. I arranged myself in Papa's chair at the writing table, pen, ink, paper, tidy bundles of bank notes, a neat heap of silver, and my own aloof expression all set before she came coolly rustling in, fresh and pink-cheeked as the African lilies Mummie had left on a low table.

'I suppose you thought we should have a little talk.' She sat down, crossing her neat legs. I hadn't asked her to sit down, and the only thing I could do about it was to stand up myself.

'Is there anything for us to discuss, Nurse – except your wages and the time of the train to Dublin?' My voice sounded frozen to me, light and disparaging. I don't know where it came from.

'My salary amounts to thirty-four pounds, six and eight. I can have my cases packed in ten minutes – and gladly.'

'Yes,' I said, still in the same voice. 'Yes.' I felt some pleasure in producing it. 'Perhaps you'd like to count these notes.'

She accepted them from me. She counted them quickly. 'Well. Thank you.' She tucked my money warmly between her apron front and the bold blue stripes of her dress. 'Will you be driving me to the station, Miss St Charles?'

'I hope Tommy can take you.' She still delayed. 'Perhaps you should start packing.'

She turned back again from the door. 'Look,' she said, 'you can't name it, and I won't name it. It's a nasty name for a nasty thing.'

'What are you talking about?' I was surprised back into the use of my own voice.

'That's all I'm going to say. Only, if I was you—'

'And if I were you I should get my suitcases packed as quickly as possible. I would rather hate you to miss your train.'

My rejoinder was both neat and dignified, but as she went

out of the room a peculiar curiosity, an unspoken unpleasant surmise, stayed with me. It was as if her body, clean and fresh as pine needles, had left a smell behind it on the air, a clinging smell, which I would rightly ignore.

CHAPTER TWENTY-SIX

The wonderful thing that came out of my decision and sacrifice was Papa's improvement. We all felt it like a radiance.

Rose had a nurse's freedom with him now. She could warm his foot, or rub methylated spirit and powder into his heel or his bottom; she could give him clean sheets every day, and freshly ironed pyjamas sometimes twice a day. One guessed that a little accident had happened, but he never looked frightened or distressed, only amused and apologetic. Rose would soak him in eau-de-cologne, disparaging to nothing that sharpish tinge of ammonia. She would brighten and tidy him with almost professional dexterity, and leave him propped on clean pillows, scented and burnished. When she went away to see about tea, he would look after her longingly. Or perhaps, as he pushed up his moustache, he was looking longingly towards the door because Mummie was coming in. She would bring a little bunch of cyclamen or a freakish early sprig of daphne, anything that smelled sweet and strong when she pinched it or threw it on the fire.

Rose and I came in with the tea. Teatime with Papa had

become a habit, now. Mummie was sitting on a low nursing chair near his bed. She was leaning back, away from him, miserably silent as he tried to tell her something. He was making a great effort.

'I say, I say, I say,' he was going on like a comic starting his patter, and Rose was just in time to share in his struggle. She put down the tray and leaned across his bed to straighten the blue bird's-eye scarf in the neck of his blue silk pyjama coat, and to mop his mouth a little. 'Beastly,' he struggled on, 'beastly, beastly . . .'

'Yes, I know, darling. I've always thought so,' Mummie answered at random, desperate for him to stop. When he lay back on his pillows like a stuffed doll, it was easier for her to sit quietly, and pinch on her verbena leaves and think of other times. But Rose, lifting him up as if she would shake words out of him, was living in the present, and lending him her strength for his effort.

'What's beastly, Major? Tell us, Major. You nearly had it.'

'Beastly – cold – bathwater,' he finished on a senseless note of memory. But not quite – Rose held the clue.

'No more cold baths,' she comforted him, 'since her ladyship have went. And no more cups with spouts neither.' She poured out his tea in a proper china cup and put in cream and sugar, both disapproved by Nurse, and fed him gently. She acted as though she had dispossessed his life of Nurse, while I had done it, and longed for him to know that it was my doing.

Mummie had been less than grateful when she heard of Nurse's departure. 'Gone? Without her wages?'

'No. I paid her.'

'You can't have, without consulting me.'

'I sold my yearling. I thought you'd be pleased.'

'You are a remarkably poor judge of pleasure.'

'Papa and Rose are delighted.'

'Oh yes. Rose will have him all to herself now. *Far* too much for her.'

'Dr Coffey thinks Rose and Tommy can manage.'

'It will give Rose far too much to do,' she said again. And then, with extreme distaste: 'Who is going to hear him if he calls for "something" in the night?'

'Can't Rose sleep in the pink room, where Nurse slept?'

'Not really.'

'Why not?'

'Oh, Aroon, would you kindly leave the matter to me. Haven't you interfered about enough?' She sounded more distressed and exasperated than actually angry.

I didn't press on. I would wait. I felt stronger. It was not happiness that was growing in me, but it was some kind of reason and purpose. Perhaps I would be the one to undertake the grim discussion with Mr Kiely; he had almost suggested it. Four days later he did suggest it. A letter enclosing three ten-pound notes and a five-pound note came for me, saying: 'We got a nice little price, didn't we? Your winnings herewith. Perhaps Mrs St Charles or yourself would drop into the office someday soon, to discuss the other matters.'

How to tell her, without saying he had written to me? Don't tell her, don't tell her anything. That became my strength and my stratagem. That was why I didn't say that I knew for certain Rose was sleeping in the pink room every night now. If she didn't have to know she would let matters take a course of their own. Rose knew that too. She had not asked for any direction about sleeping in the pink room. There she was and thank God she was, sleeping lightly, ever ready for his call, and competent in all necessities.

Soon I knew something else I was going to keep to myself. I knew the Crowhurst girls had gone away. I would let Mummie find it out. Although I could have told her this, I was learning to keep everything to myself now that I was a woman of means; no, a girl of means; no, a woman. You are a woman if you have had a lover in your bed as I have had. Poor things, always the Crowhurst 'girls,' and without any means.

'I suppose you heard the Crowhurst girls did a midnight flit?'

I had gone to Mr Kiely's office without Mummie, and with another great package of bills. He leaned across the wide top of his desk as if he would narrow the distance between us. I thought it would have suited his position in life better if he had sat upright. I was there on business. I had not come in for a gossip, or a cup of tea, or a cigarette, all of which I was offered.

'Yes. They're going to Husband's Budsworth for a month or two,' I said.

'Not the address the post office has for forwarding letters,' he corrected me. 'I happen to have a little business to settle up for them. I sold their three-year-old.'

I wasn't going to ask him about the business, but he had guessed rightly at the creep of curiosity in my mind.

'They're terrors to make a deal –' he laughed – 'but they're two great girls.'

'Who feeds the dogs?' My voice sounded tremulous to me; the news of their going was such bliss. Still, one had to show some concern for animals.

'That tinker fellow they had around the horses; he goes in every day.'

'Fancy leaving the tinker in charge,' I said. 'How *sad.*'

'About your own little trouble.' He whisked the papers in a cardboard file together. 'I think we have the worst cases quietened for the present. They'll wait on till they see how things go with the Major.'

'My father is so much better.' I felt a broad delight in being able to tell him this. It was my due. He did not look nearly as pleased as I expected.

'Ah, well,' he said, 'there's always a change in these cases.'

I put on my gloves before I said goodbye, and I gave him just the ends of the fingers. I had seen Mummie do that. It has a repelling effect.

'Pleased with your win?' he asked. I felt my face flare up. How had I forgotten to say thank you? And he had ignored my glove tips; he was shaking, no, holding, my hand beyond them. 'Well,' he let my hand go easily, 'we must chance another little gamble.'

Irritated and confused, I stumbled out of the room. Why think of him at all? There were other, less irritating, matters to consider. The Crowhurst flight for instance. The reason I enjoy other people's disasters is because they involve my understanding and sympathy in a way their successes never can – I like feeling genuine pity. Even when I know they are unworthy of my interest, I don't think I am ever ungenerous to friends more unlucky than myself. I would have loved to go and see what the Crowhursts' dear little house looked like, felt like, smelt like now.

CHAPTER TWENTY-SEVEN

Day by day Papa improved a little. His speech was better, although his mind and memory were still utterly confused. There was a touching quality in his polite acceptance of all his embarrassing dependence on Rose, and every day I was finding more comfort and order in my heart through my importance to him. I was the one who read aloud the racing correspondents.

'That fool,' he would say. And 'No. No. No,' to each of the selected runners. On the days when he was right in his contradictions we were absolutely triumphant. I thought how, when spring came, I would lead him about the place in the donkey-chaise. Papa would be pleased, and so should I. It would be delightful, taking him round like something in a pram.

I saw quite a vista of things I could do for Papa – plans and pleasures for which he would love me. Now and then I would tell him of these cheering prospects, but he did not always understand or even much look forward to them. For instance, when I planned for the future summer, days when I might drive him to the sea (in the car, of course, not in the donkey-chaise) and even envisaged the kind of sandwiches we might take with us, he grew quite fussed and angry.

'No. No,' he said. 'Awful. Awful.'

'But, Papa, think what fun. You could fish for mackerel from the pier.'

'Shan't.' He looked at me in a very funny way. 'She'd come for me.' It was quite a long sentence. He really was improving.

I encouraged him to try further: 'Who, Papa? Who would come for you?'

'Whosit. Whosit—' He seemed really upset. 'Walkin' on the water.'

'You don't mean Jesus, Papa?'

'I know who I mean.' He shut his eyes and didn't say another word.

'I could untangle your line.' He only glared at me. 'And if you felt like a little snooze in the car I could go and prawn the rock pools.'

'Poor thing,' he said distinctly.

'No. I'd love it,' I answered. 'And we could buy fresh lobsters when the boats come in.' I did so love fresh lobster. Their taste in my mind brought clearly into the present winter bedroom that day of clear September light when Richard and I ran between the cornfields and the sea: when I was so light on my feet, so sure in my wonder. The ends of my salty hair were in my mouth; his lean cold hand in mine. Now, with all my winter clothes heavy on me (it is the greatest nonsense that fat people don't feel cold) I could sustain my truthful memories and fill the time till he came back to me, as he must. Then, of course, I would put my hand in his again, and drift lightly down the aisle beside him, dressed in white satin. (No.

Parchment satin perhaps, for a big girl.) Hubert's near grave, and Papa's efforts to speak to us would be faraway things that day.

CHAPTER TWENTY-EIGHT

It was in November, when the hours light enough for painting were short, and the weather was always too wet or too frosty for gardening, and the restoration of the Crowhurst girls' side-table as good as completed, that Mummie opened for herself a new occupation – a campaign for economy.

That was the morning when I was late in meeting the postman. Rose had called me to help her lift Papa while she changed his under sheet. When that was done, I hurried across the gallery to look down through the circle to see if Richard's letter, or any letter, had come for me. I saw Mummie then, looking into the empty drawer, a bunch of unopened bills in her hand. She stood so still that I could see her breath sigh out, making a neat little haze as she looked and considered. Then she shut the drawer carefully – she was gently considerate to all furniture – and went floating down the length of the hall, the letters still in her hand, and lightly up the stairs.

'Nothing for you,' she said, as she passed me by. That was all for the moment. But at lunchtime it began. It began with the dogs' dinners. The dogs' food, meat and brown bread, soup and proper green food, was brought into the diningroom. Papa had always mixed up the dinners himself, sure of the correct quantities, and showing deference towards individual likes and dislikes. At times when he had an uninteresting guest beside him, or the talk was too boring, this rite provided him with a wonderful means of escape; it avoided bad manners, and it avoided the intolerable guest. We had no guests now. We did try to speak to each other a little, especially when Breda was in the room.

When the time came for me to mix up the dogs' dinners I knew Mummie was looking at me in the oddest way. 'What enormous dinners you are giving those dogs,' she said.

I was quite surprised. 'You must be thinking of cats' dinners. These are quite small dinners for dogs.'

'They are only twice the size of the dogs!' She spoke so sharply that I stood looking at her, and the dogs sat, looking at me. '*The* most appalling bill came from the butcher today,' she went on. 'I'm quite used to dishonesty, but this is unbelievable.' She was looking at me across the dry white chrysanthemums in the silver potato ring, and across the icy white distances of tablecloth. 'Well, why don't you feed them?'

'All right, Mummie. I've still got to chop up their spinach.'

'And another thing –' She leaned towards me, looking upwards. My enormous size, as I stooped above the dogs' dinners, filled my mind like guilt. 'Another thing I should like to know: where are all the business letters which I have so carefully put away in their usual place?'

'I gave them to Mr Kiely.'

'Do I understand that you gave them to your friend the solicitor? Don't you think you take rather a lot on yourself?'

'But you wouldn't see him, Mummie.'

'How did he know the letters were there?'

'I must have told him.'

'So I should imagine.' She tapped out the words. 'After that you proceeded to dismiss your father's nurse.'

'You know he's been much better since she left, much happier.'

'The nights are far too much for Rose.' It was like a cry coming from her.

'Rose doesn't mind,' I reassured her. 'She'd do anything. She gets up three times in the night.'

'Yes. Between you, you'll kill him – rather sooner than you think, perhaps.'

It was such a terrible thing for her to say, so unbelievably wrong, when we were doing everything for Papa. But I kept calm and reasonable.

'The trouble about nurses,' I reminded her gently, 'is that they have to be paid. And we don't seem to have the money for that.'

'Which particular fool told you so? Your Mr Kiely, I suppose.'

'Well, yes. And he says—'

'I don't wish to hear what he says. I only know that he has done little or nothing since your father's illness except by-pass my authority. As for finding any ready money, which is what he is there for, and what he is paid to do – that's the last thing he thinks of. And who economises, I ask you? Who cuts down on anything? Look at the size of those dogs' dinners –'

'Mostly brown bread.'

'– and the size of the butcher's bill. I can't look at it. It makes me quite sick.'

'I expect it goes back for years. And we do have to eat.'

'Perhaps if you were willing to eat just a little less, we wouldn't have this appalling bill; of course you happen to be a big girl.' She might as well have said: You happen to have three legs. I went on talking to the dogs. 'And all for red meat – why does it say that? What meat is not red? I ask myself.'

'Rabbit,' I told her.

'Rabbit? Then we might have rabbit more often. Not that I can eat rabbit.'

'Neither will the maids.'

'Why do we have so many maids? All eating their heads off. A little brown bread and butter is enough for me. Thin bread and butter. Perhaps you and the dogs could sometimes manage with rabbit? I'll speak to Rose ...'

Things went on from there, fluttering attempts at economies, projects envisaged and unfulfilled; penance for all was her final object. She felt we must all suffer.

'I sometimes wonder,' she said when I came into the library one evening, changed into my warmest blue velvet and wishing I owned twin silver foxes, 'where you think money comes from?' She was sitting in her own little chair. The flowers of her tapestry made a ghost summer, falling round her to the floor.

I let the question pass, changing the subject with easy diplomacy. 'That idiot Breda has let the fire out,' I said. Although I should have rung the bell, I stooped for the logs myself. I know I'm quite silly about doing the work servants are paid for.

'Stop,' Mummie said.

'But, Mummie, she's just bringing in dinner, and the fire will be out.'

'One can't help noticing how very determined you are on your own little comforts.'

'Such as?'

'Such as oilstoves burning in every conceivable corner of the house. I imagine it must have been your rather unpretty idea to put one in the PLACE.' She spoke the word bravely. 'Don't you realise that paraffin oil, like most things, costs money? And economy means a little, just a very little, self-denial.'

'The tank in the yard is full of oil, Mummie.'

'So you may think – and what about the lamps?' She went on in her most practical tone of voice. 'What happens when one can no longer see to read? Tell me that.'

'I'll tell you when it happens.' As soon as I said it I knew I should have kept quiet.

'That will be very kind, but quite unnecessary. I don't intend to allow it to happen. I'm determined to put a stop to some of this extravagance and I'm making a start with the oil-stoves. From tomorrow.'

'Won't that mean more fires?'

'Not for me. No more fires in my bedroom, or only fircones and sticks which I will pick up for myself. And I advise you to do the same.'

'My bedroom chimney smokes too dreadfully.'

'Perhaps then you will have to do without.' From the way she considered me I guessed she was longing to say: Fat people are supposed not to feel the cold.

'It's a total lie,' I said before she spoke. 'They do feel the cold.'

'My poor girl – don't let's talk about your size. There are some subjects I do avoid.' She put a final stitch into the stem of a sharp green leaf. 'They say whales can live for months on their own fat – do they call it blubber? Or is it seals?'

'Seals, I think.' The memory of a summer day came to me, unlocked and visible in that word 'seal.' It was Mrs Brock, diving and plunging and playing in the water. Kindness was the word linked with seal. Under my hand, tonight, the texture of my blue velvet dress stood up, electric with cold; this was the present, and that time, before I knew I was ugly, was a myth. Careful love, milk and biscuits, her feet buried in sugary sand, her best hat with all the roses were false assurances. Such things as they gave or promised had no material body. Tonight was real, with my cold hands on my cold dress and my longing for food, coupled to the certain prospect of Mummie's comment on my appetite. The size of anything appalled her . . .

'And who,' she was saying, 'bought that magnum of 4711 eau-de-cologne I noticed in your father's bedroom?'

'Rose needs it. It's against bed-sores.'

'Bed-sores,' she murmured. 'What disgusting thing will you think of next?'

'But it happens. Dr Coffey warned us.'

'Yes. *And* Dr Coffey's bill – can you imagine what that will amount to?'

'Dr Coffey never sends in his bill.'

'That's all you know. He charged ten pounds when you were born. It was quite a ridiculous price.' She looked through me, and back into the past. 'Nothing's worth it,' she said.

CHAPTER TWENTY-NINE

She could do it all. And she did it. The fires and stoves went out. Maids were sacked. Food became impossible. She stopped painting. She stopped gardening. She prowled the house, bent on economies. It was a game in which every vantage point represented a new economy. But as Christmas and the season of hunt balls came closer she grew solicitous for my entertainment. It was a new tease.

'Naturally I like to be alone, but I mustn't be selfish. Why don't you try to see more of your young friends? Who are your friends? What about the Hunt Ball, isn't there anyone you can ask for it?'

'But I don't want to go.'

'And you don't want to hunt – what *do* you want to do . . . ?'

What did I want to do, or to have? I wanted, beyond everything, a letter to illumine my life. I wanted Papa to depend on me more than on Rose (except for bedpans). I wanted the kind of food we used to have when he did the housekeeping. And I wanted to be warm.

Mummie kept on about the Hunt Ball, and the pity of it that I had no friends or partner. She had a list of the most inaccessible social contacts, and she whined on endlessly about people who might ask me, and probably wouldn't . . . 'I came out the same year as their mother.'

'That's some time ago.'

'Your father always went to their shoots.'

'That's not quite a hunt ball.'

'No. Of course there is a difference – they have to find men to dance with you.' The fruitless teasing went on: 'What about those Barraway girls?'

She knew that the Barraway girls lived in a sphere that was out of my reach. Even with Hubert as a talisman there was never more than a nodding acquaintance between us, a faint recognition at a race-meeting. When an invitation to a hunt ball, to be held at Ballytore Barraway, coupled with a dinner party before the dance, came for me, I was suspended between horror at the idea of going by myself into that unknown world and the longing to let Mummie know I had been invited there. I might never have told her – I was, in fact, composing my refusal – if she had not commiserated with me so gently, one evening, on my lack of friends and invitations to balls and Christmas parties.

'Poor child,' she said, stitching into the ragged edges of a pink carnation – carnations have a barbed look, sharp against the intoxication of their scent and texture – 'what are we to do about you?' She lifted her tapestry so that the weight did not pull from her hands, and settled back into her little chair. 'Without Hubert, and without Papa, what can we expect?'

I caught hold of my resolution to tell her nothing, but it escaped from me like the tail of a flying bird. 'Actually,' I said,

'I was just wondering whether I felt like going to the Barraways' party.'

Her surprise was total. She even dropped her tapestry and pretended to lose her needle while she found a reply. 'I do see,' she said, 'that you wouldn't know anybody there.'

That decided me. The next day I posted my acceptance and bicycled away to Mrs Harty, with two of my horse show ball dresses in a cardboard box strapped on the carrier behind me. One dress was pink chiffon, the other was gold lace. I brought them both because when I tried them on I found they had shrunken miserably in cleaning.

I leaned my bicycle against the wall of Mrs Harty's house. A winter jasmine grew at the door. Flowerless, only its tight, fish-shaped buds had survived the frost. As I knocked I could hear her lurching across the kitchen floor, and I shared her pause at the thick net curtains before she let me in. After my morning in the starved spaces of Temple Alice, Mrs Harty and her warm house pleased me as though she and her kitchen were a refuge and safety from wolves.

'Well, and how are you?' Mrs Harty took the box from me as if it were a Christmas present. 'And the Major, poor man? A little better . . . ah, please God.'

I stood with my back to the dirty blazing stove; the warmth of the room was sublime.

Mrs Harty put the parcel of my dresses down on top of a stuffed fox in his glass-fronted box. Fashion magazines cascaded past his improbable glass button eyes. It was a doll-like fox and I suppose it was company for her. So was the stuffed badger, curled and nailed on a board where she rested her club foot while the other worked the treadle of her magnificent Singer sewing-machine. Now, shaking out my dresses, she handled them preciously, pinching back their waists so that the skirts were blowing outwards, like those in an advertisement. I was glad to think that that was once how I must have looked to Richard.

Mrs Harty wore a stuffed satin heart hung on a corset lace. It swung, full of pins, between her breasts. I felt some connection between it and the sacred heart of Jesus flaming away in its holy picture, the constant small light burning below. Mrs Harty plucked pins out of hers and lurched about on her club foot, standing back to survey her work, or pouncing forward to remedy a fault. While the light shrank from her windows she swooped on me and round me with her scissors, and mumbled at me as she changed pins from her heart to her lips, and then to the seams of my dress; at last she staggered away . . . I could feel her dissatisfaction, and through it my bulk loomed to me – a battleship through fog. 'The wholly all about it is,' she said, 'there's not enough of it in it.'

I could imagine the wedge-shaped gaps to be filled, and the strains that the pink chiffon would not take. I knew better than to look into the narrow slit of mirror. 'Do you know what we'll do – how would it work, I wonder, if we used our gold to drape our troubles?'

I demurred – then I agreed. Panels of gold lace swept from my hips to the ground, chiffon clouded my bosom.

'And a big rose in gold and pink – imagine – on one shoulder.' The rose was not there. She sketched it on the air, and pinned the air down my left bosom. I moistened my lips and nodded agreement. In the wintry light, between the fox, the badger, and the sacred heart of Jesus, I began to feel a storybook little-princess character taking me over – possessing me.

'Now. Look at yourself.' She turned me about like a child or a dummy to face my reflection. I spun willingly round on my Louis heels. I closed my eyes, I spread my hand like a fan across my chest. I decided how I should smile – I smiled. I opened my eyes, I pulled in my stomach, and I leaned a little forwards to my reflection. Gold lace fell in points and godets to the floor. Flesh and chiffon were indistinguishable in the sweetheart neckline. I caught my breath, and for a moment I was standing alone with the beautiful doll that was me.

Mrs Harty broke the silence. She too was looking enchantedly from me to my reflection. 'Well, Miss Aroon,' I could feel her searching for the absolute word, 'wouldn't you make a massive statue?'

Statue? I knew just what that meant. And I had been feeling so mignonne and cherished. I was Aroon again – a big girl, even a great big girl. She turned away from me. 'I'll have to light the lamp,' she said, 'till I see how do it fall.'

But how could I face the statue she saw? I had to get away before she said 'statue' again. I dragged my dress over my head. I struggled in the slippery darkness of the lining. I tore my way out. When she came back, carrying the lighted lamp, I was walloping round, a great half-naked creature, searching for my winter clothes.

What panic had taken me over? I wondered, pedalling home with the frost on my cheeks, and the wheels of my bicycle sailing effortlessly under my weight. Assurance re-enfolded me as I remembered that 'massive' was Mrs Harty's word for beautiful. A rose could have a massive scent. Six yards of cobweb lace a massive quality. Statue was all right too. A nymph in a glade, perhaps.

I hurried upstairs to Papa's room, hoping that tea was still there. He was sitting up, comfortable among his pillows. In his blue pyjamas and bird's-eye scarf he looked delightfully handsome and easy as though there were nothing wrong with him. He pointed to the fireplace where the teapot was sitting. 'HOT FOR YOU.' He spoke in slow capitals, but he was smiling in his own covert way. He tried again: 'Pretty nice cake.'

Mummie had been and gone. A few drops of clear China tea, no milk, no sugar, were left in her cup, and a sprig of rosemary, pinched to death, in the saucer. Papa's good hand was wandering among the small necessaries on his bedside table. There was something he wanted.

'No,' he said when I offered him another cup of tea; and: 'Horrible – horrible,' to his barley water. 'Po cupboard.' He found the word with triumph. Oh, that bottle, and my tea had scarcely begun – but he waved that idea aside too. I looked again. One of his silver drinking cups was on top of the po cupboard. Rose kept them as bright as buttons. She thought he took his medicine more easily from them, as he could not see the size or colour of the dose. I put the cup into his good hand and hurried back to my tea. Usually he swallowed his medicine down with an exasperated flourish. Tonight, he sipped away at it slowly, looking at me over the top of his silver cup with approval and amusement.

'Good girl, good girl,' he achieved the words delightedly as I took the last scone. We both laughed. He went on shaking with laughter.

'Look out, Papa, you'll spill the stuff.' I jumped up too late to take the cup out of his hand. He only giggled at the mishap. As the wet darkened and spread through his pyjama jacket, a smell like a small cloud hung close over his warm body and bed. I sniffed at it, and at the empty cup – whisky! Papa had been drinking whisky. And whisky could lead only to another stroke, to death. Stimulants were forbidden. I was appalled. But, when I looked at him, stilled and cheered from his nervous melancholy, the thought floated to me and away from me, the thought that he required a respite from the misery that held him in terrible polite dependence on us all.

But for his sake I banished the indulgent idea and concentrated my mind on the problem of how he had got hold of the whisky. There was no more of it in the diningroom now, or in the cellar, so someone must have bought it for him. I am not exactly slow-witted, and the answer came to me in less than a minute: 'We must ask Rose if there is any more.' I nearly choked on my own diplomacy.

'Yes,' he said, 'helps a lot. Good person. Good person.'

When Rose came in to take away the tea things, I followed her out of the room, the empty silver cup in my hand. It was hard to know what to say. She had drained authority away through her usefulness.

'Rose,' I said, 'you know it's not allowed.'

'A drop left after the Christmas cake.' She sounded careless and unrepentant. 'And he needed it. And it did him good.'

'Don't you think the doctor knows best?'

'Doctors must only go by their own rules.' There was a resolute turn in her evasions.

CHAPTER THIRTY

'Possibly you may remember,' Mummie said when I told her about it (I had to tell someone), 'who dismissed Nurse and put Rose in charge.'

'It was Dr Coffey who suggested it.'

'You did it between you. I knew something like this would happen. I was against the whole idea.'

'Nurse was so beastly. So rude. Rose would do anything for him.'

'Exactly.' If she had been at her tapestry Mummie would have pinioned a flower as she said the word. But we were at the end of dinner. A Cox's orange pippin sat on her green plate. She had moved her fingerbowl and its little mat, but that was as far as she would go in eating the apple.

I said: 'Aren't you going to speak to her? It could kill him.'

'Perhaps,' she said.

'Perhaps you'll speak to her? Or perhaps it will kill him?'

She eyed her apple. 'Shall we go to the library?' She put her unfolded napkin down beside her place and pushed back her chair. I had the feeling that she and Rose were allied and I was the intruder. It was a love circle, and Rose was included.

Rose swept on determinedly, insolent and inviolable in her care for Papa. The hairbrushing, the shaving, the scenting were her business. The delicate food was all contrived by Rose, and every day she asked for less help from Tommy or from me. She was very strong, rather magnificent in her health and in her ignoring of any time off or comfort for herself.

I maintained the rota of my visits to Papa. And every evening now the smell of whisky hung clearer round him. Unquestioned, unreprimanded, the drink lifted him into a silly sort of buoyancy. I would wait a little longer before taking any drastic step. The Christmas cake whisky must soon be finished, I thought. But, after weeks had gone by, Papa was still enjoying his evening drink. He looked at me longingly across his silver cup, and I took a decision.

'You'd like another?' He nodded. 'Just one,' I said. 'I forget. Where does she keep the bottle? In here?' I tried the po cupboard.

'No.'

'In the chest of drawers?'

It was hunt the thimble. 'Fool. Fool,' he raged and moaned as I coasted about. It was rather a horrid game, but at last in the empty clothes basket I found the bottle – more than three-quarters full of Scotch whisky. I knew I was going to deprive him of this pleasure. I knew I must. Rose was buying whisky for him and I was going to prevent her. In the morning I would speak to Dr Coffey. Thursday was his day.

Next morning when he came hurrying down the steps, stockings and breeches under his overcoat, his white moustache gleaming and staring in the cold, Rose was behind him, like a nurse waiting for last words about her patient. I thought, really, she goes too far. But it was a brace of woodcock she was after.

'When were they shot?' was all she said. And when he told her, a calculation as to when they should be cooked passed clearly over her face. 'He'll enjoy them, doctor,' she said, and went away with his present, faultlessly polite and devoted.

'Ah, Aroon child, cold old morning.' He was bustling round his car to the driving seat.

'I must ask you something.' Impaled on my urgency, he stopped, his impatience melted in kindness and concern. He listened with absolute attention while I told him of my suspicions: of my present certainty that Rose was buying and supplying whisky; that in ignorance she would kill him; that she was getting above herself ... I stopped.

'Should I get you another nurse, I wonder? Of course, Rose understands him.'

'Well, she knows just how long he likes his woodcock cooked.'

He looked at me in an odd, surprised way. 'If that was all,' he said, 'she'd be replaceable tomorrow. As it is, I think,' his voice turned back into a doctor's voice, 'it wouldn't help him in his condition at all to make any change. Change is drastic. A drastic thing.'

'I do see that, Dr Coffey. All I want is for you to forbid her to give him whisky. So that it's not just me ... just me against them ...'

'Just you spoiling his bit of pleasure?' He understood more than I had meant. He put his hand on the car door. He was going. Nothing had been forbidden or decided. Then he turned back. 'My dear child,' he said, 'it makes very little difference. So long as he keeps happy, comfortable and happy – put up with things. And I'll see you again on Thursday – or any day, if you're worrying. Let me know. You're a great girl, Aroon . . .' There was no more I could do. I was set aside. Why did they ignore me? Things might have been different. I'm never sure.

There were times in the weeks before Christmas when I wondered whether Rose had exaggerated Papa's sufferings with Nurse. Once Rose and Nurse had got on very well together. So had Rose and I when we first got rid of Nurse. It had been fun, spoiling Papa. I had been happy in my practical responsibilities. When I lifted him and eased him back onto his pillows, I felt really glad to be a big girl. I could hold him quite as comfortably as Rose could. But now her progressive slighting of my helpfulness was like a tide seeping in, quietly, inexorably taking my safe places from me. She said: 'He's resting,' when I came in after luncheon for a chat. Papa was lying back with his eyes closed. I turned round from the door with no special reason and his eyes were open and lively. He was looking at Rose, who was looking at me with a kind of impatience. Perhaps Papa wanted his bedpan. I went away.

I took the dogs for a walk. I went down the drive where Papa and I had stopped to look at my Black Friday yearling – only his donkey was there, with a goat for company now. Would Richard understand that sale I had made out of love and pity?

For tea, I was back in Papa's room. I was quite determined to keep that time inviolate. Though he did not eat much of them, Papa liked sandwiches and tiny scones, and medlar jelly, iced orange cakes, and ginger cake. Mummie, of course, ate nothing, so there was usually enough for me. Mummie watched with cold disgust and Papa with pleasure as I cleared up the plates. I couldn't help myself. I hate waste. When I unfolded the day's paper and started analysing the day's racing results, she got up, hovered near him for a moment, then left the room, to go and sit under her tapestry in the library, a fresh hotwater-bottle at her feet.

Once six o'clock came Papa would get restless; his groans at the idiocies of the racing correspondents would be louder, his glances towards the door more longing. I knew it was not the correspondents – he liked nothing better than their mistakes. He was waiting for two things: Rose, and his whisky. When I heard Rose coming, strongly, neatly stepping along the corridor, I knew it was time for me to go. Because I could not allow that she had outdistanced me in the matter of the whisky, I had to pretend that it didn't happen. I had to keep up some semblance of authority. It was like putting my foot in the door to keep it open.

CHAPTER THIRTY-ONE

That winter at Temple Alice we ignored Christmas; we were too bogged down in disaster for any jollity. We kept our heads above the morass, stifled screaming despairs only by the exercise of Good Behaviour. Good Behaviour shrivelled to nothing as a support in my insensate longing for Hubert and Richard as the night of the Hunt Ball drew nearer, came so near that I was within touching distance of the event.

The afternoon hours before the ordeal were stiff with nothing to be done until the time came for bathing and scenting and strong girdling, a fortification of pink satin and écru lace, folded away since the Horse Show. At least I could light up the stove in my bedroom, filled from my ostentatiously private supply of paraffin, then I could manicure and buff my nails before the light failed and my courage too failed further from me. By then it would be teatime.

I was halfway up the staircase on the way to my bedroom when I was struck by a very practical and rather pleasing idea. It took me back to the hall and almost ran in front of me to the drawingroom door. Standing inside the doorway I was immobilised in the draughtless area of unused space; unyielding in its distance from our loves, Richard's and mine and Hubert's, the room contained a malevolent perfection of loneliness. I had not come to breathe back memories; I snatched up the small black gramophone, frozen all these months to the top of the grand piano. I had decided to practise my dancing before the ball; at least that would warm me and occupy time.

In my bedroom, I set the gramophone playing softly and set my feet moving with their own strict docility to the rhythm. Hubert always said I have an amazing sense of rhythm, and it's true. And I am lighter than air when I am dancing. I danced across my room holding the afternoon light in my arms. I was good. I was exhilarated. I rewound the gramophone. I gripped the brass rail of my bed and limbered up my charleston. I didn't hear Rose's knock on my door, if she had knocked. She was standing there respectful, watching, not quite smiling, waiting for me to stop dancing and lift the needle off the record before she spoke.

'I thought you might like to know, Miss Aroon,' she said, 'the Major's having a little rest.' That was all she said.

When she turned and went out, in her splendid, unhurrying way, I was blushing purple into the V of my shirt because she had watched me holding on to the bed rail, kicking out my strong legs to the music. She must have noticed my bosoms, swinging like jelly bags, bouncing from side to side; without words she conveyed the impression of what she had seen as unseemly – the Fat Lady in the peepshow. No. Forget the thought – a blush fails, armpits cease their creeping prickle. If Rose came back on any pretext, she would find me sitting at the dressing-table buffing my nails in a *dégagé* manner while the gramophone played softly with the lid down. I saw myself again as I was – a young girl getting ready for a very grand ball. I know I'm big, but I'm a girl, I suppose, not a joke.

At teatime I told Papa again where I was going to dine and dance. 'Ah, watchit, watchit. Pretty high pheasants,' he said. There was absolutely nothing wrong with Papa's brain when he thought about shooting.

'But I'm dancing, Papa.'

'Awful. Awful,' he said and caught my hand. I wondered if there was anything he didn't understand. Even now.

'No racing today,' I said, when he began to fidget in an expectant way. I knew he wasn't thinking of the results, but I clung to the myth of our usual evening occupation. 'They're frozen up in England.' I got to my feet. I was going to leave him before I knew I must. 'I'm changing now. I have to start early. Frozen roads.'

'What?'

'Ice.'

'Take it easy.' He was relieved to be left waiting for Rose. But when I was at the door he called distressfully.

'It's all right,' I said. 'I hear her on the stairs.' Now I felt angry.

'No. No. No.' He was speechlessly urgent. 'See you dressed UP,' he said at last. My heart melted and I floated past Rose in the doorway as though she didn't exist.

Excitement possessed me. I was dressing for somebody. As I strapped down my bosoms, I was outside my body and dressing it up with extreme care and calculation. At last I was ready for my dress. I struggled in. I looked at unbelievable me. Gold and pink swooned round, melting my size away. I stepped up to my reflection, then away from it, and I could find only surprise and delight in what I saw. Holding the rose here and there against my shoulder, I waited for a shudder of pleasure to run through me before I plunged the point of the safety-pin into the dress and shoulder straps. Last of all I took off the hair net. It would go back, of course, like the rose to its box, for the journey, but Papa must see me as I really am, every wave rigidly in its place, flawless. I was hungry for his approval as for a good dinner. I went swaying and floating round the balustraded circle below the star-filled dome, and on down the further corridor to Papa's room; I floated across to the foot of his bed, poised and ripe for his stunned admiration.

Before my moment had time to live, it fell and shattered round me. Mummie was sitting with him, as though she had guessed I would be doing just this. She sat throwing sprigs of bay and lavender stalks onto the fire and sniffing up their little bursts of flame and scent, and then throwing on another sprig.

'Aren't you starting rather early?' I might have been going to post a letter for all the notice she took of my dress.

I had meant to laugh and pivot about and show myself from every side to Papa; to kiss him and let him exclaim at my ravishing scent. But, as she looked across and smiled at Papa, I could only stand muttering about icy roads while my fever dropped from me and I loomed there, at the foot of his bed, as large as life again.

Papa was lying back against his pillows, his silver cup in his good hand. So arranged one forgot he had no arm to use on one side and no leg on the other. And almost no speech. His looks and his manner survived.

'Good girl,' he said. He looked over to Mummie to join him

and help him elaborate his admiration. She considered me with a dull obedience.

'Yes. Stupendous,' was what she said. I blushed as I had when Rose stopped my dancing, and this time I was choking on tears of pain and hatred. It was a shocking moment for each of us. The worst possible instance of not knowing how to behave.

The door knob was in my hand when a sound from Papa's bed impelled me towards him. He didn't have a hand to give me, on account of the whisky cup, and we hardly ever kissed, but his look held me before him, held me away from him in admiration. And from the dark of time in his mind a catch-word, a phrase, was snatched back and spoken distinctly: 'I'm on your side, sweetheart.' By no possibility could Mummie have avoided or escaped hearing him say it. He had restored me.

I drive well and that evening, along the icy roads to Ballytore Barraway, I felt less nervous than at any hour of the day. Phrases for the night's dancing partners slid easily in and out of my mind: 'I *am* sorry. I'm afraid number eight has gone too ... Yes, they're frozen up in England ... no racing at Sandown ... Marvellous tune ... Yes, I'd love to ... ' But as I arrived at the great, strange house an incoming tide of shyness belittled all confidence. A simple ache for Papa and Hubert filled me.

I drove under a stone archway, high as a railway bridge, on which the family coat of arms stood out, gross and gigantic. Beyond the archway, round three sides of a courtyard, Gothic battlements and towers thrust upwards and bellied outwards. Smaller archways squatted before dark doorways. Windows bulged on the vast spread of walls. It was Grimm's fairytales gone mad in stone, and, like a fairytale, light shone from all the windows. For all the light I found it hard to tell which was the hall door. Double flights of balustraded steps led to a diversity of possible entrances. I chose the largest door with the longest, widest flow of steps, and I was right. In the hall a man so aristocratic and severe I thought he might be my host put me right about his status.

'You're staying, miss?' he said gently.

'No,' I said. 'I've come to dinner.'

'Ah, your coat? Upstairs, miss. The blue room. On your right. We dine at nine.'

'Oh.' I reeled. 'Then I'm much too early.'

'Oh, no, miss. Punctuality means nothing with us.' As he said it, early and late fused in a sort of splendour.

The bedroom set apart for the ladies' coats was blue and cream and blue again. My heels sank behind me in blue carpet that touched the ivory walls. I was up to my ankles in white fur. Before the swelling kidney of the dressing-table and its winged gold mirror I sat down on a blue-and-gold stool, my feet lost in the fur rug. I pinned the gold rose on my shoulder. I took off my hair net. I smeared pale lipsalve on my pale lips and, as I did these things, every easy phrase that I had manufactured in the car became extinct, leaving not one conversational hint for me to follow.

When I waited, ready and hesitant at the stair-head, a child ran up the flight towards me. She was one of the serene, well-mannered nursery sisters I had seen at race-meetings: children who knew how to comport themselves in the saddling enclosure. Tonight she tore past me, eating something. Her jodhpurs were tight as a skin, her little man's shirt unbuttoned over a liberty bodice. 'Hullo.' I had to say something. She was halfway up the next flight before she stopped.

'How do you do?' She sounded corrosively polite. She added: 'You *are* early,' and went pounding away into her different life.

At the foot of the staircase I delayed, stretching out a minute before making my early entrance. On my arrival I had been too nervous to observe the hall. Now, as I looked round, it impressed me like a great Protestant hymn. 'Pavilioned in splendour and girded with Praise.' ... Small suits of armour sank their pointed feet in the carpet. Once upon a time someone had said: I'll just slip into my armour before we go out. Not here, I corrected myself, remembering how coolly informed Mummie was on the brief ancestry of these privileged people. Castle and title dated from the 1890s.

I stood there waiting. There was nobody to tell me where to go. I was the lost girl in the fairy story. I dared myself to go forwards. I opened a door, its architrave crowned by a bunch of swords. Then I was going headlong through a chain of rooms – large, smaller, smallest. In each room a fire was burning, not very brightly. Light came through deep parchment lampshades. Knole sofas, heavily tasselled, waited empty. Huge jardinières were filled with hyacinths and freesias. Photographs in lavish leather frames stood on every table. Photographs of children, race-horses, dogs, brides. I recognised a royal face, set apart from the rest, its modest isolation calling for attention.

At the end of the third room, from behind a closed door I heard voices. I knew I must go in. I couldn't just stand in the doorway. Suppose it was opened? What should I say? 'I'm Aroon'?

Within the room a man laughed. Nobody joined in the

laugh. Then, as I opened the door, suddenly they all laughed out together, robustly enjoying and sharing a harsh, confident amusement.

Far off down the room five or six people sat round the fire. One and all, the men wore tweed coats and grey flannel or whipcord trousers and the women Aertex shirts and the finest wool cardigans and three, four, or five rows of pearls. I had not imagined them otherwise than in evening dresses and hunt coats with varied silk facings.

Standing unacknowledged in the doorway, I felt my bare shoulders swell into mountainous acres of flesh. I couldn't find my voice, even if I could have found any words with which to announce myself. Then I realised they were all listening intently to a record – a husky thread of a voice galvanised their attention. A man got up to wind the gramophone. I felt he saw me, but I was none of his business, definitely less important than the record he was changing. I was wrong. He touched a girl whose great blond head was hung down between her shoulders; she seemed to be eating the pearls off her neck. She got to her feet and came loping across the room to me in flat leather shoes. She was as tall as I was, but her head was hung like a harebell on a thread of stem, and the length of her body shrank under her woollen clothes. Her voice was rich and concerned.

'Aroon,' she said, 'how sweet of you to come. Were the roads ghastly? Have a drink. Do you know everybody? John Savernake ... Mary Noisesome ... Ronnie Pennine ... Gwenny Fishguard ... Dominick ... Thomasine and Janine I know you know.' They all murmured, and when the gramophone stopped they got off the floor and the chairs and went out of the room one behind the other, in a private follow-my-leader sort of game.

'Oh, you *rats*,' she moaned. I thought her name might be Penelope, but I'm glad I didn't say it because I found out afterwards it was Mary Ann. She was the beautiful married sister . . . married to which of the beautiful men? And she was the very soul of kindness. 'I'll make you a warming drink.' She looked down the length of the cocktail shaker; it was as big as a tunnel for a train. 'This is all ice,' she said. '*What* would you like? Just say. I'm so bad about drinks. Oh, that rotten Dominick, gone to first bath.'

'May I have a glass of sherry?'

'No. No sherry.' She searched desperately among the bottles. 'They are hopeless. Do forgive if I don't call O'Brien now; he is so cross on party nights. Look – have a glass of champagne. Why not? Please do. Can you open the awful thing?' She stopped talking and said, 'Ooo, you *are* clever,' when the cork came quietly out – Papa had often shown me how to do it.

'Do be happy. Do keep warm. This room's icy. Do you think they'll do anything about the fire? Oh, and do be kind to Uncle Ulick. He's quite a sweet, but so peculiar. You do promise? You won't mind, will you. You *are* kind.'

I arranged myself near the fire. The day's papers and a racing calendar lay on a low table. I thought it might be nice to be found reading the calendar; it would give me something to talk about: 'So-and-so's nicely in the such-and-such with ten-seven.' But I couldn't concentrate. I just held the paper in my hand while I drank my champagne and looked round the room. I couldn't observe that properly either.

I have a wonderful head for drink – champagne or orangeade, it's all the same to me – and I was just deciding to refill my glass when the door opened and an old man came in.

He was tall and fat, and he wore patent leather shoes with bows on their toes. His huge grubby white tie looked as though he had been fumbling at it for days. Now it drooped, broken-winged; he was like a bird – not a very well bird either.

When he said, 'I live in the pigeon house,' it seemed more than likely. 'They put in some very good plumbing and all that sort of thing, but the water hasn't got to me yet. Do you have a good supply?'

'Yes, very,' I lied.

'You *are* blessed. You don't know how lucky you are. All the same I would rather live in my pavilion than in this sad Gothic building, wouldn't you? I'm all for the *dix-huitième*. May I give you a glass of champagne?' He poured out a glass and drank it himself. 'Not very nice; I can't say I recommend it.' He poured himself out another. If I had had the courage I should have got up and filled my own glass, while he sat humming to himself and drinking as much as he could, as fast as he was able.

'You're an uncle,' I said at last.

'I'm rather deaf.'

'You are Uncle Ulick,' I shouted.

'They call me "Uncle"; rather unfortunate I always think. I haven't the remotest connection with them, or any interest if it comes to that – still less since I'm writing a history of the family. I've never been so bored. I've got so far, and now I can't think what to put. Actually, there's nothing to say. Pedigrees are what I like and they don't have a proper one.'

Thinking of the assurance and beauty I had seen so often, but so distantly, and the wealth of glamour that surrounded me as I sat with an empty glass in my hand, I could only goggle helplessly at his disloyalty.

'Do you know the Crowhurst girls?' For once in my life I was glad to say that I did. 'That's an interesting family. Three lines go back to my own lot and we go back directly to Cahulahoun, the Hound of Ulster. I could call myself Prince Drumnasole if it wasn't for this rotten union baronetcy tied round my neck.'

'Sir,' I said, and it was the bravest and most successful word I had spoken yet, 'may I have another glass of wine?'

'I like that "sir,"' he said approvingly. 'Obviously you know how to talk to princes. You must come to luncheon in my pavilion. I make very good mayonnaise.' He filled his glass again. 'Not much left in this,' he said, tipping the bottle into mine. 'Too bad.' He put the bottle on a table beside my chair. I was in agony, thinking someone would come back and suppose I had drunk the lot.

'You're Beleek's daughter?' He looked at me in a hooded, private way.

'Granddaughter,' I said.

'Ugly Tom we used to call him, but I understood his girl was very good-looking.'

'That was my mother,' I shouted.

'Extraordinary.' He was talking intimately to himself. 'And all the girls here are wonderful lookers. Superb quality. I don't know where it comes from. Not in the book. Good vicarage stuff at the best. Lawyers, lawyers.' He shuddered. He got himself onto his feet as the kind pretty girl came back. She was followed by a quite splendid man – splendid, but distant to a degree that paralysed the air around him. His refuge from speaking was the state of the fire. He rang the bell. He went away. He came back with a frightened boy and a great load of logs. He directed their placement on the bed of ash. Then he sat down to turn the wheel of the fan that blew air below the flat hearth.

'I like doing this.' He settled happily to his work.

Again I was in a vacuum. At a distant table, loaded with bottles, Uncle Ulick was standing as close as possible to the one whose name was still unknown to me. I heard her say: 'Oh, Uncle Ulick, you are looking filthy.' 'It's my tie. You do it for me, my darling.' How different his voice sounded now from the tone of denigration I had heard in it before. He was imploring her youth to do something for him, to lean towards him, to be kind. Her arms were so long that she kept an airy distance between them as she retied his tie and murmured to him. 'Can't hear a word. Come closer,' he shouted.

I heard her say: '... do be kind. You do promise? Oh, you *are* kind.' The same words she had used to me, and in the same tone of voice.

'All right,' he answered with a sort of massive petulance, 'but first I must put some brandy in this.'

I was suspended in doubt, in a suspicion that soon grew to certainty. The man blowing up the fire stopped his work and pointed to the bottle beside my chair before he spoke to me, directly and for the first time: 'I bet Uncle Ulick emptied that one.'

'Well, yes.' I met his eyes, and thanked God for any link of complicity.

'Mary Ann asked him. We're short one man tonight.'

He had been asked for me – I was to be kind to him; he was to be kind to me. I felt a little sick. I wished I knew how to be rude. When she came back to me with a dish of nuts and a great champagne cocktail, my resentment forced tears up to the backs of my eyes.

At least I could honestly think her dress was quite horrid. I could pity her for that. A short white chemise, straight as a pinafore, not even a sequin to liven things up, it was high to the collar-bone, where a six-inch diamond bar held one minimal orchid. At the back it was open to a long U of brown flesh – an unfortunate garment for a girl as big (if in different places) as myself.

'Do drink. You must eat up.' She forced biscuits and nuts on me as if I were an ailing pet. 'Dinner won't be for years. Oo, you twit, you twerp, you oaf, you *person*, what a degrading fire.' She was talking to her husband now. I supposed he was her husband as he didn't answer. Uncle Ulick came and perched dangerously on the arm of my chair: 'You seemed interested in my family, so, as I was telling you, we go back to the Hound of Ulster . . .'

I faked absorbed attention and tried out a few 'Oos' as he went back through the Crusades, where his forebears had been such career boys.

'Oh you are kind,' Mary Ann murmured to me as we all stood, uncertain as to who went in to dinner first. 'Uncle Ulick loves you and I've put him beside you, do you mind? You have Kenny Norton too; be nice, don't let him drop off. Last time he broke a plate and covered his face in raspberry mousse. Too miserable. He's never been just the same since he hit the open ditch halfway up at Kempton.'

That was when I knew I was going to be near enough to touch the most famous gentleman rider of the day. It would be something to put in my letter to Richard. I wouldn't stress it, of course, but when I wrote again I was going to let him know that Kenny (I would write 'Kenny') had spoken to me. He didn't speak while we drank our soup, clear as a mountain stream, and just about as tasteless. Uncle Ulick poured a whole glass of sherry into his soup plate, on the bottom of which I could see a tortoise sprawling among weeds and water-flowers. He put down his spoon and sighed out his disgust. Then he brightened up.

'Rather a funny incident – I'm a terrible shot you know – it was when Ethelred the Unready was shooting with the Drumnasole of that day, and one of my ancestors' arrows . . .' on it went. He was too deaf for comment or interruption.

An inch of sole, in a rather delicious sauce; then terrible venison – Uncle Ulick ate his red-currant jelly with his pudding spoon, which I thought rather grand, and still I had no word from Kenny Norton. He didn't seem to be saying much to the girl on his other side either, but there was a kind of familiar happy distance between them, not the gulf of worshipping unfamiliarity that separated him and me. At last he spoke. And what he said stunned me: 'Saw Richard at Newbury.' A chasm of distance closed between us. He knew about Richard and me.

'Are you sure?' I said. 'He's in Africa.'

'Large as life at Newbury. Losing money too.' He went back to his dreadful venison and his silence. My heart raced. My hands gripped the edge of the table. He was grotesquely mistaken. I had to confirm this.

'Have you known Richard long?' It sounded so baldly conversational.

'On and off. We're some sort of cousins.'

So he must know. All the same, Richard was in Africa. 'When did he get back?'

'Long enough . . .' He stopped. 'Just back, I suppose. He was very brown.'

Just back. After weeks on the sea. That made sense of his silence. Tomorrow could bring me a letter. The next day could bring me Richard. Everything in my mind was rhapsody, Fear left me. I turned easily from Uncle Ulick. All that I had practised in the car flowed smoothly back into my head.

'What about Seamonster for the Gold Cup?' And I could remember every one of the other entries without effort.

'Funny little horse . . . funny temperament . . .' We were off and away. I had all his attention. Now I looked with confidence towards a happy evening and a tomorrow of weightless certainty.

CHAPTER THIRTY-TWO

Dinner was over. Some of the early arrivals were dancing in the ballroom.

'Promise to enjoy yourself,' Mary Ann implored me as we stood together in the respectable gloom of the hall. Through an archway Uncle Ulick came towards me. Mary Ann smiled kindly, covertly, on each of us in turn: 'I want you to have a beautiful time.' Uncle Ulick had two dance programmes dangling on their pencil strings from his white-gloved hand. 'I've put myself down for one, three, seven, nine, and eleven,' he said virtuously. 'After that I shall go home to bed. I don't know about you, I'm not very good at these modern dances, but Mary Ann will be disappointed if we don't try. Shall we?'

'What do they call this tune?' he asked me after we had made three circuits of the ballroom, our feet moving in a different world from the music.

'"The Birth of the Blues,"' I told him.

'Well,' he said, 'fortunately that seems to be the death of them. Shall we have a drink? Oh, not in the bar.' He impelled me towards the room where we had had our drinks before dinner. If Uncle Ulick had bought a drink at the champagne bar, I might have become involved and heard the magic words: May I have a dance? But no. He hurried me on to the further door, where a manservant was waiting. 'Good idea,' Uncle Ulick said. 'None of the hoi-polloi in here. Just the family. Now, can I offer you what some people call A Brandy?'

Back in the first salon, that anteroom to life and dancing, I met a girl I knew – someone to speak to. She chatted in a pleased, easy way till a man touched her arm: 'Ours,' he said, and they went off to dance, leaving me monstrously alone. A kind old man with a gammy leg advanced with gentle enquiries about Papa.

'I'm not much of a performer,' he said, 'but would you care to . . .' Halfway round the ballroom, we came to a merciful halt on two gold chairs. 'Don't really get the course,' he gasped apologetically. Later I saw Kenny Norton immersed in talk with two other men. He must see me. He never looked up. Nor did Uncle Ulick appear for his next dance.

I smiled, and hummed, and stood carelessly as the hall emptied into the ballroom and I waited, only for Uncle Ulick. Presently I took myself to the ladies' cloakroom, the classic refuge of the unwanted. I hurried downstairs again, hoping that I looked as if I were keeping a partner waiting. I stood about, smiling, compressed, submerged in politeness; aching in my isolation; longing to be alone; to be away; to be tomorrow's person; reading Richard's letter perhaps; waiting for him in reality. But there was no respite from the party that flowed round me. Beautiful creatures, men's hands guiding, just not touching, their backs passed by as they went in to dance and came back to drink. Lucky creatures, unknowing as a herd of antelope. I saw them as cherished and set apart. I saw Kenny put his arm round a girl, small and ugly as a child's pony. I turned my eyes away. A kind middle-aged couple gave me a drink and sighed about Papa with real regret before they went off to play bridge and left me almost longing for Uncle Ulick.

He came back punctually for number seven, and as we struggled in the dance his hand crept resolutely about my backbone. My backbone crept too. 'Shall we sit the next out, little girl?' We didn't get as far as the free drink. In the second salon he left me on a Knole sofa near the fire. 'Be back,' he said. There was sweat on his forehead, and he walked away as though he were sailing with great care above his feet. I wondered if he could be rather drunk.

Alone, but with a man, ardent if old, coming back to me, I felt more natural, looser somehow in my joints than I had felt for hours. I have a greedy feeling for total luxury, and waiting here alone I was immersed in its deepest textures. I took note of some ideas that I should perhaps adopt in a house that would be my own; the pale slimy satin cushions on the rougher brocade I liked, and the great basins full of white hyacinths, all their cones of bells evenly grown together, not one mature beyond another. There was a second scent behind the rich penetration of the hyacinths. I prowled the room. I found it. In a long shallow glass box stephanotis lay among its leather leaves. I smelt it, and it breathed out at me like an animal. A turmoil seized on me: the vigour that comes with the full moon.

I stopped prowling about and went back to the chair near the fire. I was safe here while the music was playing – safe to be alone and unpitied. Soon Uncle Ulick would be back. Soon I might rebuff him. I leaned across the table near me, covered in *Tatlers*, *Country Lifes*, *Bystanders*, *Punch*; I would make my choice among them. I would be reading contentedly; should any couple pass I need not see them. I chose the *Tatler* and turned to the doings of the great unknown who hunted with the Quorn and the Belvoir, who danced at hunt balls in historic English houses.

A full-page picture changed all the fugitive glamour of the chase and the ballroom to a quiet contemplation of marriage and motherhood as understood by the proper sort of English family. Here, by ornamental water, a young but solid mother sat on a stone bench. A blond child leaned against her; another squatted at her feet. The stone seat and her knee she shared with three terriers and a Pekinese. Melted far in the distance, beyond lawns and terraces, the Palladian façade of a great house filled in the picture. For me, as I looked, a transport in time took my breath. I have been here before, I have heard this before, where? when? The answer came to me clear and comfortable: Mrs Brock's happy days, and her tales of Lady Grizel and the jolly little boys, and the dogs.

Behind this picture there existed a certain past, and a future when a world of love should enclose me in just such precincts. The moment could not be endless. I let my breath go. I turned the page over.

Ah, Newbury. Next November meeting, more than likely, I would be there with Richard: nodding coolly to Kenny Norton: kindly, so kindly, inviting Mary Ann to stay at Stoke Charity: walking on careless feet from Members' Stand to Owners and Trainers, last Horse Show's days come sure and true for evermore. Now I could see without envy the photograph of just such a girl as myself, wearing the very coat Richard had given me. She sat balancing easily on her shooting-stick, Newmarket boots roughly elegant on her supporting legs. She held an enormous pair of glasses to her eyes; the man standing behind her must have lent them to her, although her own were hanging round her neck. I had a feeling he would snatch them back to read the race for himself. I felt a surge of affiliation and sympathy towards these two elegant leisured people. Then I read the caption: 'Finding a winner – Mr Richard Massingham, elder son of Major "Wobbly" and Lady Grizel Massingham, and the Honourable Alice Brownrigg, who have just announced their engagement.'

For a minute I disbelieved. I denied myself a second look. I put the paper down. I found myself hiding it. When I had done this I knew that it was true, but I could accept nothing. I was on the floor bowing my head, rocking myself against acceptance; I was a rooted thing, torn about in a volume of storm.

Not tears, but pain, seized on me, my insides griping and loosening. The absolute need of getting to the lavatory possessed me. Even my terrible distress had to find this absurd necessity. As I walked carefully down the long, warm room, I had the idea that the light had changed like a short winter afternoon, and the room and my life were both spread with sand and salt.

Back in the hall the fun of the party was blazing up now. I ploughed my way through the drinking, chattering, easy people to the foot of the staircase. The crowd was as impervious to interruption as the crowd at a race-meeting, where faces known and unknown float and pass one by, occupied and avoiding recognition. So I saw, without a nod or a smile, Mr Kiely standing with some of his friends. I didn't have to know he was there. I breasted on. Kenny Norton put a hand on my arm: 'Come and dance,' he said. The miracle was late.

'I'm sorry, nothing left,' I said. I felt his appalled stare following me as I flogged on up the stairs to the salvation of the lavatory. I had to get there; pain was twisting in me again, and above it the dreadful childish call: I'm going to be sick – sick in the basin. Partly in the plate holding the Bromo, partly over my dress, into my shoes, on the floor, I was sick. I must escape before it was found, get myself into my coat and run, with this taste in my mouth, and the smell under my coat going with me.

In the hall the crowd had thinned. Music was playing and those lucky ones who danced to it were distanced from me, far and foreign. I was at the hall door, almost on my way home, but the door was locked. I turned the handle violently. This was the last cruelty; I must get out. The studded door loomed. I shook the lock with both hands. A voice beside me said: 'I think Jody Kenny in the bar has the key.' I looked round and down at Mr Kiely, immaculate in his black tail coat, his white tie just too large. 'Are you on your own?' he said, when he had opened the door for me into the blessed frozen night.

'Yes. I was dining.'

'Ah. So you didn't enjoy the party?'

'Goodnight.' I kept my voice cold and steady against his familiarity and his helpfulness. 'Thank you so much.'

'Drive carefully,' he cautioned me; 'the roads are all ice.' He went back into the house, into a great gulf of light.

I was escaping. I was running from Mary Ann's terrible kindness, from Uncle Ulick's talking and groping and desertion; I ran from the indifference that was shown me through the endless hours, timed by the numbers of dances when I did not dance and could not hide. I would be alone now with my pain. I would take it home with me, and go to bed with it, and suffer it always, for it would never change, I knew. Grief possessed me, but I would and must behave. No mourning. No whining.

At last I was in the car, pulling the rug round me. It was familiar. Soon I would take off my clothes and get into bed; that was all there was for me.

And not even that, it seemed, because I could not start the car. I was sobbing before I gave up – waited – tried again, waited again, hoped, despaired. There was no attendant among the parked cars; it was too early for departures and largesses. I would try the starting handle myself, though I was afraid of it. And rightly so; the kick nearly broke my arm before the engine gulped and quenched.

'Ah, you poor little thing, it's a pity about you,' a voice spoke near me. 'You got a great knocking about.' It was the wrong kind of voice; that was my first impression before I recognised Mr Kiely in his overcoat and tweed hat, and dreadful scarf. 'Sit in out of the cold,' he said, and I obeyed, although it was just as cold in the car. After ten minutes, he gave up.

'I'm afraid,' he said, 'you're here for the night.'

'Oh, no.' I knew I could never face them – not if I had to sit in the car till the morning.

'Or, if you prefer it,' he said, 'I'll drive you home.'

'Oh, would you? Would you really? It's miles out of your way.'

'Ah, come on.' He took the rug off my knees and wrapped it round the engine. 'I'll tell the garage to collect the car in the morning.'

He thought of everything. In his car I leaned as far as possible away from him. As our bodies and our breath warmed the air I was conscious of the sour little smell creeping about under my coat and beneath the rug. When he offered me a cigarette and lit one himself, I guessed a whiff had drifted from me. I must say something to take his attention off it.

'What a good party.' My voice shook.

'Was it? I wouldn't know.'

'You didn't enjoy it?'

'No. Did you?'

'Yes. Awfully.'

He waited. 'Kenny Norton was there,' he said unexpectedly.

'Yes. I sat beside him at dinner. I'm afraid I cut one of his dances.' It was almost true. It was true. It sounded impossible.

'He has the ride on Seamonster at Leopardstown.'

'Kenny? So he has.'

'Should the two of us go up and see the race?'

How to answer him within politeness? No one could possibly call me a snob, but some situations promise only total embarrassment. Papa's friends and the kind Mary Anns would pass me by with a word, or without a word. None of them, none of us, knew Mr Kiely.

As I cringed in my corner of the car, hesitating for the final refusal, I saw again two other pictures: the easy ardent girl at Newbury, intent for the moment on horses, and the calm young woman sitting by water with two glorious children. Tonight, for a minute out of time, these had been pictures of myself, in the world belonging to me, in the world lost to me.

In the shape of the word 'lost' my grief bore me down – what had I lost? Nothing, for I had nothing, and my heart was bursting for nothing. But burst it would, and into loud crying.

'I am so sorry,' I apologised, almost whispering, I was so ashamed.

'Better now?' He was whispering too, as again he tucked the rug neatly round me. 'What you need,' he let down the window an inch or two on his side, 'is a man to look after you. How would you like the idea?'

I couldn't see him, sitting there beside me, but his voice had the wrong texture, the wrong colour; it was as wrong to me as a false note in music. Ashamed of myself as I felt, his sympathy was unattractive, even alarming. He stopped the car before the gates of Temple Alice and put his hand on my knee: 'When you need someone,' he said, 'will you think of me?'

One of Mummie's phrases came to me and I spoke it in her voice: 'You must be out of your mind,' I said, and I knocked his hand away. In spite of my heartbreak and tears, I was, after all, Aroon St Charles, and I felt it too. He didn't answer, and when we got to the house he didn't get out to open the car door for me. He didn't even answer my 'Goodnight.' Perhaps I had really hurt him?

In the cold of the hall I loomed to myself, a great creature within limitless suffering. I took off my shoes before I went upstairs. Step by stockinged step I padded past Mummie's door. Lemon-shaped above my head, the dome held the perfect form of winter air, as it had held the light and breath of summer evenings. Within this hollow of cold and truth I gave up my dream, its core of fact, its wings of hope, shrivelling to absurdity; I knew that here stood the changeless me, the truly unwanted person.

A streak of light under Papa's door made a faraway sliver in the darkness. It made a small change and lift in my heart too … If he was awake he must need something and I was here to give him whatever he needed. I put down my shoes and my bag, using both hands to turn the door knob softly, in case he had fallen asleep with his lamp still lighted.

He was not asleep. He was leaning back, hollowing his wall of pillows. His eyelids were loosely downwards on his cheeks, and in his entire expression there was a grave concentration of pleasure. Rose sat beside him, her head bent low as if she were whispering; her hand was under the bedclothes warming his foot – his phantom foot that felt the cold as much as his real foot. Rose snatched her hand from under the sheets, and Papa opened his eyes to look up and towards her in a surprised, questioning way. He didn't see me standing in the doorway. Only Rose saw me, and her eyes blazed, raging, across the bed.

'His feet are perishing.' She spoke in a curiously apologetic way as though I might not see or understand that she was warming his feet. Papa did not even try to say goodnight as I went away. He heaved a little on his pillows, turning as much as he was able towards Rose. Before I shut the door I caught the breath of whisky on the warm air.

What must I do, I thought, standing in my own room again, what must I do now, tomorrow and for ever? I put my hand down my bed to where my hotwater-bottle lay, cold as a fish. Here was something I could change, something I must give myself, for without it I would never get to sleep.

Passing Papa's door, I looked away from the slit of light; passing Mummie's door I held my breath. Then I was on the staircase, and turning off it down the back stairs with its muffled household smells. In the kitchen my candle expelled the light of the sky and the dark of the trees coming through the unshuttered windows; it made its own giraffe-shaped shadows up the walls. I had a slight feeling of adventure, of getting level with Rose, in this kitchen which was hers. I moved the top ring on the range and put the kettle closer to the heat of the fire. When it boiled up I had a longing for a cup of tea. Why not? I found the thumb-bruised tin where they kept the kitchen tea, and, near the window, a milk jug wreathed in dull roses. I sat on a chair near the heat, waiting a minute for the tea to draw.

In the space of waiting there came a reunion with a moment nearer than the present, when mice had flickered in their cages and I could smell the faint appropriate marriage of hot milk and Marie biscuits. Then love and trust had swelled the air round me, and there had been a wild nonchalance expressed by a hat flung down with its wet pink roses. For a breath I was held in that time before love and trust had failed me. Now, as before, the moment broke into ugliness and terror.

It was Rose, plunging along the passages, crying, calling; throwing her body across the kitchen table, howling; dispossessed of all authority, a wild creature, just as Mrs Brock had been on the evening of her drowning.

'He's going . . . he doesn't know me . . . ' she was gasping.

'What have you done to him?'

'Ah, it's just a little turn he took.' Her minimising was frightening; it was on a different scale from her grief. She was hiding something.

'You've killed him.' I stood above her; her head was down on the table between her spread arms.

'He wanted it,' she said.

'I told you whisky would kill him. I told you, didn't I?'

She looked at me from a distance. 'Yes,' she said, 'you told me.' She said it gratefully as if my accusation were some kind of reprieve.

We went back to his room together. He was breathing in a knotted, groaning rhythm. She stood and looked at him. She had been his nurse and washed and dressed him like a doll, and sat him up and laid him down. Now she stood apart from the difficulties of death, accepting all the strife and pain he was in as necessary before death; nothing could ease him, so she stood apart looking on as though at the death of an animal. I felt the same. He was changed. Changing and lessening every moment from a person to a thing. I agreed with her. It was futile to lift him or bring him any comfort. In fact I was afraid to touch him, and Rose leaned far away at the foot of the bed, staring, waiting for him to die. Half an hour ago she had been giving him whisky and warming his feet.

'Mummie?' I whispered to her. 'Shouldn't we tell Mummie?'

She shook her head. 'He wouldn't like it.'

I knew she was right. Papa would spare her anything.

'I'll get Dr Coffey.' I had to speak more loudly against his dreadful breathing. Then I remembered I had no car. 'Tommy can go for him,' I said. 'I'll wake him.' I turned away from Papa. I was at the doorway when I felt the change behind me – a stillness, filling the room to its walls. I turned back and looked at Rose. I didn't want to look at Papa. 'He's better, isn't he. His breathing's better . . .'

'He's gone.' Rose's voice was half its size. She stood there far away from him, gripping the bed rail. Then, as though it were an immediate necessity, she rushed across to the window opposite his bed, rattling back the curtains, pushing up the lower sash, and reaching up the strong length of her arms to tear down the top sash. It was as if she were opening a way to nowhere and waiting for something to pass. If Papa had a spirit she was giving it freedom. I knew it was an ignorant Roman Catholic superstition, and I felt it a gross impertinence. I wished I could think of something to keep her in her proper place. But all I could think of was that she should be the one to tell Mummie.

'I'll tell her with her morning tea,' Rose said firmly, 'when I have him looking nice.' She looked away from me as though I were of no account, and almost eagerly, I thought, at Papa. I wondered what she was going to do to him now that he was so completely her doll. I had to be grateful for her competence; for her recovery from the creature that had lain across the kitchen table, torn this way and that way before my eyes. Now her ability was a raft on empty waters. I needn't think about what she would have to do for Papa.

Out again in the dark corridor, alone with the thought of my cold bed, I felt a sick shivering go through me. I thought what a crash there would be if I fell, and I almost wished for a disturbance that would bring me some pity. But there was no such thing. Only good behaviour about Death. So I sat down on the floor before I fell down and waited for the weakness to pass over. Sitting there I felt my grief for Papa and my lost love for Richard as joining together. Only Papa had known that we were lovers. Now half my despair was my own secret. No one could take it from me, or lessen it, or tell of it. My great body had been blessed by love. True. It was true. Some merciless shaft had been ready to pierce me with denial. I must run from it, and keep that truth whole for myself. I could hear Rose stirring busily, sure-footed, behind Papa's door, and the idea that soon she might be going to the bathroom for water got me onto my feet.

As I stood up I thought of that pot of tea sitting on the kitchen stove and my wish for it felt guilty in all the tragic circumstances. But, the more unseemly I thought it, the stronger came my wish for a cup of hot tea, perhaps a slice of bread and butter, and my hotwater-bottle – how had I forgotten that? They were three necessities, and I was glad of them. There was someone I could help, if it was only myself. But I was relieved to think that there would be nobody there to watch me drinking tea and buttering a slice of bread.

CHAPTER THIRTY-THREE

Mummie was rigorously set on perfect behaviour. She was eating some breakfast when I came into the diningroom. She put down her knife to write something on the back of an opened-out envelope. 'There's such a lot to be done.' She spoke in her ordinary voice. 'So many things to remember. One has to be businesslike.' She wrote something down. '*And* put out the spirit-lamp,' she said, 'when you've had enough breakfast.'

Eggs and bacon and coffee, the dogs' porridge and the winter sun coming in on long slanting prongs through the high windows – except that the world had stopped, things were going on much as usual.

'What must we do this morning?'

I had to break the indecent noise of shovelling down eggs and bacon; my swallowing had an immense sound.

'I,' she repeated, 'I have sent Tommy for Dr Coffey. Rose says that is the first thing to be done. After that he can go on to Kildeclan and get your friend the solicitor to help me about—' she looked round the table, unable to say 'funeral' or 'coffin.' Instead she said: 'Rather a pity about the car. But you mustn't blame yourself. Really not.'

'She wouldn't start, Mummie. It was freezing.'

'Of course,' she said, 'it might have made no difference. One never knows, does one?' She wrote something down on the envelope. 'They said someone was waiting to see me.' She pressed the little mother-of-pearl bell on the table, and when Breda answered it (all importance and restraint), she said: 'What did I want? Who is waiting?'

'The steward, madam.'

'Oh, yes. Tell Foley I'm ready to see him now. In the hall.' She got up and walked out of the room with brisk intention. She must have forgotten the envelope and pencil beside her plate. On my way to give myself a second cup of coffee I looked at it to see what plans she had outlined for the day. The envelope was covered with doodling scribbles and isolated words, making no kind of sense or guide. Really rather silly.

When I went through the hall to call the dogs in to their breakfast Rose, not Mummie, was in consultation, not with Foley but with Mr Kiely. She had the kitchen scribbling pad on the table and I could see it was written over by her in tidy lists of necessities, marked: 1, 2, 3 – very different from Mummie's envelope. I read: 1. Near Mr Hubert. *Not* the vault. 2. Millinery department, Switzers, Grafton Street. Send three black felt hats on appro. 3. Wreath from the staff.

'Good morning.' Mr Kiely looked very brisk in his smart little overcoat. 'I heard the sad news about the Major so I came along to see if I could help about the ... arrangements.' It was a relief to hear someone speaking in an ordinary voice – the first I had heard that morning, except for Mummie's. His businesslike tone conveyed a discreet denial of our contacts of the night before. Perhaps I had imagined things, I was so sick and blinded then.

'Thank you so much,' I said. 'It would be a great help.'

Rose picked her pad up off the table and came a little closer: 'Madam is so grateful to Mr Kiely for his prompt attention –' she spoke very grandly – 'and I have this list for him of her wishes in all matters.' Mr Kiely looked from Rose to me.

'Maybe you had better come to my office and telephone?' he suggested. It was as if he had told Rose to stand aside. He took the list gently out of her hand, and read it aloud to me. His action made nonsense of her presence, and this pleased me. I stood beside him, looking down the list, while I made further suggestions.

Rose left us, going quietly away, as a servant should, but returning, within a few minutes, shepherding, shadowing, almost compelling Mummie towards us down the cold distances of the hall. She stood behind Mummie, as if to support her, or to supply a tactful hint, or a helpful reminder, should they be needed.

Mummie gave Mr Kiely the tips of her tiny, straightened fingers and bowed her head briefly at his condolence. 'Rose thought there were some other questions to decide about tomorrow.'

'It can't be tomorrow, Mummie,' I said. 'There won't be time.'

'Perhaps, Aroon, Mr Kiely and I had better discuss this. Shall we go into the library, Mr Kiely?' She turned away, expecting him to follow, and he turned towards me.

'I made arrangements for the garage to collect your car –'

'My car. How kind,' Mummie corrected and commended him.

'– and to send the account in to my office.' Mr Kiely was still speaking to me.

'If only the car had been here last night.' Mummie spoke as though each word were drawn out of her by pincers. 'However,' she added, 'we mustn't think about that.'

I was stunned by the assumption that Papa might have lived but for my idiot incompetence or neglect over the car. If I had gone for Dr Coffey as Rose came howling into the kitchen, Papa would still have died in less than an hour. There was a pause until Mummie said: 'Rose, would you come with us and bring our list?' Rose threw me a polite, pitying look as she shut the library door.

Because they had shut me out I was still standing in the hall, raging with my grievance, when Dr Coffey arrived.

'My dear child, it wouldn't have made a blind bit of difference if I'd been with him all night.' Instead of being in his usual flurry to get away to his next patient, he seemed to have all the day's leisure to hear what I had to say.

'I know she was giving him whisky,' I insisted. I had to say it. 'I told you before, didn't I? That's what killed him. Wasn't it?'

'Whatever she gave him,' Dr Coffey said, 'made no difference. And if he died happy, what about it?'

'He didn't die happy. His breathing – if you'd been there . . .'

'He was unconscious, my dear child.' He took my hands strongly in his. 'We all did our best for him. God rest his soul, he was a grand man.'

'And will you please tell them the car made no difference?'

'I will, of course. It's only the truth. Try and put the whisky out of your mind too. It was death from natural causes, and Rose was a great nurse to him.'

'Oh, I know. She was sitting up warming his bad foot when I came in last night, this morning, whenever it was.'

'Death from natural causes,' Dr Coffey repeated with more certainty. He said no more about Rose. My admission of her devotion seemed to stop him.

'I'll run up and see the Major,' he said, just as if this were one of his frequent visits. I almost expected there might be a brace of woodcock in his car. It was just the weather for them, I thought. As I stood and shivered in the familiar cold of the hall, the dogs came dispassionately towards me. They seemed unattractive and dispirited. I was just in time to prevent one of them from peeing on the baize hall-door curtain, their favourite cold-weather lavatory. They conveyed to me a clear picture of myself: the unmarried daughter who doesn't play bridge, letting out the dogs for evermore. Mummie and Rose would be in power over me, over Temple Alice, until I was old, or middle-aged at best, beyond even the remembrance of time past. They may starve me too – the idea filled me with panic. Mummie doesn't eat and Rose won't cook for me alone. They will enjoy starving me. It will be called economy. Daughters at home are supposed to do the flowers. Mummie does the flowers . . .

Mr Kiely came out presently. Somebody shut the door behind him. It would be Rose, and she would overlook us through one of the windows on either side of the hall door, a fox behind glass. As though he realised this he hurried past me to his car. 'Everything sorted out now, I think.'

I could not be ignored again. I must know, so that I need not ask Rose for the plans.

'Thursday. Two o'clock. I'll ring the *Times* and the *Irish*

Times, and I'll send off the other telegrams ... Switzers ... flowers – what about your own flowers?'

So they had forgotten to put me on the list to the florist. 'Please,' I said, 'not chrysanthemums.'

'Not chrysanthemums,' he wrote it down. 'I'll see to it they send something good.'

Later in the morning when our car came back, its presence invoked and concentrated a sad hostility. Too late now, all the eyes seemed to be saying. Heads turned from me accusingly, pityingly. As the day crawled on, hushed and cold, I felt more wronged, grieved, and unwanted than ever before. My sorrow for Papa and my agony over Richard were hooked and linked. I could see no possible end to unhappiness. Besides, I was wolfishly hungry all the hours before luncheon. And, when luncheon came, I could feel Mummie's eyes sad and unbelieving, on my plate. It was fish. Delicious. Rose brought Mummie a creamed egg in a minute earthenware pot. Waiting in the diningroom was Breda's business, but today things had no proper order, servants whispered and revelled in the sad change.

'Try and eat it, madam; it's only the bantam hen's.' Rose looked accusingly at my half-empty plate. 'I knew you'd never manage to swallow the Major's fish.' I felt like a cannibal, a hungry cannibal, and very unloveable. They looked at me in satisfied derision as I finished what was on my plate.

'I couldn't let anything pass my lips,' Rose said, 'but a cup of tea. Light tea.'

Next day telegrams came. Relays of boys brought them in sheaves from the post office. Rose piled them together on the writing table in the library, sombrely pleased at the multiplicity of the tributes. Mummie looked at the heap of telegrams with a sort of blind disgust: 'One must open them, I suppose.'

'Would you like me to do it?' A share of the love and sympathy was mine, and opening envelopes is always nice.

'No, thank you.' She sat down at the writing table. Then I heard her say in a sharp, decisive voice: 'Most certainly NOT – the very last person I wish to see.'

'You needn't see anyone, need you? Everyone must understand.'

'He won't. He means to stay. Read it.' She handed me the telegram.

'"Coming to you for funeral. Wobbly."'

Wobbly – Richard's father. Papa's friend. I felt myself going red with longing to see him.

'The silliest friend your father ever had.' She spoke patiently. 'His wound –' even now she didn't say Papa's wooden leg – 'his wound was all because of some mad wartime escapade of Wobbly's. *And* he loaded Mrs Brock onto us. Then Hubert . . . ' She put the back of her hand up to her mouth. She was on the brink of not behaving beautifully, but saved herself just in time. 'I shall simply wire: DON'T COME.' She wrote it down. 'Get that to the post office for me.'

It was the first and only thing she had asked me to do, and it meant for me the loss of a last contact. In the dark of the post office, as I copied her message onto a form, it occurred to me how easy to substitute DO for DON'T, but I overruled the temptation. They would find out. As it happened it made no difference. Late that afternoon another telegram arrived, saying: PLEASE MEET BOAT TRAIN LIMERICK JUNCTION THURSDAY MORNING. WOBBLY.

'What shall I do?' Mummie said to Rose, who brought her the telegram. When she asked Rose a question it was as though she laid a burden down.

'He'll have to come for the funeral,' Rose decided, 'but he won't be staying. After he sees the yellow room, he'll be laying his plans for the night mail.' Their eyes met. Something like naughtiness flashed between them.

'Perhaps that would be best,' Mummie agreed, 'and Miss Aroon can meet the boat train – that would be cheaper than a taxi. Not that petrol's cheap. And all these telegrams – the porterage must be in pounds and pounds.'

'Ah, don't upset yourself, madam,' Rose said. 'It will only all come out of the estate.'

I kept quiet. I was so worried that any show of agreement from me would change their decisions. However deeply it might hurt me, a longing to hear about Richard, to keep in touch, throbbed in me as regularly as the ticking in a poisoned finger. Besides this – to see the companion of Papa's youthful rampages would be to explore a bright place where Papa belonged by right, a place where I could see him far distant from the patient doll he had become. The doll I was not allowed to play with. I had fought for my rights of possession in him and I suppose I had lost. Clearer than the memory of his hobbling run across the fields to save me when Hubert's horse had hopped it so ungovernably came the other memory: his betrayal of our hour, his agreeable subjection to Mummie's quiet derision. The ghosts and whiffs of disloyalties stirred in that past air, hinting at pity, not at love.

On the night he died, when in my distress I looked in for the comfort of helping him, Papa had needed nobody but Rose – Rose who had killed him with her spoiling and her whisky. I would have given him anything except whisky. Surely he might have needed me most.

CHAPTER THIRTY-FOUR

I stood with unknown travellers in the cold of the gloomy station waiting for the boat train. Steam plumed the air, fortified by the hissing of water on hot ash and hot iron. A small, sedate engine made a supreme effort and set off with its train and its few serious passengers. The emptied rails and lines assumed a magnificence. Over my head the iron stays and echoing unfurnished arches of the station became part of the empty spaces within me. I stood waiting in their cold shelter, sometimes wetting my lips and sucking them in, folding them under and over. It was a relief. It was companionable.

Presently the daily business proceeding inattentively round me proved a sedation; the ceremonial surrounding trains lifted my heart by its very distance from myself. A magnificent ticket collector, stuffed man of the moment, strode unseeing towards me, removed, like a great toy, from real life. I felt the moment had come to inquire about the boat train. He only shook his head. He conveyed a mystery he could not probe.

'She's late,' was all he told me. The train might have been coming in across miles of steppes, followed by wolves; he would not answer for her. I decided I had time to go to the ladies' lavatory, and it was from there that I heard the sounds of the boat train rushing to its standstill; gasping out steam; its carriage doors clanking open and banging shut; calls for porters; willing responses; barrows rattling beneath the frosted window of the lavatory; footsteps making their coherent passage to an immediate purpose. Above the common noises, a voice, direct as a child's, flowed and floated on the air: 'Is the bar open?' it asked.

'It is of course, sir.'

'Ah, splendid. And can you tell me at what time the five-thirty boat train leaves for Cork?'

'At half past five, sir.'

'Ah, splendid. That's what I thought.'

'Are you being met, sir?'

'I hope so. Just look after this stuff, would you? And keep an eye on that. Don't touch it. Just watch it. I don't want to take it into the bar . . .'

The voice could only belong to Papa's friend. When I came out his porter was still standing beside a lavishly preserved leather suitcase across which a camel's-hair rug and a dark overcoat were folded neatly. Placed on top of the lot, as though on a newly plump grave, was an enormous wreath of orchids, sustained on wire and moss and backed by a hedge of variegated holly. Orchids for Papa, I thought; what a rehabilitation. With the orchids came a clear picture of Papa at hunt balls, the exotics yearning round. Although he couldn't dance because of his gammy leg, and never talked much, and would be silent now for always, his enchantment was imperishable.

Tears pushed into my eyes again, tears for himself, not for

his death. I swallowed them strictly down before Major Massingham, Papa's forbidden friend, who had once flogged Richard, and from his distant magnificence had paralysed and frightened Mrs Brock, came bundling towards me. I saw an elderly gentleman in a tweed coat and a soft brown hat worn at his own sacredly absurd angle. He took my hand.

'How dear of you to meet me. You're –? You're –?'

'I'm Aroon.'

'Of course. What a girl, bless you, aren't you? Ghastly day for you. End of an era for us all, actually. Let's get my stuff into your car, shall we, and then perhaps something to steady the nerves. Look OUT—' he shouted as his porter picked up the orchids and holly. 'My dear fellow, don't hold it like that, you're going to drop it and ruin the whole thing.' He picked up the wreath gingerly. 'I took a separate cabin for this last night,' he said, 'only one berth in mine. How do you like it?'

'It's beautiful.'

'Yes, I think so.'

When we had shut the car door on the wreath and the luggage and he had given the porter a small tip (doesn't do to overdo things) we went back to the bar.

'I shall have a glass of port and brandy,' he said decidedly, 'and I'm going to make you one of my specials. Have you a lemon about you?' he asked the woman behind the bar. 'Good girl. Splendid. Now we need a large measure of brandy and a small bottle of dry ginger ale. Oh, capital. I feel it's called for. Now, tell me if you like it.'

'Yes, I do,' I said. We sat near the fire at a marble-topped table with iron legs.

'I suppose we shall be in time for this five-thirty train,' he said, looking unhappily at the clock, which said eleven-forty-five.

'How far is Temple Alice? And the funeral is at two o'clock? I suppose we couldn't hurry things on a bit? No, of course not. What time do we lunch? That's a question. Quite a question.'

I had no answer for his question so I asked if he'd had a good crossing.

'My wife was rather against the whole thing,' he said absently. 'The heart, you know, the old heart. Your mother didn't want me to come either. I expect she always thought I was a poor influence.'

'Yes,' I said.

He gave me a jackdaw glance. 'You'll miss him all right, poor child. We all have our difficulties. And Hubert. Too dreadful.' He put his hand on the back of mine, then took it away again. 'I shall have to get into the right kit before luncheon. Shouldn't we go?'

'It's warmer here.' Everything was expanding for me. Ease soared from me and flowed back through me. I was going to say it. It was easy. 'How's Richard?' I had said it.

'Oh, my dear, my dear,' he looked at me; there were tears in the red-veined blue eyes, 'he's in a ghastly pickle.'

I was going to be generous. 'She looks wonderful,' I said.

'The whole thing's beyond me,' he said.

I was going to be more than generous: 'I expect they'll be terribly happy.'

'If that's his idea of happiness—'

'He must be happy.' I wanted to hear him deny it.

'Wrong from the first.' He shook his head and looked into his glass. 'Reading books in trees. Nannie was right – unhealthy stuff. Then there was that governess – we sacked her. She was in it somehow. Queer person. She found things. Gave a couple of good winners too, but it got a bit much. Mrs

Who, can't remember.'

'Mrs Brock. She drowned herself.'

'Did she? Did she really? Sad. Then that footman, quite harmless of course, but we sacked him too. Nannie thought he was a poor influence – one does one's best. Trouble at school. Who hasn't, after all? Forget it, I always think.'

'But he'll be happy now,' I insisted. I must hear him contradict me. It was my right.

'How do I know? No use asking me. Terribly upset about Hubert. That was unfortunate – we hoped this damned expensive safari would help that. Now he comes home with some wonderful heads and horns and gets himself into this fix. Poor girl, she's pretty upset.'

My heart could not contain the hope filling it. How to ask? 'Do you mean . . . ?'

'Yes. I do mean.' He looked like an angry blue-eyed baby with a pain it can't explain. 'Broken off his engagement, broken up the entail, upset his mother, and taken himself off to farm in Kenya with Baby Kintoull.'

The glory drained, the hope failed – always the same. The post comes daily and no letter for me. I was licking my lips, alone again. Baby Kintoull – I could see her in whipcord trousers and an open-necked shirt, blond and sunburnt. I might as well know the worst: 'I suppose she's beautiful?'

'Good-looking,' he corrected me.

'Married?'

'Married?' His blue eyes dropped open. 'I don't think you quite have the riding of it,' he spoke gently. He paused. 'They were in the same house at Eton. Let's have another drink,' he said.

He went across to the bar and left me under an arching of

the sky. Now I knew why the station roof soared and vaulted upwards. It was to give space enough to the volume of my happiness. When he put the drinks down on our table my being leaned out towards him as if I leaned far out of the window that was myself into a sunny day.

'Thank you,' I said. I wanted to thank him for a moment only comparable to that flying moment when Richard had kissed me, but my acceptance of the drink had to do instead. He drank his third glass of port and brandy as in duty bound and looked doubtfully at my glass. 'What time do we lunch, did you say? Perhaps we really ought to be making a move.'

'Oceans of time,' I said. I wanted to sit on and on in this warm, kind place where the moments went dimpling, sliding by, and even the bottles on the shelves looked so more than real, so more like bottles than bottles, so true to themselves. Truth was so easy to see and speak, entirely believable when spoken. My elbow slipped off the edge of the table. I put it back again.

'I shall have to change out of these clothes before luncheon.'

'If you want to know –' words loomed out of my mouth – 'I don't think there's going to be any luncheon.'

'Oh, I can't believe that.'

'And another thing you won't believe –' I was free; I could say what I pleased – 'Richard loved me.'

'I'm so worried about catching that five-thirty train.'

'Don't you believe me?'

'I know you'll do your best to get me there in time.'

'No question.'

'Then drink up, like a good girl. Let's get going.'

He didn't take in what I was saying, a bit muzzy probably

after all that port and brandy. I felt clear as a bell myself. They would toll a bell for Papa. 'You heard what I said?'

'I wonder if they would make us a ham sandwich?'

I'm not a greedy person about food and drink. My theory is: if it's there, I may as well. 'What a good idea.' I accepted it. 'And you do believe me?'

'Of course. Absolutely. Did you say we're twenty miles from Temple Alice?'

'Nineteen and three-quarters; we'll do it easily.' I spoke distinctly, repeating three-quarters carefully because I really didn't think he was making much sense. He went across to the bar, and not too steady on his feet, I thought; good thing I'm driving. He came back with a plateful of ham sandwiches and a pot of mustard. He put the plate down in front of me.

'Blotting paper. And that very kind girl tells me I can change in the station master's office. There's a huge fire going in there, she says, and he'll be simply delighted. I think that's best, don't you?'

'Then you needn't see Mummie, or only just.'

'That's a point too. Eat up like a good girl. Is your car locked?'

'I forget if it does lock.'

'Oh dear.' He looked at me. 'This *is* a rampage. Give me the key in case.'

'If I can find it –' I spoke with proper weight and responsibility – 'you may certainly have it. But don't lose it.' After a search in my bag I remembered distinctly that the car door hadn't locked for years, but I gave him the ignition key as he was looking anxious and I wanted everybody to be happy now that I knew Richard was not going to marry any glorious girl.

If he would come back to me across the world I would wait through a thousand safaris.

What would he say? Now I wondered what he would say when he came for me. I could not decide, but I could clearly see myself in a low (though roomy) thatched house in the foothills of Kilimanjaro with dark servants bowing low, cooking exquisitely. Some happy years in the high air and the sun, then, when Mummie died – my breath came sharp across my teeth – we would come back (with our two jolly little boys) to Temple Alice. Perhaps I would give Rose the furthest gate lodge, but I would not put in a lavatory and she could go to the well for water and pick up dry sticks for her fire in the ash plantation. I saw her, an old woman stooping under frozen trees. She would get a new cardigan every Christmas from me. I felt myself hover over the future, all time between lost. The thought of Papa brought me only happiness. How glad I was that I had told him Richard and I were lovers, especially now that he could never question or betray me.

'Would you bring me another of these?' The girl behind the bar looked doubtful.

'A small brandy, miss?' she said rather miserably.

How little she knew what I was celebrating: 'A large brandy, please, and give yourself a drink as well.' My kind feelings for everyone overpowered me. 'Do be happy,' I said to her. 'I want you to be happy.' She put the drink and a little bottle of ginger ale on the table beside me and skipped nervously back to the bar. With careful and delicate precision I poured the ginger ale, just enough and not a drop too much, into the brandy, and stretched my feet to the fire.

Presently Richard's father came back. He was leaning over me. 'Can you get up?'

'You needn't shout.' I didn't want everybody to realise he was what Papa calls a bit foxed. 'I can hear you.'

'Come on then, my dear girl; we're going to miss the whole thing.'

'Yes.' I allowed the words to crawl out agreeably: 'We mustn't miss Papa's funeral, must we?' I looked him over. He was wearing a dark overcoat, so cut and contrived as to take at least a stone from his weight. I thought of Napoleon. No. A Russian officer. The thin stripes in his trousers fizzed together and separated before my eyes. 'I'm glad you look so splendid.'

'You've a worse head than your father.'

'Don't insult my father. I love my father.' I couldn't feel angry.

'That's all right – so do I. Always have.'

'Always shall. Say it.' I put my hand over his and he gripped it and pulled me to my feet. I towered over him laughing. So funny, I didn't mind being tall. Rather nice. But there was something I must do. I must pay for my drink. I must be meticulous. At the bar I gave the girl a pound note.

'No, no, no.' He wouldn't allow it.

'No, no, no.' It was my turn to say it. 'This was my own idea.'

'Don't be silly.' He stuffed the note back into my bag. 'Sure you're all right?' He looked so bleak with worry that I began to laugh. Dizzy from happiness and laughter let free, I clung to a pillar. The station seemed top-heavy; it needed more support. At that moment I could have borne the world on my shoulders. My strength and certainty were so immense. Even when I slipped and fell on the ice outside the station I went down forgiving its treachery, and when I tried to get up I laughed and moaned together at the shocking pain in my ankle.

'Now we *are* souped,' he said. 'I can't carry you, can I? Out of the question. Stay your ground while I find a strong porter.'

So I sat there on the flags, still as a mouse, warding off the pain, until, as if past trees in a wood, I heard his returning voice: 'My friend's rather under the weather. Broken something now, I shouldn't wonder. Can't put a toe to the ground, and I see very little prospect of luncheon before *or* after this funeral.'

'There's a restaurant car on the five-thirty; you might get a cup of tea.' It was an official voice. The station master loomed above me, illumined in gold braid.

'Perhaps a couple of poached eggs?' Major Massingham insisted.

'It's a sad occasion for poached eggs.' The station master meant Papa I knew, but why sound so disapproving?

'Thank you,' I said, 'we'll miss him terribly.' I spoke very clearly.

'The poor thing—' the station master said accusingly to Major Massingham.

'All my stupidity.' I thought it was kind of him to feel responsible for the ice and my fall. Very kind.

'If you both put your arms round me,' I said, 'I expect I can hop as far as the car.'

'And why not?' said the station master.

Gently and kindly they sustained each step. The comfort of their support went through me. I leaned on each in turn, distributing myself as fairly as I was able. Major Massingham smelt delicious. The station master smelt like the station: scalding steam on hot iron, hot feet on cold flags. I leaned on him more trustingly to show that I felt no preference either way.

'Easy does it,' he kept saying, 'take it easy.'

Major Massingham left me in the station master's arms when we had hobbled as far as the car. 'It's not an original T model, is it? It can't be. I've never driven one actually.'

'We might get a boy from the garage.'

'Oh, *no*. What fun. Do let me. I've always longed to.'

'My eleven-forty-two is due now, it's ten-after-twelve.' The station master sounded as if he were going to leave us. I held him more closely.

'Don't give it a thought,' I told him. 'You've been so kind, so wonderful.'

When they had lifted me into the car and wrapped me in the blue face-cloth rug with its undefeated fur lining, tears eased into my eyes.

'Let go his hand; we really must get on.' Major Massingham settled himself excitedly behind the steering wheel. 'Which of these jobs is the accelerator? Don't tell me, don't tell me. What fun. Clutch? Ah, I have it. Bang in for low gear? Don't worry, I've read about it. Hand brake? Right. We're off—'

Papa's orchids leaped and subsided on the seat behind us. 'Never look back,' I said to myself, 'and don't distract the driver.' Not that I could. The pain in my foot had eased, and a hot, sugary warmth filled me. As though he knew how happy I was, Major Massingham sang as he drove along: '"Whispering while you" . . .' he whistled the next bar and I was carried back into a September evening . . . past, future, and for always, please God let it be like this, let time be lost, and pain and doubt.

'Come on – wake up, wakey-wakey – pull yourself together.' He was shaking my head off his shoulder. I opened my eyes. The demesne walls darkened the winter road. The bare trees released the winter light. We were near the church and the lodge gates. 'Sit *up*,' he insisted. 'Please.' He had been so kind I tried to obey him. I sat upright in a dignified way as we drove through the waiting crowds at the church gates and on up the drive to Temple Alice.

'We've made it,' he said. 'Hate to be late. So rude, I always think. Feeling better?'

'Wonderful,' I said. 'Really wonderful.'

He stopped the car on the further side of the gravel sweep from the house, then scrabbled up his orchids and got out to stand rigid and bareheaded, waiting, forgetting me, his eyes only on the farm cart drawn up at the foot of the steps, its paint blue as eucalyptus leaves, the spokes of its wheels crisply pink in the morning light. Volumes of breath from the quiet horse stayed low on the air while four of the men on the place carried Papa down the steps; slowly, awkwardly as great crabs, they went sideways, directing each other in ordinary voices.

When Major Massingham moved away, intent on depositing his orchids, I nearly called out to him to wait for me because I knew, although I was floating and weightless, that my ankle might crumple and give if I walked alone, no station master near, no sweet-smelling stranger on my other side. But I had my new reality. I could live on, assured in hopefulness. I felt certain that if I could get nearer to Papa, even reach the farm cart before they drove him away, he would know the blaze of my happiness as he had before, when I told him Richard and I were lovers.

My weight, when I dared to put it on my foot, was bearable, I could have walked straight across the gravel if it had not been for the cold bright air, which affected my movements, strangely muffling my knees. The men were looking at me in an odd way and I saw Wobbly hastily prop his orchids against a wheel before he came to put a hand under my armpit. Then I had the cart to cling to; steadying myself against it, I tried to remember what I wanted to say to Papa.

I was too late to say it, for Mummie was coming out of the house now, coming between us as always. As they settled Papa in the straw-filled cart, she stood on the top step, composed and still. Strong, careful, neat as a packet of black pins, Rose stood behind her; behind Rose I saw Mr Kiely and two men in dark clothes waiting, burdened and wreathed in flowers, until Mummie, looking over her shoulder in the most natural way, signed to them to precede her with their loads of neatly labelled tributes.

She was at the foot of the steps now, her new black hat bending round her face, subject to her feeling for the perfect angle, its veil seemed less than air about her cold face. Her hand in a black glove held her old loose coat up to her throat; her mourning was economically perfect.

Still close behind her Rose came, watchful and ready. Except that she had no veil, she was black as a second widow. Her outfit must have cost her as much as six months' wages. We were near now; Mummie's face, shocked and grieved, swam up to mine, and Rose's face, in some way pleased, was joined with it. It was then that my ankle gave way and neither Major Massingham's support nor my hold on the cart could stop me falling. I felt like a house falling, and through the fall I heard his voice saying: 'Terribly, terribly sorry. My fault, my fault, absolutely.'

And Mummie's voice, her usual voice to me: 'Would someone be very kind and carry her into the house?'

The two men in dark clothes came forward. They carried

me up the steps and into the library, easily, professionally; they knew about handling bodies in all sizes, I suppose.

'Footless, poor thing,' I heard one of them say to the other as though he spoke over my dead body. Mr Kiely was putting a cushion under my knees.

'Oh, you *are* kind,' I said, remembering Mary Ann. But they were turning away, they were going to leave me on the library sofa, alone, out of all the fun. Not fun, of course. 'Don't go,' I said, holding their hands.

'You get a bit of a kip and you'll be all right.' It was Mr Kiely's voice.

'Yes – you bundle up there, my dear, and sleep it off. That's your best bet,' Major Massingham advised before anxiety for his own problems repossessed him. 'End of an era. End of an era.' Their voices removed to connive in the hall. '. . . and I don't see the smallest hope of luncheon . . .' That was the last I heard before the sound of cartwheels on the gravel caught me in their heavy turning. I breathed together with them and then I fell asleep.

It was Dr Coffey who woke me up. His hand was on my shoulder. How kind people were. It could never last. 'Let's have a look at the poor old foot,' he said. While he was taking off my shoe, I fumbled for my suspenders, and as I rolled my stocking over my knee I remembered what the day was all about. They had been burying Papa. It was evening now, four o'clock, perhaps. The thickness of rain was beyond the windows. A thaw had come and in the changed light I felt all the lone vacancy of the morning. I knew my hope was precarious. Certainty fell away from me as though a loved person dropped my hand in indifference.

'How was it?' I asked.

'Very cold.' That was all he had to say about Papa's funeral, as if he wanted me to think I hadn't missed much. He was examining my ankle and I squeezed my dimpling knee against the pain I expected. I hoped for more pain. I longed for him to say my leg was broken.

'Only a little sprain,' he said, and I burst into tears.

'Don't upset yourself, child. What is it all only passing through life?' Did he mean Papa, out there in the cold, or was he thinking of the future days for me with Mummie in power and Rose to abet her power? The hope that had flown me up in the morning to an air-borne delight was seeping away now. I was carried on fluctuating, fractured currents till I reached the ground.

'Don't mind me at all,' he said. He was strapping my ankle. I wished the turning and gripping of the bandage might continue endlessly.

'I do feel so awful,' I apologised.

'It's just the reaction hitting you now,' he said. 'You won't repeat the experience.'

'I hope not,' I said. 'It was that icy spot that did it.' He gave me a funny look.

'They'll be here any minute now. They're walking up from the graveyard.'

'In the rain?'

'I came on to straighten you out. Jim Kiely told me you were in a poor way.'

'My head feels pretty ghastly. I must have hit it when I fell.'

'That's right. You could have a touch of concussion. Let's say you have too. I must be off now. I have a patient in labour up the mountain.' He took a step back towards me from the doorway. 'Take it easy now. And I left a brace of woodcock on the hall table for you and your mother.'

... For you and your mother ... But would Rose cook them as she did for Papa? Crisp skins and pink flesh – a little blood leaking onto toast? Buttered crumbs and wafer potato chips and a wine sauce? I wondered. Mummie couldn't bear woodcock.

I had a premonition of future luncheons and dinners: spaghetti with a little melted butter cooling in the depths of the silver sauceboat, and a few crumbs of grated cheese. There would be plenty of baked apples, and stewed rhubarb with junket, roast beef on Sunday, and apple tart, or a grocer's jelly with preserved ginger chopped through it. The house would grow colder because Mummie never felt the cold; she would paint her peculiar pictures and rub her little hands and fiddle out into the garden and back to her tapestry. Whether she was painting or gardening or stitching, her disgust with me would enlarge as I grew older.

As we lived on at Temple Alice a ceiling cornice would fall or a dog would die; those would be the interests and tragedies to mark passing time. And as time passed there would be new devices invented and contrived for my restriction and humiliation. I could see myself hungry. I would keep my dress allowance to buy food; it was a cosy secret idea. Water biscuits (high-bake) and gentleman's relish and anchovy fillets, perhaps a bag of sugar for an occasional grapefruit, all to be stored in my bedroom, with a bottle of sherry now and then. But Rose would find out my store, and a scene to satisfy them both would be organised. I could imagine no escape from them or from myself in the interval, and it might be a very long interval, of waiting until Richard came back to me from Kenya – if he came back to me.

Feeling like a rat in a trap, and too big for my trap, I sat on in my overcoat, staring at my bandaged foot, discouragement possessing me, and a disconcerting embarrassment linked with Dr Coffey's half-spoken excuses for my fall, my double fall. We had agreed that I must have hit my head. I still felt slightly concussed and that was the truth I was going to maintain. 'Dr Coffey thinks I have a bit of concussion,' I repeated the words as I heard the returning voices in the hall, quiet voices not yet turned back to ordinary heights of speech. Only one voice sounded clear and natural above the shuffle and murmur.

'I shall certainly say goodbye. She must be feeling quite awful.' I felt a pause of silent dissent behind him. I put my leg up on the sofa, and I wished there was a bandage round my head too; the look of the thing would have been a great help.

'Slept it off?' he said. 'Good girl. Good girl. I'm all right too. Very kind fellow with a sharpish sort of car says he'll put me on the train – drive me on to the boat if it comes to that, shouldn't wonder. And that nice housekeeper of yours is making me a few sandwiches. I'll be all right. Don't worry about me.'

'But what about me?' – it came from me in a sort of roaring protest. 'What can I do?'

'That's quite a question. End of an era and all that, my dear. We just have to hack on regardless, don't we?' He looked uncomfortable. He was leaving me without a word that mattered. Didn't he want to hear about my concussion? Has he forgotten all we had said to each other? About Richard? About Papa? Was I less to him now than an object beheld and passed by on a train journey? I must run beside the moving train, press my face upwards to the hastening glass.

'Give my love to Richard,' I said, 'when you write.'

He looked at me; he put me at a distance. 'We don't write,' he said. Then he turned back from the doorway, eagerly, warmly, to say something I must hear, I felt sure of it. 'One thing,' he said, 'my orchids looked absolutely terrific, well worth all the bother.'

Mummie came in alone. She looked tall, as a small dog can sometimes convey a false impression of size. She spoke to someone behind her, so I knew Rose must be near.

'I think perhaps we should light the lamps. He says he wants to read something ... We have to let him, I suppose.' Her voice trailed away in a kind of disgusted obedience to ritual, easier to accept and ignore than to disobey. She came nearer. 'Am I asking rather a lot, or could someone have kept the fire alight?'

'I was asleep. Dr Coffey thinks I concussed myself when I fell.'

'Other people, my dear, think you were blind drunk when you fell.'

'I suppose you mean Rose thinks so.'

'I'm afraid Rose was not the only one who thought so; Major Massingham thought so too. And he's a remarkably good judge.'

'Mummie – it's not true.'

'It happened and I don't want to discuss it. Not today.'

I didn't say: It's because you hate me. It was in my mind. I only looked at her.

She looked back at me. 'Please,' she said, 'you do rather exaggerate.'

'Oh, what shall I do?' I said.

'Your home will always be here with me,' she said patiently.

'And another thing – now that all the responsibilities and decisions for Temple Alice are mine I hope perhaps in small ways you may be more – shall I say – loyal.'

'Mummie – what do you mean?'

'You must know perfectly well what I mean – for instance, no more private arrangements with your friend the solicitor – after all, not quite of our class.'

Rose came in with a cardboard box full of kindling wood. She paused near Mummie. 'You're perished, madam,' she said as if she had touched her. But there was a wide respectful distance between them; only her concerned voice crossed it.

'Oh, Rose,' Mummie said. Her voice was quite changed. It was an appeal to an outer force, a strength to which she could yield, and still not yield from the astringency of good behaviour. Again a circle was forming – it had already formed. I was back in the diningroom on a summer night, on a hot September morning; the circle was closing to hold me out. Now the fire rose and blazed triumphant. Complacent in her success, Rose swept up the hearth.

'You shouldn't be doing this, Rose. Where's Breda?' Mummie went closer to Rose's fire, feeling at her hands. 'Perhaps better bring the lights. He has to read me something, so he says.' She looked at me, sitting beyond the heat of the fire, the winter afternoon darker every minute behind me. 'Rose could help you to your bedroom; that might be best – that is if you feel quite all right.'

Heaving myself up from the sofa, one hand grabbing at its arm, I towered, at last on my feet, toppling in my own dreadful height and world. 'If you would bring me a stick from the hall,' I said to Rose, 'I can manage. Please.' I cried out, '*Please*,' in my pain.

Rose put an iron arm round me. 'Ah, what stick, what nonsense,' she said. 'Lean on me. You'll be all right.' She was like a nurse of steel, a wardress in power. There was refuge in her great authority, but I would refuse that refuge, I would resist the abyss of yielding. I pulled myself out of her arm and stood alone.

'Oh, hold on to her, Rose,' Mummie said plaintively. 'She'll break that other leg of hers if we're not careful.'

'Come on.' I might have been a refusing horse, Rose's voice was so urgent and impersonal. 'Bed's the place.' Her hands were on me again.

'Let me alone,' I said.

'I wonder would I tell Mr Kiely come in?' Rose looked to Mummie, speaking across me as if I were not there. 'She might go with him.' Mummie nodded some silent meaning. Their meeting eyes frightened me. I stood there between them, and the shape of my future blew up, nightmare large in its certainty of their conspiracy.

'I'll ask him so,' Rose said, 'and when we have her settled I'll bring in the drink tray.'

'The *other* sherry, I think,' Mummie said, 'not the you know.' She didn't speak after Rose had gone. It was as if she retreated into her quiet, well-behaved sorrow. She contained it for herself, hid it beneath good manners. Her clothes dressed it gracefully, distinct from everyday clothes, but not flamboyantly widowlike. When Mr Kiely came in, her unchanged voice forbade any thought of mourning.

'Ah, Mr Kiely?' she almost questioned his identity, as if she were kindly recognising a lesser person, successfully remembering his name, putting him at ease. 'And I hear you are most kindly driving Major Massingham to the station. We mustn't let him miss his train, must we? So shall we be very quick—' She looked at the briefcase in his hand.

'I have the document here,' he said. 'If we had a lamp I could read it.' The darkness came a pulse nearer at his words, our grandeur and our poverty joining in our discomfort.

'Yes, yes, of course. They're just bringing the lights. I wondered if you would perhaps give my daughter an arm across the hall – I expect she can manage when she gets to the staircase and the bannisters. It would be kind.'

'Of course. Delighted. No trouble.' He didn't even speak to me. I stood there, some sort of animal, hopping lame, that had to be housed and cared for and put out of sight. Mummie looked at me with agonised distaste.

'Mr Kiely will help you,' she said to me, and I knew the dismissal in her voice. But he took me by both hands as if dancing with a child, to guide me back to the sofa.

'There are a couple of small legacies and gifts,' he said, and he looked from me towards the door. 'Rose Byrne is mentioned too. They should both be here.'

'Must we really have all this now?' Mummie implored, shrinking away from him, putting her feet under her and her hands on the arms of her chair as if she must get up and say: Goodbye, so kind, but another time would really be better. Before she could perfect her avoidance of the moment Rose had come with the silver tray of sherry and the smallest glasses, followed by Breda with the brass lamp and the silver lamp, lighted and smelling faintly of paraffin, ready to be dropped into the baskets of their standards. They made a new kind of dimness in the room, quelling the afternoon, while simmering in the great spaces of uncurtained light.

'Leave those curtains.' Mummie spoke quite sharply to

Breda, who was going about her usual evening ritual as carefully as on any other day. Now she reared her head like an insulted hen. 'Just leave them,' Mummie said more politely, 'till later. Thank you.'

Rose turned towards the door too, accepting the dismissal with propriety. Mr Kiely looked up enquiringly from the papers he was sorting under the lamp, but before he spoke Mummie's voice encircled Rose: 'Stay with us, Rose. There's a message for you.' Rose turned from the door, waiting respectfully without eagerness, her sense of good behaviour matching Mummie's own. I was the only one to fail the code. Tears, squeezing through spasms of anguish, bounced off my cheeks and fell onto my hands. My own despair surpassed any love I had known, for Richard, for Papa, for Hubert. At that moment I knew myself entirely bereft. The sofa murmured and creaked under my sobbing.

Mummie glanced at her watch: 'Aroon, please. If we don't get on with this he's going to miss the boat train.' She was keeping strictly to the day's essentials; things must be done, masks against any vulgar intrusions of grief. I felt like a child who wets her knickers at a party. Nowhere to hide, no refuge from the shame of it. Rose moved a step nearer.

'Miss Aroon,' she said urgently, 'think of your mother.' I sobbed, gulping on, regardless.

'Well,' Mummie said hopelessly to Mr Kiely, 'if you can make yourself heard . . .'

Mr Kiely stood up near the lamp to read from the papers he had sorted out; he needed the light, improving now beneath its beaded shade. His dark overcoat was still tightly buttoned. He looked like a priest in a cassock and I was as inattentive to what he read as to the voice of a clergyman in a cold familiar church. I was still sobbing and rocking the sofa when he stopped. In the silence I caught my breath, and caught it again. Something had happened. The silence had nothing to do with good behaviour. It was astonished. It was unbelieving. Rose had crossed her distance. She stood behind Mummie as if to shelter her.

'Actually,' Mummie was speaking to Mr Kiely, 'I think there must be some silly mistake, don't you? Because Temple Alice happens to belong to me.'

'You made it over to your husband five years ago, didn't you? The deeds are in my office.'

'That was just a temporary arrangement. And this is an unfortunate misunderstanding – it can all be cleared up.'

'I'm sorry, Mrs St Charles. Everything of which he died possessed, with the exception of those small legacies to yourself and Rose Byrne, is left to his daughter, Iris Aroon.'

'That's my name,' I said.

'Yes. Do you understand? – He's left everything to you.'

I wondered if I could go on breathing naturally, through the delight that lifted me. Twice over now this euphoria of love had elevated my whole body; I was its host. Then the vision changed; it was as though the face of my old world turned away from me – a globe revolving – I was looking into a changed world, where I was a changed person, where my love was recognised and requited. Through the long assuring breaths that followed my sobbing I drew in the truth: that Papa loved me the most. Explicit from the depths of my breathing, like weed anchored far under sea water, I knew a full tide was turning for me. Love and trust were present and whole as they had been once on a summer afternoon. Inexactly present, inexactly lost, the memory fled me as a seal slides into the water with absolute trust in its element. A disturbance on the water closes and there is nothing again. I particularly wanted Rose to hear it again. I was claiming what was mine – his love, his absolute love. I wanted them to understand that he had loved me most.

'Would you read that bit again, the bit about me?'

Mummie moved suddenly in her chair. It was as if she gulped back something she could not swallow. 'Don't read it again. I understand perfectly. I can explain it to my daughter – later, when she is calmer.'

Mr Kiely turned from her to me as though he hadn't heard: 'To my dear daughter, Iris Aroon, I give and bequeath . . . '

Rose moved closer and closer still to Mummie while he was reading. I thought she was going to put her hands on her shoulders, but it was only her breath I could hear when Mr Kiely's voice stopped. Her breathing was like a shadow round Mummie. They must be minding dreadfully. Empowered by Papa's love I would be kind to them. Now I had the mild, wonderful power to be kind, or to reserve kindness. I looked at them with level, considerate eyes.

Mummie looked at her watch. 'I'm so dreadfully afraid you may miss that train.' Her voice was full of anxious consideration, but the dismissal, as she rose to her feet and faintly held out her hand, was obvious. I got up too. The pain in my ankle was gone, due to the bandaging, I suppose. I walked over to the tray of drink.

'Do have a glass of sherry,' I said. And to Rose I said: 'This seems very nasty sherry. Would you bring us the Tío Pepe?'

'Ah, no thank you, not now.' He refused the drink. 'I really must get off. Come in and see me in the office and we'll look into things.' I gave him my hand quite warmly, because I felt he was in my employment now. Then I walked easily across to the fire, throwing out all its heat to me from the chimney breast. I stood there waiting to say something beautiful to Mummie, when Rose should have gone. She stayed on, as though she were needed, until I remembered Dr Coffey's woodcock. 'We'll have them tonight,' I told her, 'and you may take a glass of sherry for your sauce. It's better than nothing. Thin potato chips and an orange salad, don't you think, Rose? And would you ask Breda to bring us the Tío Pepe.'

'I know you like it best,' I said to Mummie when I was left alone with her.

'I don't want it, thank you.' Mummie had sunk back into her chair. She looked smaller and her eyes looked smaller too. Her pretty hat, worn so concisely, had changed its perfect angle.

'But you must. It will do you good.' When Breda brought in the sherry I filled Mummie's glass to the very brim, and, walking soundly across the room, I stood above her, shrivelled back again in her chair, and I spoke to her in a voice I didn't know myself – a voice humid with kindness: 'Drink this,' I said, 'and remember that I'll always look after you.'

She took the glass and looked up at me from under the absurd tilt of her hat; in an odd way her look reminded me of a child warding off a blow.

'Yes. Always,' I reassured her firmly.

VIRAGO MODERN CLASSICS

The Virago Modern Classics launched in 1978 with the radical aim of rewriting the canon, bringing women's voices and stories into the spotlight – and into conversation with each other – and expanding the definition of a classic.

The name Virago means a heroic war-like woman – or, as the thesaurus has it, a dragon, fury, hussy, spitfire or tigress – and signalled the founders' intent to challenge, entertain, enrich, raise eyebrows and revolutionise the literary landscape. Our Modern Classics are chosen with the same ambition, and the list itself continues to evolve, finding new ways to champion works by women and authors of underrepresented genders. With introductions by some of today's very best writers, these are books that speak to each new generation.

'The Virago Modern Classics list contains some of the greatest fiction and non-fiction of the modern age . . . Still captivating, still memorable, still utterly essential reading' SARAH WATERS

'The Virago Modern Classics list is wonderful. It's quite simply one of the best and most essential things that has happened in publishing in our time' ALI SMITH

'The Virago Modern Classics have reshaped literary history and enriched the reading of us all. No library is complete without them' MARGARET DRABBLE

VIRAGO MODERN CLASSICS

AUTHORS INCLUDE:

Maya Angelou, Elizabeth von Arnim, Beryl Bainbridge, Pat Barker, Nina Bawden, Caroline Blackwood, Vera Brittain, Angela Carter, Willa Cather, Barbara Comyns, E. M. Delafield, Polly Devlin, Monica Dickens, Elaine Dundy, Nell Dunn, Nora Ephron, Janet Flanner, Janet Frame, Miles Franklin, Marilyn French, Stella Gibbons, Charlotte Perkins Gilman, Rumer Godden, Radclyffe Hall, Helene Hanff, Josephine Hart, Shirley Hazzard, Bessie Head, Patricia Highsmith, Winifred Holtby, Zora Neale Hurston, Elizabeth Jenkins, Susanna Kaysen, Molly Keane, Rosamond Lehmann, Anne Lister, Rose Macaulay, Shena Mackay, Beryl Markham, Daphne du Maurier, Mary McCarthy, Gloria Naylor, Kate O'Brien, Grace Paley, Barbara Pym, Mary Renault, Stevie Smith, Muriel Spark, Elizabeth Taylor, Angela Thirkell, Sylvia Townsend Warner, Mary Webb, Eudora Welty, Rebecca West, Edith Wharton, Antonia White